DANGER ZONE

DANGER ZONE

MAURICE SHADBOLT

Hodder Moa Beckett

Maurice Shadbolt

Maurice Shadbolt is the author of four books of stories, several works of non-fiction and ten novels, including some now seen as New Zealand classics. His most recent novel *The House of Strife* was the third in a trilogy which began with *Season of the Jew*, winner of the Wattie Book Award in 1987 and selected by the literary editors of *The New York Times* as one of the best books of 1987. It was followed soon after by the much applauded *Monday's Warriors* (1990). His autobiography, *One of Ben's*, has been called the best literary memoir by a New Zealander.

'A magnificent writer' *Newsweek*

'Dramatically original' *The Washington Post*

'A master storyteller' *Los Angeles Times*

ISBN 0-340-379537

© 1975 Maurice Shadbolt

First published in 1975
Reprinted in 1985

This edition published in 1995 by Hodder Moa Beckett Publishers Limited
[a member of the Hodder Headline Group]
4 Whetu Place, Mairangi Bay, Auckland, New Zealand

Printed by Griffin Paperbacks, Australia

For my son Sean, who couldn't sail; for Stephen Becker, who would have; and for Jim Cottier and Grant Davidson of *Tamure, Spirit of Peace,* and *Greenpeace III.*

Know that life is unreal and death also is unreal. Only what you experience is real.

The Tibetan Book of the Dead

The sea is like music; it has all the dreams of the soul within itself, and sounds them over. The beauty and grandeur of the sea consists in our being forced down into the fruitful bottom-lands of our own psyches, where we confront and recreate ourselves...

C. G. Jung

One

Perhaps Blair's phone call found him in the right mood
that morning. Or at the right time of life. For Blair's voice
made the past reverberate. He afterwards marvelled that his
reply had begun to shape itself so swiftly. Years since he and
Blair had spoken at length. Never more than casual meetings
since, things of chance, wry words quickly spoken. He should
have been more surprised. It was Monday morning too. On
Monday mornings he often felt vulnerable, and that Monday
more than most. The weekend had been no success. There
was a dinner party on the Saturday, the guests largely theatrical
friends of Helen's, and one or other of them, or both, drank
too much and too damagingly along the way; there were angry
words flung across the debris left by the departed guests. Then
more than words were flung. On Sunday there were in-laws.
Finally an indifferent television play which did nothing to heal
the weekend. Nor was there reconciliation in bed. Her farewell
that morning had been frosty.

And then Blair on the phone, early. Like a crack appearing
across the trivia on his desk.

'I expect you're surprised to hear from me,' Blair announced.

'Well,' Stephen said, 'yes.' His first thought, a reasonable one,
was that Blair was in trouble. Had outreached himself, at last.
Perhaps his glass towers had begun to shatter and tumble.

1

Stephen was used to telephone calls delivering diverse problems first thing on a Monday morning: arrests for drunken driving, sudden marital separations. But Blair? He had never turned to Stephen before; he could afford more expensive assistance in any case. And Stephen's reputation was unlikely to further any cause of Blair's.

'Everything all right with you?' Blair asked.

'More or less. Yes.'

'Settled again?'

'Fairly.' Stephen's second marriage was years in the past anyway.

'And you've coped with your fortieth birthday gracefully?'

'I should like to think so.' It was almost a year gone. He and Blair were the same age, contemporary almost to a week.

'A dangerous time,' Blair observed.

'So they say.'

'I read somewhere that it has to do with a man accustoming himself to the idea of his death, a mid-life trauma he has to survive, or go under.'

'That sounds reasonable. A bit dramatic, perhaps.'

'I imagine a young wife helps. Like yours.'

'Possibly.'

'If anything does, I mean.'

There seemed some depression at work behind those words. So Stephen experimented.

'Oh?' he said. 'Say on.'

'I mean – well, I mean a man has to face up to whether his life amounts to anything anyway. Whether all he's done, or tried to do, adds up to more than sweet bugger all. And the answer is, or seems to be, God knows.'

'I see.'

'I'm speaking generally, of course. Not about myself. Not necessarily.'

'Fair enough.'

'And I'm certainly not thinking about you. You must take some satisfaction in what you've done.'

'Thanks.' Stephen saw himself, briefly, as Blair might see him. As a liberal lawyer, say, who involved himself in marginal and radical causes too often for his own good. Which was all that Blair, or any outsider, might see. Never that by far the greater part of his life was lived in a rut of received wisdom, with conveyancing and civil claims, compensation and petty crime; the rest only made it all tolerable. And then not always.

So what did Blair want? Obviously preliminaries. And?

'I mean it,' Blair insisted. 'You must have some real satisfactions.'

'At times,' Stephen allowed. He wished himself more plausible at that moment. Detail on his desk began to grow distinct again; he also had a brief court appearance that morning. 'Look,' he said suddenly, 'what's it all about, Blair? This call, I mean.'

He did not want to sound brusque. But perhaps he did. There was a brief silence, as if Blair were taken aback.

'Well,' he said finally, 'to tell the truth I've been thinking a lot over the weekend.'

He didn't have that alone; perhaps Blair could feel vulnerable on Monday morning too. Another pause.

'Yes?' Stephen prompted.

'On my yacht,' Blair explained. 'It was nice sailing yesterday, out in the gulf. That brought you to mind, you see.'

Stephen didn't see, altogether. It was twenty years since he'd sailed with Blair. Not competitively, and never with more than modest expertise; it had been a fairly boozy student enterprise, that old 14-footer they mutually owned. Blair had graduated to larger and more luxurious craft. Stephen had seldom sailed since. The link was remote.

'I wasn't,' Blair went on, 'just thinking about us both being past forty now. As a matter of fact, I was thinking about another danger zone altogether.'

'Oh?' Stephen was baffled, briefly.

'The one around Mururoa atoll. The French nuclear test zone. Are you with me now?'

'Not quite,' Stephen said, still puzzled. He was aware, of course, that bombs were again to be detonated soon at Mururoa; the news would have been difficult to escape anywhere in the South Pacific. Routine diplomatic protests had been passed over. The French had just restated their intention to warn off shipping and aircraft from a large stretch of international waters. Inquisitive journalists were being tipped out of Tahiti. Rumours agreed that the French were trying for their first hydrogen blast. It was still at a confused distance, so far as Stephen was concerned; at the margin of his concerns, rather, where most things drifted when he felt personally powerless. Little enough could be done within the crunch of the everyday, much less within the crunch of the larger world. It was all he could do to plead usefully, say, for some Polynesian prisoner who bashed a warder out of despair with language and close confinement; Stephen's eloquence might be no more than a kind of lubrication. For the wheels still turned; the sentence was still passed, if less savagely. Something had been seen to be attempted, and possibly conscience had cleaner hands.

'Well,' Blair announced, 'I'm thinking of going up there. Sailing up there. Into the danger zone.'

'No,' Stephen said, without thinking, surprised. Blair? It was unreal.

'You're welcome to try and talk me out of it, if you like. But I wouldn't give much for your chances.'

'You're not really serious.' Of course he wasn't. A whim. A wealthy whim. Sprung from boredom or booze, on an idle weekend. Blair's youthful schemes had never been less than spectacular. Twenty years ago they had been going to circumnavigate the world twice together. First with the wind, then against it. Ashore again, though, he found the winds of commerce more tempting; he tacked out of Stephen's life.

'I expected something better than that from you. Of course I'm bloody serious. It was this protest boat idea that started me off. Then I thought, why not? I've got this big bloody sloop. It sleeps six comfortably. A ton of storage space. A new diesel auxiliary. It could do the trip easily.'

'That's hardly the point. Doing the trip easily. It's more than a trip, a jaunt. Or so I'd imagine. The protest boat notion, as I understand it, is to get in the way of nuclear tests. Block them, if possible. At the least call international attention to fallout hazard, with the risk of being in the vicinity.'

4

'I thought you'd take all that for granted,' Blair said. 'Of all people.'

'I'm just wondering whether you do.'

'Give me a chance.'

'In any case,' Stephen went on, merciless, 'these protest boats haven't amounted to anything yet. They break down, give up, lose heart, get towed away. They never seem to make it. Be realistic. Small boats have enough problems out there without the French too.'

'There might be more than one or two protest boats out there this time,' Blair argued. 'That might make a different story.'

'Nice to think so anyway,' Stephen said. It was true there had been talk of a small armada this year. But most protest boats remained promises. One had left New Zealand, and a couple of others were struggling to follow. The only really resonant protest so far had been ashore; a Molotov cocktail tossed into a French consular office. The rest was anguished outcry, and Gallic indifference.

'I expected to find cynicism elsewhere,' Blair said. 'Not from you.'

That shook Stephen for the moment. 'Perhaps I'm just tired.' He paused. 'Look, Blair, I'm in favour of anything to save the world. Provided it's well meant. I'm not convinced that it's not something you'll have forgotten by lunchtime. Apart from anything else, can you really afford to go? I seemed to be reading last week about your latest takeover.'

'That's my business,' Blair said sharply.

'True.'

'Anyway it's as good as wrapped up. I can afford three months. Perhaps four. I'll get a good radio on board. I won't be out of touch.'

'And it's a long way. It must be two thousand miles without a stop.'

'Two thousand five hundred,' said Blair. 'The quickest way.'

'The equivalent of an Atlantic crossing. Only no landfall. You've got the same distance back again. Five thousand all told.'

'I've thought it all out,' Blair insisted. 'You're way behind. It's on. All on.'

Stephen was beginning to concede the possibility. 'So what about this political thing?' he asked finally. 'I see you're becoming involved again, with this talk of your name in the ring for a Parliamentary seat.'

'That's nothing,' Blair said. 'Beside this.'

'You sure?'

'Of course I'm bloody sure.'

'At the least, I suppose, it wouldn't hurt your prospects.'

Stephen meant the observation as a test. There was a small, predictable silence.

'What do you mean?'

'I mean the progressive young man of industry, and all the rest. Sailing a protest boat up there wouldn't hurt you. Rather the reverse. Provided it comes off, that is.'

Blair's tone was tight. 'I can think of easier ways to cultivate an image.'

'I don't doubt it.'

'And besides, I don't see that a moral conscience is exclusive to you liberals and leftists.'

'Fair enough.'

Stephen began to regret the imputation. It was only fair to take Blair at face value. Or try to. But what did he want? Stephen's liberal blessing? Reassurance from the past? Acknowledgement that he had a conscience after all? Perhaps all three.

'And if you still don't take me seriously, read the paper tonight. I've already announced the thing. These nuclear protest people have already been on the phone, offering provisions and volunteers.'

'I see. So it's gone that far.'

'Of course. I wouldn't be talking to you otherwise. And I'm not really ringing just to get your reaction. I'm ringing to ask would you come along and crew.'

'Me?'

'You. Why not?'

'I haven't sailed for years. And that was pretty safe stuff. You're talking about an ocean. You need experience.'

'I also need congenial company.'

'Blair, it's twenty years back.'

'We got on well enough, as I recall.'

'True.'

'Golden days.'

'Young days. The world's shrunk a bit since then.'

'All the more reason. You were the first person I thought of. I mean that.'

'I appreciate it. All the same –'

'Yes?'

All the same, it was impossible. Out of the question. He could list a score of reasons. Not least among them Helen, his faltering marriage. And a dozen large and neglected duties among the papers piled on his desk. Among the rest of the routines, the rituals.

'Well –' he began, and paused, perhaps fatally.

'I thought you'd be on like a shot,' Blair said. 'Just your thing. You're always on about the condition of the world. That environmental fight you had a month or two back with all those bloodied noses. Take that as an example. What's the difference?'

'There is a difference,' Stephen insisted.

'Sure,' Blair said. 'In one case you only have to put words on the line. Win or lose. Only words. Don't tell me I've called your bluff.'

'Look, Blair, I've had years of good causes, protests, deputations. I haven't noticed you around for a long time. You want my support? You've got it, all the way, if you're serious.'

'I'm saying I want you along too.'

'And I'm saying that's different.'

'Why?'

'Because I've got an office here, for one thing. I don't have a dozen understudies, and I can't run the place by radio.'

'You have a partner.'

'I can't unload everything on to him. As it is, I can only get a couple of weeks off in summer. You're talking about months.'

'You could fall ill for months. What then? Same thing. This

is an emergency too. The French will go on testing up there until people start making them sweat.'

'I'm not that important.'

'You're people.'

'Right. So you won't be short on other people, volunteers with far more experience.'

'And you are important to me. I've been trying to make that clear. I've got to have some kind of mainstay, someone aboard who can think clearly. I don't want to be landed with a whole crew of wild-eyed protesters, or scruffs with a death wish. Apart from which, I may need some legal expertise anyway. Without you, I might have to rethink the whole thing.'

'Then you should have got in touch first.'

'I was certain you'd be on. Can't you see? We could manage it together. We left something unfinished back there. Those old days needn't be wasted. They could have been rehearsal for something like this.'

That idea wasn't without appeal, though Stephen resisted it. Blair's plea had the colour of the past, of days under sail in sun or storm, lonely landfalls and cheerful survivals. Of drift-wood fires, fish frying in an old black pan, long twilit dialogues on lives usefully shaped, effectively lived. 'Don't bulldoze me, Blair. Give me time to think.'

'Go ahead, then. Think.'

There was a few moments' silence.

'Well?'

'I'm still thinking.'

'You want me to hang up? I'll call again in five minutes.'

'That might help. No, perhaps it's all right.'

Strange. For the reasons why he couldn't go were uncannily shaping themselves as reasons why he should. To say no to Blair might be to admit himself prisoner of his life, another victim, more closely confined than most. To say yes might not make him free, but it might at least provide for the possibility that freedom still existed. The kind of knowledge some sought in desperate and despairing love affairs past the age of forty. Or in war. Only there was no war. And he had begun to forget what love affairs were like; there seemed only ever to have been

8

the one, and death insisted that was long in the past. And the hell-bent world might confess itself less evasively out there, more tangibly; a seething and exclamatory tower of fire, satanic upon innocent ocean, ignited by human arrogance, fuelled by human indifference, and perhaps by impotence such as his own. Man tugging apart the tiniest, most minuscule particle of his world, as if taunting the universe to protest, merely to discover what dramatic damage he might yet work, what ingenious terrors he might yet inflict on his kind. To sail toward that in challenge could be to put trivia behind him, to travel into the teeth of his time. The temptation was real; he was surprised by its size. Surprised? Staggered. And dismayed. It was if every lack in his life now rose in conspiracy, took power, and sat in judgment. Regardless of Blair, or Blair's motive for the thing; that was irrelevance. The satisfactions he won from his work began to seem excuses for living, apologetic signals offered after surrender. Given still more austere interrogation, he might even confess that as the truth, entirely.

'You mean you might be on?' Blair said. There was an edge of anxiety now.

'Yes. Possibly.'

'Good. Now let's –'

'I have to think the thing through. It's not going to be easy.'

'I never said it was.'

'I mean, getting away. There are difficulties.' But he was already beginning to see difficulties as details. Even Helen. He couldn't begin to imagine her reaction. He didn't try.

'If it's financial, I could help.'

'It's all right.'

'What then?'

'Probably nothing I can't sort out, given time.'

'I can't give you much of that. A week. Perhaps two, at most. We've got to get up there before the French blow the big one. Otherwise there's no point. The sooner the better.'

'I see.' That, of course, might have advantage too, all things considered. Especially Helen considered.

'What about a quick lunch today? Then I'll take you down to see the boat.'

9

'I think I might manage that,' he agreed.

Ten minutes later, while he prepared to leave for court, the telephone rang again. A journalist this time. 'I believe,' he said, 'you may be accompanying Mr Blair Hawkins on his voyage to Mururoa.'

'Then,' said Stephen, 'you know more than I do.'

It had begun. When he had got rid of the man, he was tempted to blast Blair. Instead he saw that he had to call Helen, before the thing went any further.

'Listen,' he said when she answered, 'there's something I'd better warn you about.' And went on to explain, as briefly as he could. Too briefly, as it turned out.

'So that's it,' she said. 'I knew you were stewing over something again all weekend. And that's why you took it out on me. It's always the way. Your faithful chopping board.'

He had never quite been able to cope with unreason.

'I'm telling you the truth,' he insisted. 'It's only just come up in the last half hour. I'm on my way to court. We'll talk about it later.'

'You'd better,' she said. But her voice was small.

They had a swift counter lunch in a bar near the boat harbour.

'You didn't need to mention me to the press,' Stephen said.

'A misunderstanding,' Blair apologized smoothly. 'Your name was supposed to be off the record – just as a possibility. Sorry about that. What did you tell them?'

'That I was still thinking about it. No more.'

'Fair enough.' Blair kept glancing at his watch. He seemed under pressure, but that wasn't unusual. 'Well, we'd better get down there.'

Blair looked a fit forty. His large frame still didn't appear to carry much fat. His face and hands were well tanned. He had trendy sideburns now, and his vivid black hair had lengthy trim. He could pass for a vigorous thirty anywhere. And his personality was as imposing as ever. Legend said he was a bull in some of the boardrooms he inhabited. Stephen had always needed irony to keep his distance from Blair. He might have more need of it now.

10

They clambered into Blair's sports car and drove down to the boat harbour, through a maze of masts and rigging and cradled vessels. 'It went up on the hard this morning,' Blair explained. 'We have to throw some paint over it.'

'I haven't even asked its name.'

'*Moana Nui*. Big ocean. It used to have a reputation as a racer. We should make fast time up there, if that appeals to you.'

'Don't count me in yet,' Stephen suggested. 'I'm still deciding.'

'Of course,' Blair answered mildly. 'I keep forgetting.' And then added, 'Here she is.'

Suspended above the shore, *Moana Nui* was long, narrow, sleek. There were people moving about the deck, and clustered below.

'What's all this?' Stephen said.

Then he saw one of the figures carrying a film camera, and a sound recordist arranging his gear. A television crew. The others? Journalists, no doubt.

'My God,' Stephen said. 'You might have told me.'

'Told you what?'

'About this gang. I thought we were going to have a quiet look.'

'It's a surprise to me too,' Blair said.

'Of course you bloody knew about it.' He remembered Blair looking at his watch.

'Well, not precisely,' Blair lied cheerfully. 'Though it's fairly predictable.' He swung the car into a parking place. Two or three in the crowd began to approach.

'I'm staying here,' Stephen announced suddenly. 'I'll have a look some other time.'

'Don't be ridiculous. You'll only draw more attention to yourself. You'll look like the bloody secret service, sitting here.'

'Hell.' Stephen, with a sigh, supposed Blair right. He seems in a trap of Blair's devising, and now had to make the best of it, see it through and keep his cool. He should have known what Blair was like. Should have remembered.

Blair had already jumped from the car. With bland smile, he held his hand out to the first of the approaching journalists. Stephen followed cautiously. Then, seeing a gap, he swerved past Blair and the journalists and walked on toward the boat. He hoped Blair might be sufficient distraction for the media men. 'In about ten days,' he could hear Blair saying behind him. 'If we can get it tidy and provisioned. And the survey through.' Then, 'Yes, it's definite. You can put a ring around it.' His voice was loud and confident above the muffled questions. 'I'm sorting out a crew now. Yes.'

Stephen walked around *Moana Nui*. True, she was a craft of exciting appearance. Fast and slender line, yet not in the least frail; he could imagine her lively upon the sea with spinnaker full. His hope that he might miss recognition was, though, quite brief. As he climbed the ladder to the deck, he felt a touch on his shoulder. 'Mr West?'

'Yes.' He looked around. A reporter familiar from the courts.

'We understand you're considering the voyage.'

'That's all, at the moment. Considering.'

'Could you clarify your motives?'

'I think that would be more appropriate later. When I've decided.'

'When are you likely to decide?'

'I think that's a personal matter.'

'You wouldn't mind us counting you as a likely crew member – as someone mentioned.'

'It seems that's being done already.'

'And relate it to your more obvious public concerns – the environmental issue, say.'

'Whatever you like,' he said irritably.

Then he was swamped, overtaken by the arrival of Blair and the others at the foot of the ladder. 'I bought it about eighteen months ago,' Blair was saying. 'The price, if you're interested, was twenty-five thousand dollars. This, by the way, is Steve West incognito. He's here to look the boat over. Don't lean on him too hard. He's still making up his mind. That right, Steve? Or has *Moana Nui* grabbed you already?'

12

Stephen made no answer. Anyway Blair didn't appear to need one.

'I'm working through a list of volunteers at the moment. I need a good navigator, for example, and a skilled radio man. I should be announcing others in the next couple of days, as soon as Steve's found whether it's possible for him to get away. As I don't doubt he will. I need hardly stress his value to us – not just as a capable crewman, one with whom I've sailed in the past, but also as a dedicated citizen of this country, one who has frequently demonstrated the courage of his convictions. Also as a lawyer who should be able to keep us advised, at all times, of our rights in international waters. There may be some tricky navigation there, and we'll be telling the world as we go. Right. Now where do you want me exactly?'

'Somewhere on deck,' said one of the television men. 'Maybe in the cockpit, if you like, by the wheel with some rigging behind.'

'Fine. Anywhere you say.' Managing the media was everyday work for Blair.

Up on the yacht, it was even more difficult for Stephen to keep his distance; he was crowded close to Blair as he arranged himself before the television crew and looped a microphone around his neck. He needed no deep breath to begin as the camera rolled.

'In continued atmospheric testing of nuclear weaponry we are confronted with a species of insanity,' he announced. 'A nationalist insanity; a human insanity. The genetic risk is well known. It's a distinct possibility that millions of people now living, let alone those not yet born, may have their lives shortened by indiscriminate release of radiation into the atmosphere in the past three decades. If the governments of the world, through the United Nations, can't bring the madness to a stop, then it's up to individuals to act.'

'What do you mean by that?' asked the interviewer.

Blair smiled wryly. 'I'm a do-it-yourself man, always have been. Even self-made, as you all probably know. If diplomacy can do nothing, then I think it's time to do it ourselves. I mean for ordinary people to confront the mad bombers. To tell them to leave the Pacific alone, and give the human race a chance.'

It was altogether impressive, and convincing. Blair had done his homework thoroughly at some time in the last few hours, as efficiently as he might for any commercial proposition; he went on to quote Nobel prize-winning scientists and statistics precisely to the decimal point in elucidation. Yet Stephen wished himself more overpowered. Perhaps it was Blair's fluency. And that Blair was saying these things at all, after years of apparent indifference to anything beyond his personal condition. Why now? Possibly it didn't matter, if he was saying the right thing at the right time. More than saying; doing. That was the point, surely.

'You'd go right in under the bomb?' said the interviewer.

'Right in. No point otherwise. We'd be wasting our time.'

'You see your voyage as a direct challenge, then?'

'I can think of no larger challenge for any human being,' replied Blair.

Nor, at that moment, could Stephen. He wished he could.

Afterwards, walking back to the car, Blair slapped him on the shoulder. 'Look,' he said, rather surprisingly, 'I know you've got your reservations about me, these days.'

'Well –'

'Just trust me. That's all.'

'I'll do my best.'

'Fine.'

'Tell me one thing, though. Why you're doing it. You're talking to me now, not to television. Why?'

'I should think it's obvious.'

'Oh?'

'Because,' said Blair, climbing into the car, 'I want to do one good thing with my life. Will that do?'

It had to.

The afternoon was manic. His secretary was late back from lunch, he had a crowded appointment book, and his telephone refused to stop ringing; he had to fight through to the end of the day to find time to talk quietly with his partner. That wasn't easy either. They left the problem of his prolonged absence swinging until the next day.

That night, home late, and before they had a chance to talk, he sat with Helen and watched Blair on television news; their son had been put early to bed. She was subdued enough until the camera panned from Blair on to Stephen's face, and he was named as probable crew member.

'So it's gone that far,' she said.

'I'm sorry. I didn't know about that. I mean it.' He found himself angry with Blair again.

'You're no fool. At least I still like to think so. You must have known.'

Did he? He couldn't be sure. He could have kept himself clear of Blair, while Blair talked, and out of camera range. Until he settled things with Helen, as he was evidently about to do now. He rose and switched off television.

'Hard for you to back out now, isn't it?' she said into the silence. 'Or is that the idea?'

'No. No at all.'

'Well, don't,' she said.

'Don't what?'

'Don't back out, on account of me. That's what it would amount to at this stage, wouldn't it?'

'Not necessarily.' He might, though, have to concede the point.

'As for me, I'd hate to deprive Blair Hawkins of his first choice. Why you anyway? Are his other friends too fat and bloated? Does he want you along as a portable conscience?'

That possibility wasn't remote to Stephen either; he had seen it several times through the day. He shook his head, all the same. 'I allow for the chance that Blair has one himself. That he means what he says. He may be rather more complex than he appears.'

'I don't doubt it. I still think he's a big mouth.'

'Well, his big mouth seems to be saying the right things at the moment. He's serious, so far as I can see. And if he is, it's reasonable to assume he may make a useful protest. A highly effective one.'

15

'I can't see him risking his precious carcass near a bomb. He's too much in love with it.'

'You don't know him. There's a reckless quality in Blair. Risk made him rich.'

'Always for himself. So don't tell me this isn't too, right along the line. An altruist overnight? I don't believe it.'

'Of course he may see mileage in it all. Even so, there are easier ways to earn it. Allow for the possibility that men move for more than one motive. There may also be an old streak of idealism at work. The idealism that took him into the Communist Party, then out of it, when he was young. I was an interested spectator at that time, I remember. I also remember the idealism being real enough.'

'You think he wants you along to remind him of it?'

'Possibly.' Stephen shrugged.

'A house-trained liberal. Or respectable radical. That's what he needs. Especially your reputation. He needs that most of all. To prove he's on a genuine crusade.'

'All that might be true,' he conceded. 'But it still doesn't matter a damn if he's doing the right thing.'

'You baffle me. I look at people first.'

'I look at what they do. And even if the worst is true, it's all the more reason to go.'

'Why?'

'To make sure he keeps doing the right thing.'

'That's as fascinating a piece of rationalization as I've ever heard. Are you sure it's not a holiday from life? From me? From the tediously ordinary problem of living with other human beings? That's likely to be more fatal than any bomb test, and you know it. No one knows it better.'

'That's hardly fair.' More and more it seemed his first marriage was fated to shadow his second; he might never be free.

'It's your bloody indifference. That must be what drove her to it. I couldn't see that before. I can now. Your work, your brave causes, it's all excuse.'

'For what?'

'For being only half alive.'

'I see.' He was unwilling to argue. He could sit it out. He had before.

'I suppose I could live in hope that a bomb might thaw you out. In which case the trip might be worth it. If you came back alive, really alive.'

'And that's all you've got to say?'

'Almost.' Had she hardened herself to this moment, to make it easier for him? God knew. He fetched himself a drink from the liquor cabinet. It was true his first marriage had left him gutted: with a vacuum, often, where feeling should have been. He had hoped, with Helen, that gap might close. But it never had, altogether. Perhaps it was fear of feeling. Fear of further large human demand. Anyway he had never really relaxed with Helen as he should have; perhaps he was perversely manufacturing the same demand again, in another guise.

'It's not that I'm against the protest,' Helen went on, 'or against the voyage. I'm for it. It's just that, quite naturally, I should sooner someone else went. Someone else's lover or husband. Do you really want to go?'

'I think I do. Yes.'

'Then go, if you need to. Just tell me why. If it's not too much trouble; if you have the time to waste on your wife. Why?'

'I suppose,' said Stephen, trying for truth, 'it may be because I'm more than half way through life –'

'Like I said. More than half way through life and only half alive.'

'All right. Perhaps something like that. I still feel I've never been tested. Not really; not to the limit. And in every way.'

'I thought that was what marriage was about,' Helen observed quietly. 'But never mind.' She sounded sad, but no longer bitter. 'It could be worse, I expect; I might have married some monotonous bloody mountain climber out every weekend. Instead of a male who has to cut his slice of machismo just the once.'

'It's a bit more than that.'

'Of course. And I'd sooner you went. I mean that.'

At the end of the evening, anyway, it seemed he was going. Helen made love that night with more than ordinary fervour, perhaps still in search of explanation, and his body offered what it could. Which finally was both more and less than he felt. Next morning he woke in fright at finding his life so swiftly changed, the world so strangely coloured, but nevertheless was soon talking on the telephone to Blair.

Two

THE COOL WINTER SUNLIGHT WAS ALL FRACTURED SILVER AMONG
the jetties and piles of the boat harbour, the moored craft
rocking lightly on the risen tide. Volunteers scraped and painted
Moana Nui. Others were working on the deck, and on the
rigging. Blair stood commanding at the centre of it all, checking
through a list on a clipboard. There was a noisy electric drill
somewhere inside. A newspaper photographer clicked his way
through the commotion. When Blair saw Stephen, he gave him
a hand up on to the deck.

'It's coming together,' he said cheerfully. 'We might even
have a crew soon. Meet our navigator. Peter Lee, Steve
West.'

There was a lanky, brown and bearded individual in oily
shorts and unravelling sea-jersey beside Blair. He shook
Stephen's hand.

'Peter's been around,' Blair explained. 'We'll be leaning
heavily on his experience. He knows the area, and he knows
his navigation. We won't get lost. You should try to get to
know each other before we go.'

Peter Lee looked likeable enough, at least. Amiable blue eyes,
open smile. Just as well. They would have to find each other
tolerable soon. Peter was similarly eyeing Stephen. Then he
spoke, with slight North American accent.

'So you're the lawyer who's going to bail us out of the Bastille,' he said. 'Good scene.'

'I'd like to tell you both to go off and have a drink together,' Blair said. 'But I need Peter at the moment. We've decided to put you in charge of provisions, Steve. You'll know where everything is when we're at sea.' He paused. 'You getting things tidied up?'

'Yes,' Stephen said. For it all seemed to be happening regardless. Work, marriage, responsibilities; everything appeared to be sliding into distance already. 'So where do I start?'

'You mean you're free to help?' Blair said, surprised.

'Why not?'

'God help us,' Blair said. 'You're keener than I thought.'

The rest of the crew did come together. Blair shared his decisions with Peter, who had most sailing experience, and Stephen, who was supposed to consider character and conviction. Rex Stone gave them their first problem. He didn't volunteer formally; he just arrived out of a rainy afternoon, and said he was going to join them, as if his acceptance could never be in doubt. He was perhaps sixty, lean and balding, with a conventional business suit under his dripping raincoat. When they questioned him in the cabin, he couldn't offer any special qualification for a yacht voyage; he admitted never to having hoisted a sail in his life. That ruled him out, but then he went on to speak about his years at sea, in earlier life, in naval ships as engineer's mate. And at length his name had resonance. Rex Stone, war hero, his once familiar features now as faded as those old newspaper and magazine stories. So far as Stephen could remember it, he had worked in a burning engine room, mates dead and dying around him, after some surprise attack; and had not only managed to subdue the fire, but also to give his ship sufficient power to escape a trap. A dramatic affair; he had been called to Buckingham Palace to receive the Victoria Cross, and been much celebrated. Stephen recalled all this for Blair and Peter after Stone had departed.

'Well,' Blair said, 'at least he's a man with guts.'

'It was thirty years ago,' Stephen observed.

'And he's going to be much older than the rest of us,' Peter said 'There's that too. He'll be an odd man out. At that age, there could be a health problem.'

'He looks vigorous enough to me,' Blair said.

'And no experience,' Peter added.

'He might be useful with the diesel.'

'We're sailing up there, not motoring.'

'All the same –' Blair was clearly keen on Stone. 'What do you think, Steve?'

'It's your decision, in the end.'

'That's no answer.'

'I suppose not.'

'What's the trouble, then?'

'I'd like to know more about him.'

'You just told us about him.'

'That was war. I mean, in the peace.'

'Let's face it. We're never going to be able to check anyone out wholly. To some extent we have to take each other on trust. Anyway he told you what he was doing now; he's a customs inspector.'

'Which tells us nothing.'

'Except that he's prepared to walk out on some reasonable sinecure to join us unpaid. It indicates some conviction.'

'I hope so,' Stephen said.

'All right.' Blair looked at Peter. 'What's your verdict, navigator?'

'I'd like to see another man with open sea experience. In small boats, not frigates. You haven't got it; Steve hasn't. And he'd be a third. It leaves me lonely.'

'We'll all learn,' Blair argued. 'We're not fools.'

'It's not just learning. It's survival out there, friend, before we ever reach the danger zone. And a crisis a day doesn't keep the doctor away. I don't like the idea of an old man.'

'Steve and I aren't young.'

'You aren't old either; you'll do me.'

'So I'll have to decide,' Blair said.

'It looks like it,' Stephen agreed.

It was never in doubt. By the end of the day Rex Stone was

with them. Or not so much the man as his Victoria Cross; Blair now had a certified hero aboard as guarantee of his good faith. And more headlines for *Moana Nui*. The voyage was already a public relations triumph; they hardly needed to sail.

Stephen took consolation in Peter Lee, in his competence, as they worked together on the boat. Blair gave the appearance of vast activity; Peter did the work. He was seldom flustered or irritated. He had a master's ticket, but had never used it. He had sailed most of the Pacific as a sea bum, hitching his way along easily, from yacht to yacht, with his knowledge of navigation. When ashore, as lately, he taught navigation as livelihood. He had no real home, unless the Pacific, and next to no possessions beyond his sextant. He was still short of thirty, but well weathered, prematurely wrinkled, with sun-bleached beard. He had a distinctive smile, with crooked teeth, a smile with which Stephen was soon familiar; his long and loose body, under a large flow of fair hair, already seemed to have become part of the craft as he padded barefoot around it. In a sense that was true; he slept aboard. He had nowhere else. As soon as he heard of the protest boats he hitch-hiked from the remote inlet where he was temporarily and lazily resident, in some old fishing shack, and volunteered. Stephen asked if it was just another voyage to him. Not quite, he replied. It was a chance to be useful. He had always thought himself a pacifist, but had never had opportunity, or cause, to prove this one way or the other.

'I never thought pacifists had to prove anything,' Stephen said. 'I thought that was the point.'

'It means staying sane, as much as you can, in an insane bitch of a world,' Peter explained. To own anything, belong anywhere, was to share the insanity. So he didn't own anything, belong anywhere. It was extreme to Stephen, but he could envy so unequivocal and austere a vision. Not that all was austerity. There was a guitar propped behind the head of Peter's bunk; he plucked at it, apparently finding comfort in its sound, when they took a coffee break together.

At length Stephen asked, 'How do you feel about Blair?'

'Do I have to feel anything about him?'

'You're going to sail with him.'

'He's got this boat. It's a good one. That's enough for me, friend. I can make it go where he wants it to go.'

'And that's it?'

'That's it,' Peter agreed. 'So long as I don't have to do much talking.' He took up his guitar again, in emphasis. 'He can talk. You can. I'll get on with it.'

'I see.'

'We only have to agree on one thing. Where we want to go. Not why. Where we want to go is somewhere around twenty miles off Mururoa atoll. International waters begin at twelve miles, and I allow at least eight for drift. Depending on wind and current. Out there, friend, it's all wind and current.'

'And a bomb or two.'

'Maybe so. But we don't have to think about that.'

'Why not?'

'Because we're behaving as though we're sane. To prove the sons of bitches setting them off are insane. Once we start worrying about their bombs, they've won, we've conceded their point, we're as mad as they are. You must see that, friend.'

Stephen didn't, even obscurely, but he allowed the point to pass. They were soon at work on the boat again. And Stephen admitted pleasure to himself in his tasks. It was years since he had worked on a case or cause with such pure and single purpose. He could already feel the deck beginning to move beneath him, though *Moana Nui* still sat high on the hard. He slopped paint around; he worked on fresh fittings in the cabin; stowed bags of flour, rice and potatoes in the forward hold, and cans of food down in the bilges under the bunks, carefully arranged and marked, lest they lost their labels at sea. Blair, most of the time, was coming and going, fetching professional advice and help, checking his lists, issuing deadlines and press statements and revised departure dates. He handled things with all the verve of one of his takeovers.

The next crew member was the radio operator. This time Blair allowed himself to be overruled with seeming reluctance.

Perhaps he felt this necessary after the decision on Rex Stone; perhaps his reluctance was, in any case, only apparent. He retained his gift for stage management anyway. Choices eventually came to two: an operator with experience of coastal cargo shipping, a man in his early fifties; a long haired and densely red-bearded student radio ham of some vehement conviction and slight sea experience. Peter and Stephen, with Rex Stone in mind, voted for youth; Blair's bother seemed to be that the younger man had the colouring of the conventional protester. Difficult to say; he didn't make his doubts plain. He just reminded them that they were going to live with their final choice, quite literally, for three or four months. That was no news. So it had to be Blair's image-building which was really the issue. One beard aboard the boat was enough, perhaps, and Peter's was reasonably trimmed. 'We're here to sail a boat,' Stephen felt obliged to observe, 'as efficiently as we can. Not to please suburban sensibilities.'

'Anyway,' Peter said, 'we're none of us going to look like roses out there. Or smell like them, friend, in rough weather.'

So Blair gave in. He allowed that the student, Barry Purchase, was more experienced in the handling of the sophisticated radio equipment he was installing aboard. He became, then, fifth crew member.

'There's one thing, though,' Blair said. 'This sixth place. We've room for one more.'

Peter argued against it; there could be too much strain on food and water.

'You got someone in mind?' Stephen asked.

'To tell the truth,' Blair admitted, 'various media people have been pressing. No lack of volunteers there.'

Stephen might have expected it; he hesitated to push an opinion.

'In a sense,' Blair went on, 'it's all part of the communication problem. If we're going to take on the French out there, we should make sure the world knows about it. Otherwise we lose the value of what we're doing. If we can't actually get in their way, we can at least shame the bastards. As a lawyer, Steve, you should see the point. We're making a case; the court is

24

world opinion. We need someone to make sure the court gets the story. Right?'

'It sounds like so much bullshit to me, friend,' Peter said. 'Two pints of water per man a day is a bare working minimium. Six people mean we go below that. Either we're sailing a yacht, or parading for the press. Me, I'm sailing a yacht.'

'The problem is reconciling the two things,' Blair said. 'True, it puts a strain on the enterprise as a purely nautical one. There's also the question of safety out there in the zone. The more attention we draw to ourselves, the less likely it is that the French will get rough, the more we'll pose them a dilemma.'

'And each extra man increases the risk we won't get there at all, friend. It means one extra chance of appendicitis on board. Or injury and sickness. Or breakdown. Or that we don't get on with each other. It means six risks instead of five, plus the extra strain of less space, less water.'

They looked at Stephen. It seemed he was expected to consider the two arguments, show a preference. A successful voyage versus ambitious publicity enterprise? He could see that moral gestures, these days, apparently had no point unless before cameras. And he did not much like what he saw. For most gestures seemed to exist for the cameras, protests choreographed and tailored for television, protesters who became props of the media, no more. After all, he had prepared and edited more than a few protest scripts himself. Where were the gestures made because anonymous men could no longer stomach what they saw? Perhaps there were still such in society, though it had become difficult to believe.

'I'd like to think' he offered finally, 'that we were doing this for our own satisfaction.'

'Of course,' said Blair, not entirely taking the point.

'Which means shaping the voyage to our own satisfaction, not to the needs of newspapers.'

'I'm not sure what you're trying to say.'

'Nor am I.'

'Well –'

'But I expect it has something to do with a German I once read about, in Nazi uniform.'

'Oh?' Blair said with some impatience. 'And just how does he figure?'

'I think he was a Corporal Schmidt. Ordinary man. Ordinary name. But involved in transporting Jews to the gas chambers or something of the sort. Doubtless there were others as sickened as he. But he acted alone. He helped Jews escape, perhaps only a few dozen out of a few million, until he was gassed and incinerated himself.'

'A good story,' Blair conceded. 'But so what?'

'He didn't need anyone around reporting on his humanity and heroism. We don't really know who he was, what he looked like, what he ate for breakfast. We mightn't even have his name right. We just know he said no to a nightmare. And that's all we need to know. That a man, one man, could do it.'

'All right,' said Blair, more impatient. 'I still don't see where you're at.'

'I think I'd sooner we just sailed and said no, in our own way, if it's possible. And left the rest to look after itself.'

'You know that's not practical,' Blair argued.

'Perhaps not.'

'Or sensible. We need allies.'

'True.'

'And your ideal way of doing it, if you really think about it, is bloody selfish. So we can live with a personal moral glow, and nothing really changed. With the bombs still tested, and the world writing us off as idiot adventurers on a suicide trip.'

'Doubtless Corporal Schmidt was written off too.'

'Well, he didn't change anything, did he?'

'He proved men might be more than a bad smell. To us, that is. We'll never know what he proved to himself, or if he did. But no, he didn't change anything. He was a failure, if that's what you mean.'

'I'm trying to make damn sure this trip's not a failure. That's all.'

'I can see that, Blair. So don't get heated.'

'I think we should leave obscure German corporals out of this, and get down to the practical side. Whether we sail with five or six. And if a sixth, who?'

'Five,' Peter said. He paused. 'Unless an experienced yachtsman. That might just sway me.'

'And if I turn up a journalist who'd be more than a passenger?'

'That might be different,' Peter agreed, though without enthusiasm. 'Anyway it's your boat.'

'That's beside the point,' Blair said briskly. 'We must have general agreement. And no recriminations afterward.'

Later Stephen realized that the voyage, in a real sense, had begun. Next day *Moana Nui* went gently into the water. It was cleared to leave.

Three

THERE WAS CHOP IN THE CHANNEL AND DARKENING WEATHER
ahead. The motor cut as the mainsail rose and swelled with
breeze. Behind were the maritime suburbs of the city. The
green islands of the gulf began to pass to starboard in seemingly
single long line. *Moana Nui*, lifting her nose from wave to wave,
was swift towards open sea.

It seemed they were free at last of decisions and doubts and
delays and cameras. Even free, more slowly, of farewells from
the wharfside and then escort vessels, as these drifted away
across the widening water. There was some boyish exhilaration
aboard. Blair, already barefoot, down to shorts and parka,
wrenched open a bottle of whisky in celebration; he left the
wheel to Peter Lee, and flipped the cork on the bottle over the
side. 'I think we can kill this one now,' he announced. 'A day
like this deserves a fatted calf.' The bottle moved from hand to
hand as he began to talk.

'I'm leaving decisions on the course to Peter,' he went on.
'We'll have two hour watches revolving among four with either
Peter or myself as spare men on stand-by. Barry may need to
forgo a watch or two while he sorts out radio routines. Today,
though, I think everyone should take a turn at the wheel, just
to get the feel of it. We'll start regular watches at midnight.
Any questions?'

There were none, yet.

'And if anyone's feeling queasy,' Blair added, 'get below and sleep it off. Don't hesitate; don't be shy.'

First to leave the deck was Barry Purchase, after one gulp of whisky. He didn't look in the least interested in establishing a radio routine. Next to depart was Mel Cross, their last-minute crew member, the journalist with yachting experience Blair had promised. Only Blair had met him before they gathered on the yacht that morning. He was rather thin, quiet and severe, neatly clad, his jeans still showing a price tag, and bespectacled. And Blair had been obliged to confess that Mel's yachting experience was rather slight after all, but that this disadvantage had no significance beside his international contracts; the story of *Moana Nui*'s voyage would be reported under his by-line in a number of countries, even in France itself. Too late to argue; it was an amiable deception.

'So much for communications then,' Blair said, when Barry and Mel went below. 'You might fetch up some hot food, Peter.'

Rex Stone followed Peter to the galley. That left Blair and Stephen alone in the cockpit.

'Old times,' Blair said.

'Yes.'

'Take the wheel. Feel the surge. Good?'

'Interesting,' Stephen said presently.

'That's sailing. Real sailing. Don't over-correct. You'll enjoy it soon. That's more like it. Easy to port. Good. Who'd have guessed it?'

'What?'

'That we'd ever be putting a big one like this into open sea. After all these years.'

'Not me.'

'Nor me. Life's twists and turns. Jesus. And here we are.'

'Yes.' He was content to let Blair talk, while he got the measure of the wheel.

'It could be the biggest thing we've done with our lives.'

'So you said.'

'And the best. You realise that? We might even make a little history out here, something for people to remember.'

29

'Everything's possible,' Stephen agreed. For it seemed to be.

'Survival,' said Blair. 'That's the name of this game. We're going to survive this ocean whatever happens. Easy now. You're still swinging too far to starboard. Ease it back slowly. That's it. We'll survive all right. And we'll survive the French too, if it goes that far.'

'If it goes that far?' said Stephen, wondering.

'Anything could happen,' Blair said. 'Anything.'

'True.'

'We don't know, do we?'

'No.'

'We could turn over in a storm tomorrow. And that, brother, would be it.'

'I can see that.'

'So it's survival from now on. Oceans don't come any bigger. All right, so it's a protest voyage too. We don't forget that. But that's about the survival bit too. Survival of the human race, no less. Causes can't come any bigger. You seem to be getting the feel of the lovely old bitch now. Sweet?'

'Sweet,' Stephen answered. 'She's humming along.'

They were passing out of the channel. The gulf islands shook out into separate clumps of land, with growing vistas of broken water between; Stephen began to find delight in the wheel, in the opening horizon.

'We'll jibe,' Blair announced. 'Start bringing her round. Not too fast.' He freed the mainsheet, hauling in the boom. They ducked as it swung over briskly, and the main ballooned again. *Moana Nui* was now headed toward the open Pacific. By nightfall they had seen the last of land.

Stephen slept heavily, uncomfortably, and at midnight took the wheel again, from Peter Lee. 'Steering o-five-three,' Peter announced. 'All the way to Mururoa. How does that grab you?'

Then he dived below to his bunk and Stephen was left with the wheel and faintly lit compass. The sky was too clouded to steer by stars. He had no sight of the sea either, just faintly luminous flashes of spray as the boat pounded into the waves rising huge around; they were doubtless best left unseen. It needed concentration to keep on course. Barry Purchase and Mel Cross were seasick below, and even Rex Stone had surprisingly confessed to queasiness; perhaps it was sleep which had saved Stephen so far. And a certain tension; his body was an arrow lately fired, still to fall. He certainly had still to feel the sea.

Then he did. A wave slammed over the cockpit, into his face; it had a quite stunning sensual sting on his flesh. And he swallowed salt with relish. 'My God,' he said to himself with awe. He was almost drunk with the sensation; his entire body prickled with pleasure. Like a lover's.

He could never have imagined himself like this, lonely, at the wheel. With such a night, the heaving sea. Nor could he have imagined himself so far from indifference so soon. It was like gathering up a gift. For he wanted, quite despairingly, to live. More than he had in years, perhaps more than in a lifetime. This might be the treasure to be chipped from the stony heart of survival. And if that discovery was less fresh truth than platitude, it was still a singing one.

A parka-clad figure groped awkwardly up out of the darkened cabin. Too soon for Stephen to be relieved on watch. Then who? Rex Stone, it appeared.

'All right?' Rex asked.

'Yes.'

'Couldn't sleep. Big day. Mind if I keep you company?'

'Not at all.'

If Stephen did, it might be kinder not to say so. The man eased himself into the slight shelter offered by the canopy at the forward edge of the cockpit.

'Yes,' he went on. 'Big day. Still hard to believe.'

'For all of us, I expect.'

They still did not know each other, really.

'Yesterday I was walking the street. Now this.'

He sounded bewildered.

'You sorry?' Stephen asked.

'Christ no. Me? Sorry? Never.'

'That's good, then.'

'I only need to look at those other people in the street. Walking up and down. Running to offices. Running home to their little houses.'

'I see.'

'They'll never know. Never bloody know.'

'Know what?'

'What it's all about. Never.'

'And what is it all about?'

'Not that. Not that anyway. Jesus no.' He spoke as if he saw the pit. Perhaps he did. 'What does it amount to? Television. Weeds in the garden. A yarn in the boozer, with a mate or two, to kid yourself you're alive. I don't know what life is, but that's not it.'

'And this?'

'This is more like it. Whatever we do, whatever we don't. It has to be. Doesn't it?'

'I don't know,' Stephen answered honestly. 'Not yet.'

His first view of Rex Stone had been of someone angular, stiff, lost, perhaps lonely. He still had no cause to discard it. But the man at least could talk with passion to a stranger in the dark. Possibly the ocean made them intimate, the loss of land.

'I'll take the wheel if you'd like a break,' Rex said. 'I don't mind an extra watch tonight. I'm too churned up to sleep. Not my insides. My mind.'

'It's all right,' Stephen said. 'I'd sooner be here too. Don't mind me. Go ahead. Talk, if you want.'

He did. Since the war, since he left the sea, things had never gone bloody right. Farming had been a bust. City jobs finished in fights with the boss. He was lucky to get his last, but now it looked as if he might have thrown that away too. If there was one bloody thing he knew, it was that he should never have bloody left the navy. Because now he was too old to go back.

'Still,' Stephen said, attempting consolation, 'you had your share of excitement. The war.'

'What would you know about that?' he asked, with sudden suspicion.

'Not much. Too young.'

'Then you wouldn't know.'

'Not really. No.'

'At least we knew what we were on about, then. At least we knew what we were alive for.'

'I can understand that.'

'Can you? Buggered if I can. All I know is that I never had a job since that made sense. Why should it be like that?'

'Some adjust again,' Stephen offered. 'Some don't. Obviously.'

'I look around. I see men at the top. Cushy jobs. Fancy homes. No better than me in the war, and most a bloody sight worse. They slap me on the back at reunions. Good old Rex, poor bastard, he's never come right, buy him a drink. Then they bugger off quick. Then these journalists, they come along. Whatever happened to Rex Stone, they write. Bastards.'

This time Stephen could find nothing to say.

'I'll tell you whatever happened to Rex Stone. What happened to Rex Stone is he's a little customs creep peering in bags, next door to a copper, waiting for a pension so he can call it quits. Pissing up of a Saturday. Listening to his wife snarl all Sunday. With two kids he doesn't even want to know about. And a Victoria Cross he'd like to lose like a bad smell. Every time I've tossed the bloody thing out in the garden, I've sobered up and gone to look for it again. God knows why. It must be all I got. A bit of bronze with my name on the back. Me. But not me. Doesn't make sense, does it? Nothing does. That's what happened to Rex Stone. But that's not what they write. They wouldn't want to know.'

'Probably not.'

'They had a different look on their faces last week. After I volunteered.'

'I suppose they did.'

'Bloody poufters. They wanted to know my motives. Motives, they said, but what are your motives? As if it was their bloody business. I showed them the door.'

'Still, it was a natural question.'

'Nothing's natural about those wordy pricks. They twist a man's life around like he can't find it again.'

'Well, what are they?'

'What are what?'

'Your motives.'

'The same. Nothing's changed.'

'The same as when, though?'

'The war, of course. The war.'

'I don't quite see that.'

'You're not very bloody bright for a lawyer. It's a fight, isn't it?'

'In a sense, yes.'

'Don't fart around. A fight's a fight. Germans then. The French now.'

'But it's no war, all the same. Almost the opposite. A peaceful protest. Even the French would argue that they need their bomb for the sake of peace.'

'I'll tell you this. There's going to be nothing bloody peaceful when we get up there in the danger zone. They'll want us out. They'll try and get us out. And I'll tell you something else. No French bastard is going to fuck around with me. Or tell me who's boss.'

'I see.'

'I mean that. I'm not joking.'

'I didn't suppose you were.'

'If we're not here to have the French on, then it's all a bloody waste. Isn't that right?'

'Up to a point, yes.'

'Otherwise it's just a pleasure cruise, with us thumbing our noses and pissing off again. Bugger that.'

'There's probably a limit to what we can do. I daresay we'll discover that limit.'

'You're just talking bloody words. Say what you mean.'

'I mean we're vulnerable. A yacht. A half dozen men. Against a navy. Our strength is a moral one. With the world outside watching. It should embarrass the French.'

'The first French prick to show his face on this deck is going to be more than embarrassed. I'll tell you that.'

'What can you do? Punch him in the face? Throw him overboard? I can't see much future in that.'

'I'll shoot the bastard,' Rex Stone said suddenly.

'With what?'

'Never mind.' He appeared to regret having spoken.

'You've got a gun?'

'Never mind.'

'Then you have.'

'All right,' he confessed. 'So I have. And so what? Just a war souvenir. From a U-boat captain. That's all. And some ammunition. Why not? I don't know what I'm getting into on this trip. I'm entitled to protect myself.'

'Hell,' Stephen said. He froze under his wet gear; the boat swung on a heavy wave and slipped sideways into a trough. He fought to bring it round again, on course. His concentration was gone; he was over correcting. They went into a wild swing downwind, threatening to jibe. It was a minute or two before he had it steady. And could think about Stone again. And the gun. He could instantly and profoundly regret the loss of shore.

'You should have thought what it means,' he said coolly. 'What it could mean. Trouble. Pointless trouble.'

'I shouldn't have to tell a lawyer about the law of the bloody seas. Any bastard boarding us in international waters is a pirate. We can treat him like one.'

'It's not quite that simple. And there are other people involved. Beside yourself.'

Perhaps Stone took the point. Difficult to tell. 'I'm not a fool,' he said suddenly. 'I don't need a lecture.'

'So forget about it. Better still, toss the thing overboard.'

'And let them do what they like to us?'

'There's a limit to what they can do. All this international pressure. They're sensitive.'

'They can still do what they like. They can piss all over us, and what can we do? Nothing.'

'Perhaps. But a gun's only going to make it uglier.'

'No bastard's going to board us with a gun shown on deck. Or try to put us under tow. I know what I'm doing.'

Stephen then had to consider the possibility that he might. It wasn't, though, a possibility he cared to contemplate long. The point of the journey was, after all, a confrontation; and it wasn't easy to see how that might shape. Until now, and

35

doubtless for some time to come, the journey itself was sufficient for the imagination. Or his imagination. Not for Rex Stone's.

'This isn't a war. We have to remember that.'

'So we give in as soon as the French say boo?'

'Not quite,' said Stephen vaguely. 'We make our point.'

'Bugger that for a joke. I'm not here to make points. I'm here to do something. I didn't walk out on my job for nothing.'

'There's always the risk it may amount to nothing. We may never get there.'

'We're doing our best to get there.'

'True. Depending how we all make out.'

'You're in it for real, aren't you?'

'I like to think so. Yes.'

'What about Hawkins, then?'

Stephen was briefly silent, shaping an answer.

'Too much the glamour boy for my liking,' Stone added.

'Blair's all right,' Stephen said quietly, but wishing for more conviction. 'He means well.'

'What if the French throw a scare into us? You think he'll turn tail?'

'I can't answer for anyone but myself,' Stephen said. 'I'd like to think I wouldn't. I'd like to think Blair wouldn't.'

'He talks too much.'

'We have to trust each other. I have to believe you mean what you say. Blair too.'

That seemed to silence Stone; he grew quieter, perhaps thoughtful. A spiky, rather sad old man. In a buffeting world which had use for him once, but never again. Until now, possibly; and that had still to be seen. Anyway Stephen failed to see menace in the man, despite the gun. It might be no more than a personal comfort, like a pipe and can of tobacco. Nor was there much point in telling Blair or anyone else about the weapon. If need or crisis arose, perhaps. But not until. No point in breaking the peace prematurely, arousing angers and anguish; they could be coping with an explosion before they ever saw the danger zone.

'And,' Stephen said, 'don't talk about that gun again. I'd sooner not know. I'll forget it if you do. Fair enough?'

'Fair enough,' Stone agreed. And after a time he added, 'I think you're all right. I think you'll do me.'

It began to seem they might be allies, as the boat bashed on into the night.

Next morning the ocean overtook him. His stomach emptied his breakfast over the stern. There was a huge following sea, a blasting westerly with frequent rain. The main was reefed right down by mid morning; later they ran only on storm jib. Blair was stricken too. Barry Purchase and Mel Cross were still helpless on their bunks. Peter Lee and Rex Stone did extra watches.

It was a purging, the seasickness. The farewells of flesh to land. Or like labour pangs, before rebirth upon the sea.

So he told himself, when it was finished. For it did finish. Rather marvellously, miraculously. He was quite intact. Not only that; he had never seemed so solid. Or more aware when he found himself back at the wheel, on watch once again, with waves bulky across the horizon, a creature of these roaring waters, this ocean called Pacific.

Four

ON THE THIRD DAY THE WEATHER BEGAN TO MODERATE, BUT the wind was still keen under the brittle blue sky, and the ocean lumpy. Though with only scant sail, a well-reefed main or slender jib, they had made more than two hundred miles in the right direction. A reasonable beginning, but for the casualties. Barry Purchase and Mel Cross were still mostly limp in their bunks; Barry had been able to establish only perfunctory radio contact, and Mel Cross had sent no message at all to his employers. So much, then, for public relations.

For the others, now, the discomfort was in the dampness. The spray and condensation in the cabin invaded clothes, sleeping bags, bunks, pillows. There was no relief from the clinging cold, just as there was no escape from the crashing sea. Rex Stone, always awkward, had collided with most corners in the cabin or cockpit; one side of his face was badly bruised and swollen, and the bald crown of his head gashed. He didn't complain or seek attention, so the others affected not to notice either; Rex could persist in his stoicism without embarrassment. Blair looked shaky – perhaps Stephen looked it too, for all he knew, since he consulted no mirror – and certainly the edge of Blair's enthusiasm was gone, or at least badly blunted, as they settled into the dour routine of voyage in wintry southern sea; anyway he was already a Blair shrinking to amateur seaman's size, far less commanding a figure aboard. Their cool and thoughtful centre had soon become Peter Lee, perhaps predictably; out on the Pacific his efficiency was always clear, at the wheel, changing sail, cooking a meal, taking shots, and working over log and charts; it had fallen on him to hold the enterprise together with the first shock of the sea, and all would surely have been demoralized chaos without him, probably yet another abortive protest mission. He did double watches, with others ill, and often watched over Stephen, Blair and Rex in the night too; his eyes were reddened from lack of rest. Yet he showed slight testiness, and that mostly with Blair. Changing sail, with sheets swinging and winches working, he was quietly patient with Rex and Stephen as they slithered around mast and boom and wildly tilting deck, trying to follow his instructions with the wind too loud in their ears. An idiot blunder might undo them out there, shred the main or part the rigging, but there was sustenance in his reassurances; they seldom went into panic, or made for further peril, when they fumbled or misunderstood. If he was different with Blair, perhaps it was because he had expected more; their skipper was revealed as no blue-water sailor, but rather as coastal dabbler, familiar with drifts from one boozy haven to another, and often still painfully without knowledge of his expensive craft.

And there was, besides, an issue. Their first upon the Pacific. Peter wanted to take larger advantage of the prevailing weather, the wind; he wanted more sail to make more distance while they could. After all, he argued, wasn't time now the need of the expedition? If they were in earnest about getting alongside Mururoa before the French detonated their hydrogen bomb, then they put as much of the Pacific as possible behind them while they had the weather. 'We can't waste a blow like this,' he insisted.

Blair agreed in theory, but objected in practice. There was already enough discomfort aboard. More sail would only mean they took a greater pounding in the sea. They were thundering along as things were; why push it?

'The way I see it,' Peter observed, with a twitch of irritation, 'is we're pushing it anyway, friend. The whole bit, I mean. This voyage. If anyone's pushing their luck, we are. So let's talk sense and get there.'

Perhaps it was tiredness talking too, impatience with a lame and awkward crew. He deferred to Blair in the end, to the comfort of the craft, but had his way with the course. Instead of travelling obliquely northward, towards warmer waters, they were running with the weather, straight out from land, and were now more southerly in latitude than when they began. This course, and the strength of the westerlies, compensated to some degree for lack of sail; later they might pick up a change in wind to move north again. Blair had no enthusiasm for prolonging their stay in temperate waters, but finally didn't argue the course. 'Let's keep moving,' Peter said. 'It wasn't meant to be a tropical jaunt.'

The three of them, Blair, Peter and Stephen, were together over the chart table; Rex Stone was on the wheel; the others were quiet. That was when Rapa was first mentioned. Rapa? The name was alien. But it fast began to dominate their days.

Peter's parallel rule moved across the chart, demonstrating their new course. Then his weathered forefinger, with blackly bruised nail, fell on a point to the east. 'One interesting thing about this course,' he said. 'This island. Rapa. We go very close. I've been looking it up in the pilot book.'

Rapa, according to the chart, lay alone in the South Pacific. No other islands near at all.

'I've never called there,' Peter said. 'Hardly anyone does. Well off the track. The most southerly island in French Polynesia. Only three or four hundred people in a pretty primitive state. Not even a French resident. Really isolated, just a boat every three months or so, and a little radio contact with the other French islands. I found all that most interesting. Suggestive.'

'Of what?' Blair said with impatience.

'Of the possibility of using it. Calling in there.'

'French territory,' Blair was quick to say. 'A big bloody risk.'

'No way, friend,' Peter said. 'Like I see it, we just call casually. Do some quick barter, stock up on fresh vegetables and water, take a refresher ashore. Rapa's supposed to have good crayfish.

That turns me on. Also we can check out the boat thoroughly before the last leg to Mururoa. There's a good harbour, safe anchorage. We could be in and out before the French knew a damn thing, or could do a damn thing.'

'Well,' Blair began cautiously, and paused. 'What do you think Steve?'

'I like the idea of those crayfish.' He also found the prospect of his feet on any shore vastly tempting; and something which might become more so, with Rapa still two or three weeks away.

'I mean technically. Legally. The risk we're taking.'

'I think we'd just be yachtsmen in need, technically. The only risk would be if there were a French ship around. Any hint of that and we turn tail. Otherwise I trust Peter's judgment. So long as he doesn't think we're likely to prejudice the whole voyage.'

'I don't like the idea,' Blair said, 'of being held in some primitive prison on a phoney charge until the bomb tests are finished. All for the sake of a spell on some fancy tropical island.'

That thought briefly entertained Stephen. Blair sulking in some grass hut with a faded gendarme on guard. Hardly a fit residence for a hero, still less for a rogue elephant of commerce and prospective politician. An unfair thought, of course. But then Blair had the knack of making Stephen think unfairly.

'Rapa's no tropical island, friend,' Peter said. 'A freaky place, by most accounts. Bleak. Most tropical things don't grow there. No coconuts, no breadfruit. Barren hills. A mysterious place, they say. But nothing like the Easter Island statues. Just strange old fortifications up in the hills. Syphilis killed off most of the history of the place. And Peruvian slavers killed off most of the people left. The ones still around are mostly old.'

'Now you're making it sound something like hell,' Blair observed.

'It possibly is. I wasn't promising paradise. Just offering a practical proposition, friend. A chance to see everything's right before we go into the danger zone; God knows how long we're likely to be hanging in there.'

'All right. I'll buy Rapa. You too, Steve?'

'Me too,' Stephen agreed.

So Rapa was bought. In imagination, at least. At the wheel alone they could feed on the likely shapes of land ahead: hills, rocks, a quiet shore. Emptying cans for a meal they could contemplate fresher food, joke about crayfish to come. Most of all, in those thudding seas, they could consider their craft at rest in still water. The silence. An end to the creaking and pounding and lurching. Peace for a day. So Rapa was no longer a tiny name on a chart. It was a hope, a vision, a luminous thing.

For there was little else in their lives. Turns at the wheel, changes of sail. Pumping out bilges. And eating, of course, and elimination over the stern. No one washed; it was still too perilous a business on the bucking deck. And there was small point in changing clothes often; one lot of clothes was as damp as another, and in this weather nothing dried on deck. Difficult to believe there was single and substantial purpose in this endless animal existence. Animal? It seemed to Stephen finally that they were more vegetable than animal, sodden and mildewing, feeding the whims of their always crashing craft; it lived off their separate energies, using them carelessly and cruelly for sustenance, an indifferent creature of gross appetite. And in truth they soon all looked thinner; they had begun to lose weight. And the boat rumbled on. The voyage was purpose. The voyage was existence enough.

And the ocean, of course. The sea dun. The sea bright. The sea puckered up under prickling rain. The sea showing how solid waves could be. A bird or two, wheeling, departing. Waterspouts marching along the horizon. Whales heaving in dense school on some migration. Rainbows vivid across their course by day. Pallid moonbows, a ghostly surprise of the Pacific, by night.

Otherwise there was only sleep. That was never difficult, not after a watch. Stephen sometimes just fell on his bunk in his wet gear, too tired to strip. Sleep was easy. Rest was not. Sleep, banging back and forward in his narrow bunk, was as bruising an activity as any other; and there was never enough of it anyway. He never woke refreshed; he always craved more. But it was time to eat, to take another watch. Doubtless the dreams had something to do with it too. Perhaps the motion of the boat shook these startling shapes out of his subconscious. Because who, if not himself, was scripting the dreams so intricately? Once begun, they became larger, starker, kaleidoscopic; their casts were no random assemblages, but infinitely specific, laceratingly relevant. The symbols were mostly blatant, absurdly insistent on themselves, if he could choose to consider them. He didn't choose. He had no choice. He walked through wars; he strayed into dry deserts; he stood in paralysis in the middle of a city street with traffic murderous around him; he was in his office, and the place was empty of all other human presence, even the slightest particle of paper, but for the telephone ringing, trying to tell him something, if only he could find where it was hidden; a log-jam of images, colliding, ricochetting. Perhaps there was a single message to be salvaged from this confusion. Perhaps the dreams were trying to remind him that he wasn't after all anonymous, not yet; that he still had a past; that he was still Stephen West, for better or worse. He might need reminding.

Barry Purchase revived. He was shamefaced about himself, his seasickness. He began to work the radio in the aft cabin, establishing a regular routine at last, to Blair's relief. For Blair had his world again, his companies and investments, and market trends; all seemed safe elsewhere, his lifeline functioned, his identity too. Barry, something of a Maoist, stiffly of the left, didn't appear happy about becoming vehicle for this information, but the skipper was the skipper and Blair had to be indulged for the purpose of his boat. Otherwise the messages which passed from land were even more mundane: Helen sent her love, among other things. Strange how little Stephen had thought of her as land and his life receded: perhaps there hadn't been time, perhaps the yacht had become everything, with only his dreams telling him different; anyway marriage was a wilting irrelevance. Hadn't he wanted to test himself to the limit, at least once in his life? It was possible he was doing just that, with the danger zone still unseen. A conceivable corollary was that he had become self-centred; another as credible was that his self no longer had centre at all. Too soon to say. But at the wheel he wondered about Helen. About how long, for example, it would take her to find a fresh sleeping partner, or partners, as his absence lengthened; he didn't doubt she would. There was no twinge, no jealousy or melancholy at all; there was even perceptible relief at the idea of her getting on with life, her life, leaving him guiltless. His infidelity lay in trying to keep this erratic craft on course, trying to voyage out of indifference. So let Helen have her lovers as consolation.

Was he trying to tell himself something, then? Probably. It was a devious way of admitting his marriage a mistake. Not his first. His second. His first marriage might have been tragedy; his second merely a mistake. A word without dignity at all. A whimper of a word. He couldn't afford another one, another mistake. This voyage, say. Perhaps a third marriage, with the features of his bride still indistinct, lacking colour, some vague moonbow of the mind.

His watch was almost finished. Peter Lee climbed into the cockpit beside him, bearing cups of cocoa.

'We still surfing?'

'More or less. But not so hard to keep on course.'

'Perhaps the weather's slackening off.' A hint of dismay. 'The wilder the better, friend, if we're going to make good time. Not that I complain, not so far. Seven days out, and we're holding together. No one at anyone else's throat yet. I must say I wondered.'

'Me too,' Stephen understated.

'A motley lot, friend, if you look too hard. I don't try. Too freaky for me. The first week's the worst, breaking in a crew. You seem to have the idea now. Cranky old Stone too.'

He discreetly avoided naming Blair. Had some other issue arisen?

'And the other two might come right,' Peter went on. 'Anyone can. That kid seems to know his scene with the radio, so that makes him better than a passenger now. Maybe I won't be happy until we've made Rapa and those crayfish. If we get there in good time, it's just a matter of easing up into the danger zone.'

So they talked of Rapa, the safest of subjects, until Stephen finished his cocoa and went to his bunk below; and delivered himself again to dream. There was no safety there, no Rapa, no oasis in the wastelands he too often wandered. Unless it was to be found, from time to time, and fleetingly, in the curious sensation he had begun to have of Jacqueline's presence. His first wife. He had never had sense of her in his dreams since her death; but then he had seldom dreamed memorably at all until now. It was as if familiar words, in a familiar voice, had been whispered against his inner ear; and he searched for sight of the speaker.

But there was no speaker, no more than there was any precise meaning in what he heard. Just a tone, a sound of some colour, like a lingering song in an alien language; yet an unmistakable presence. And he woke to the yacht racketing on into the starkest and emptiest of oceans.

Mel Cross was by far the last to find his legs. He glided rather ghostly about the cabin one morning, bloodless, thin, grimly taking hand holds to keep himself upright in the more sickening surges. He hunted out a pen and notebook, and tried to set a typewriter on the cabin table. No use; the lurching of the yacht defeated him. Yet his persistence was admirable enough; he was trying to recall his purpose here too. Finally he braced himself in his bunk and began, shakily, to write in longhand. Whatever he was attempting took him the best part of the day. He deleted, tore out pages, frowned, pursed his lips, polished his spectacles, sometimes abandoning the affair altogether, falling back on his pillow and closing his eyes. Peter gave him no duty out on deck; he was plainly still weak. Blair, though, took much interest in Mel's welfare; he sat some time on the edge of Mel's bunk, giving him material for a mid-ocean interview. Stephen, on watch again, couldn't hear what was said. But late in the afternoon, his first and belated report in hand, Mel groped across the cockpit and down into the tiny aft cabin where Barry Purchase was making radio contact. They were down there some time.

Then, after Stephen had given the wheel to Rex and gone to help with the evening meal, the two arrived back in the main cabin. Mel quiet, Barry angry.

'Tell this bastard to go take a running fuck at himself,' Barry announced loudly. To no one in particular.

'What's wrong?' asked Blair, awake on his bunk, sitting up.

'I want to know why we've got this creep aboard, man. That's what's wrong.'

'Come now,' Blair said. 'Cool it.'

'I'm not sending any of his shit back. I'm not helping him. Not my bag, man.'

'What are you talking about?' Blair showed irritation now. He swung out of his bunk.

'If he wants to piss on us from a great height, I say we tip him overboard fast.'

'For God's sake,' Blair said. 'Talk sense.'

'He refused to put my story through,' Mel offered, though that was already obvious enough. 'I was just wondering if he had authority to act as censor, so far as you're all concerned.'

'No one has authority to act as censor,' Blair insisted. 'You're a free man.' He looked at Barry. 'Well,' he said blandly, his boardroom manner evidently beginning to surface, 'let's have your hang up, Barry. I'm sure it's nothing insurmountable. We can all talk it out, with a little patience.'

'I got no hang up, man. I'm just telling you this bit of bad news is trying to do dirt on us. That's all. You can let him get away with it. I'm not. For starters, he called us quixotic. A quixotic protest voyage, he said, in that thing he wanted me to put through.'

'So?' Blair said. 'It sounds a harmless journalistic adjective to me; I've heard it before.'

'You've got to be joking.'

'Personally I should prefer, of course, that Mel saw us as a little more realistic. But he's entitled to his viewpoint, as are we all. And he doubtless has publishers and readers to consider; he wants to write something bright and appealing. Many of them may indeed think our voyage quixotic. That's unfortunate, naturally, but it's also the way of a cynical world. People need something to justify sitting in armchairs in front of the telly while we're out here in the cold.'

'So what are you trying to tell me, man? That we have to make them feel good?'

'Ask Steve there. He's been rocking boats all his life; he's had his share of mockery. But he also knows you can't win a fight if no one knows you're fighting.'

Stephen, though, had nothing to say; he resisted the invitation to take a side.

'Quixotic means tilting at windmills,' Barry insisted stubbornly. 'I thought we were tilting at a bloody bomb. Tell me if I'm wrong, man. Tell me if I'm freaking out. Tell me if we're slogging through this shitty weather for sweet bugger all.'

'I'm not defending the word. It's his, not mine. His viewpoint. We must allow him that.'

'The hell we do. He's sharing this ship. He's eating our food. We've even been nursing him while he's down. For what? So he could report from our ship that we're a quixotic pack of fools.'

'I'm sure you're being extreme, if you think about it. I'm sure Mel didn't say we were fools.'

'I didn't,' Mel agreed. 'I also begin to regret the adjective quixotic. But I'm not prepared to withdraw it under pressure.'

'Well then.' Blair paused, at an unusual loss, looking from Barry to Mel, apparently hoping for a truce to arrange itself.

But Barry wasn't looking for one. 'It's more than a word. It's his whole tone, man. One long sneer. The creep's lucky I didn't lay one on him.'

'Look,' Blair began, attempting to remain amicable while his patience crumbled, 'Mel has quite a considerable reputation as an objective journalist. That's why I wanted him, why I got him. Because people are likely to pay more attention to what he says. I didn't want anyone obviously partisan. I had enough of those on offer.'

'Out here,' Barry said, 'he's either with us or against us. No in betweens, ifs or buts or howevers. We're in this for real or we're not. I think he should make up his mind, man. Now.'

Intellectually, Stephen supposed himself on Blair's side. Emotionally, though, he was on Barry's, with a bruised and aching body in emphasis; there were enough sceptics ashore without one surfacing in mid-Pacific too.

'I'm committed to being as fair as I can,' Mel announced. 'I can't do more than that. It's been clear from the beginning.' there was a quiver in his voice; perhaps he was feeling the sea again.

'You mean you've put your reputation on the line, that it?' Barry said.

'Yes. In a sense, yes.'

'Out here we put our lives on the line. Maybe you haven't noticed. We aren't here for a good story.'

'So you're entitled to tell me what to write?' Mel now looked in appeal to Blair. 'We did have an understanding,' he said. 'At least I thought so.'

That forced Blair to assert his grip, if he could. 'All right, Barry, I think we've talked around this enough now. We've got a yacht to sail. Let's get on with it. I'm telling you to put Mel's story through, regardless of your feelings.'

'And I'm telling you,' Barry answered, 'to get knotted.'

That reply produced distinct enough silence. Even Peter stopped scraping potatoes and seemed to be listening with interest for the first time. They all appeared to be waiting on what the silence said. Even Blair.

'You're what?' he said presently, treading carefully on unfamiliar ground.

'Telling you to get knotted. If you think I'm going to be a message boy for that crap merchant; I'm not out here for that.'

'You will,' Blair said, his voice rising, 'go back to that radio, establish contact again, and put Mel's story through. We've had enough of this.' He looked to Stephen, then to Peter, as if for support. 'It might surprise you here, but the world's out there. It wants to know how we're making out; Mel's with us to tell them. That's his job. You have yours.' There was an edge of desperation now; the weather had them ragged enough.

48

'We're here to get on with it. Now get on with it, for Christ's sake. Go back to the radio and put that story through.'

'I'd sooner put my foot through the bloody thing.'

'You'll do what I say.' Perhaps it was the largest defiance Blair had encountered in years; he seemed unable to cope, except reflexively. This scruffy student was a threat to the voyage as one tuned to his world; Stephen could see that clearly enough. With the best yacht his money could buy, Blair was now probably regretting not having bought his crew too.

Because Barry answered, 'I'm not on hire, man. I'm out here because I volunteered for something I believe in. If Dial-a-Cynic here isn't with us all the way, I vote we dump him at Rapa. The French would fly him in the best radio they've got.'

'It sounds as if we'd be better off dumping you,' Blair said. 'I should have known you were a mistake.'

'So try it. That's pretty sophisticated equipment you've got back there. There might be someone else up to it. But you'd be lucky. And I meant that about putting my boot into it first.'

'I don't doubt it,' Blair said coldly. 'Try that and I'll sue you.'

'That would make a good story too,' Barry observed.

Indeed, Stephen thought. And that, more or less, was the end of it. Mel Cross's first and only story on their voyage was never sent; Blair was blocked for the first time; and again the voyage took shape from the voyagers. That at least was never news.

Bright skies, bitter wind, random squalls; the boat banged on. Always with an austere and loveless masculine world in that cockpit and cramped cabin. Their world; the only world. Bare feet, unshaven faces, ritual obscenity, sweaty underwear, festering cuts, slow healing sores, unwashed bodies, clutters of wet gear, damp bunks, whisky off watch and functional food. The one relief from intimacy was on watch at night, while others slept, unless there was need for sail change in a squall. Mel Cross, demoralized, now evidently considered himself out of the running as a voyager; he was withdrawn in his bunk most of the day, and ate his food in silence. Barry remained competent at the radio, with weather forecasts and other information coming through, and now took his full share of watches too. He and Mel kept distance from each other, so far as they could; Mel appeared to flinch if Barry came near. Rex Stone, supposedly the weak link, instead managed in most crisis without complaint, always alert to lend a hand; and Stephen, impressed, did his best to offer imitation. Peter, now with more sleep, was the one who revelled in the wild southern run, indifferent to the cold, the damp, the daily discomforts. While the others teetered clumsily about the craft, Peter was always light and fast on his feet. On watch, long hair flicking in the wind, or methodical over the chart table, calculating distance travelled, his poise was always reassuring.

Blair was the puzzle. He grew quieter by the day. Possibly the weather. Possibly the first large clash on the yacht. Certainly frustation. Stephen watched him with such interest as he could muster; he was short on mental energy for prolonged speculation. A leader, a skipper? The Pacific left Blair merely a man among men. A stranger among strangers, even to Stephen. Their shared past, Blair's sentimental bait, shrank as soon as most things left ashore. To Peter, Barry, Rex, and possibly even Stephen now, Blair was a rich bastard with a boat. They deferred to the boat. But that didn't mean deferring to Blair. The television cameras no longer framed his face, the microphones no longer caught his heady pronouncements. He was stuck with the drear and gritty days of voyage, a reality he possibly hadn't quite foreseen beyond the cameras and microphones. Unlikely that restless Blair would ever find himself fulfilled in the trivia of an ocean journey, however satisfying to most men.

It was one of Stephen's routine tasks to listen to news bulletins on a transistor radio, to report on them to the others and interpret them, if he could. Thus he was able to pass on, for example, a message that two other battered protest boats had already turned back in defeat from the Pacific; another was altogether out of touch, possibly lost at sea. It was evident they were likely to be on their own. Unless they completed their voyage, reached the danger zone, all would be farce again. More fodder for the cynics. Yet this news appeared to stiffen the others, perhaps the challenge, the higher odds; only the indifferent Mel and puzzling Blair were without reaction.

Otherwise all Stephen could tell them was that formal international protest was again growing as the annual testing time for French nuclear weapons arrived. An unofficial report from Tahiti suggested there had already been some postponement of this year's programme. None of the French nuclear fleet had yet departed Papeete for the testing ground, a reliable indication.

Blair seemed more interested in this news. When Stephen went on watch, Blair followed him up into the cockpit.

'Well,' he said, 'what do you think?'

'Nothing much. The report's unofficial.'

'It gives us more time.'

'True. But we left things late anyway.'

'I'm wondering about our course.'

'Oh?' That was surely to be discussed with Peter, not Stephen.

'Whether it's worth freezing our arses off down here in this weather.'

'It's miserable,' Stephen agreed. 'But Peter thinks it necessary.'

'What I mean is, perhaps it's less necessary now.'

'Then have a word with Peter.'

'I wanted to see how you felt first. We've all been taking a beating out here, and God knows what there is to come yet.'

'What are you trying to say, then?'

Blair paused. 'That if we've got a chance to ease up for a bit, why not?'

'I see. Then you'd best talk it over with Peter.'

'I just don't want anyone to think I'm chicken. You, especially. I'm still in this all the way. You see that, don't you?'

Stephen hoped he did. 'Of course,' he replied. They seemed to have come a long way from that highly coloured first day out, with Blair breezily passing the wheel to Stephen, and land beginning to scatter behind. And they had, in truth, come a long way.

'Besides,' Blair said, 'we'd all like to be warm and dry for a bit.'

'Sure. No one's arguing.'

'I think we could win Peter over.'

'We?'

'Together we might make the point more effectively.'

'It's your boat, Blair.'

'Right. But I like to see you as our political brain aboard. Well, not a commissar, exactly. But something like. Someone who can weigh up the practical pros and cons of our tactics.'

This was new to Stephen; he tried taking it in. As Blair's portable conscience, in Helen's acerbic view, he had so far been satisfyingly neglected; he had been content with trying to command the rituals of ocean survival, the craft of seamanship, as just another voyager. Absurd, he supposed, to imagine there might not be more.

'Don't think I'm trying to pass the buck,' Blair added hastily. 'You know that's not my style.'

Possibly true enough ashore; that other world. But here? Reservations were all too possible in this world, even if left unspoken. 'I still think it's your affair,' he insisted. 'Between you and your navigator. It's not as if life is at risk. Or that there's any question of turning back. That might be different. Easing up seems a relatively small issue.'

That, at least, cheered Blair. 'Good. I'm glad you see it my way. I didn't want you to think it might be the thin edge of the wedge. That I might be starting to back out. So you'll talk to Peter with me?'

'If you think it's necessary, then.'

'Great. Incidentally, I wouldn't say our problems are small altogether. This communication problem. And friend Mel seem near some nervous breakdown at the moment.'

'You brought him aboard.'

'I wasn't to know Purchase would turn out such an unreasonable young bastard. That's another point I was coming to.'

'Oh?' Points were coming to the commissar thick and fast suddenly; more might make a thorn bush.

'I'd like to drop one or both of them off.'

'Where? Rapa? That's not on. You heard what Peter said.

They could be there months before being picked up, and God knows how they'd finish up. The French might treat them as spies; they've already made noises about protest boats really being cover for espionage.'

'I've looked at the chart. If we headed north into warmer waters now, we could take a break at Rarotonga. Friendly territory. Pleasant island. A bit of healing ashore for a day or two. I might even find myself a new radio man. At least drop Mel off if he's no better. No use heading into the danger zone with this situation aboard.'

Blair sounded altogether reasonable; but then he usually did. Later that day they conferred over the chart table with Peter. Blair eloquently put the case for a new course to Rarotonga instead of the present one to Rapa, and stressed Stephen's agreement, given the evident delay in the year's nuclear testing. Stephen found it unnecessary to say much at all. Obvious that Blair only required his presence. Perhaps Blair sensed some trust and respect between Peter and Stephen, something he might use to help his case; perhaps too he was singed by Peter's suspicion. After all, it wasn't the first time Blair had pleaded for the comfort of the yacht.

Peter listened patiently enough. 'First, friend,' he replied, 'we can't be sure this isn't some French trick. To delay protest boats making for the danger zone while they get on with it.'

'You think we're that important to them?'

'A nuisance. Maybe even a big nuisance, if we play it right. They know we're coming. Sure; it might be worth a phoney report.'

Blair found it necessary to catch Stephen's eye at last. 'What do you feel, Steve?'

'I think,' Stephen said slowly, 'that it's more likely the French are going to pretend we don't exist. Until they have to. Until we're actually there. After all, the Pacific's on their side too. Three other boats are out of the running. Any luck and we might be.'

'All the more reason for getting there fast,' Peter said.

'Or all the more reason for making sure we get there at all,' Blair objected. 'You can't call it a happy boat. The way things are.'

Peter didn't counter that. 'That's your business, friend. Mine's getting the boat there.'

'So I think we need to reorganize ourselves,' Blair said. 'Offload one, maybe two. Get this communication thing right. Sorry, I can't see it any other way.'

'Another thing,' Peter said. 'When we move up to Rarotonga, we get into the trades. More time lost. We'll be fighting into the wind all the way to Mururoa. When there is wind. I've been becalmed a fortnight up there. Down here we've got the wind on our side.'

'But what have we got but Rapa?' Blair asked.

Peter tired of debate suddenly. 'True,' he agreed. 'Okay, friend. We'll play it your way.'

'Our way,' Blair insisted. 'We've got to be in this together. At least the three of us. There's more to all this than seamanship; we have this human problem too.'

'Who hasn't?' Peter said.

A new course, a fresh tack, more sail. They were moving north, towards the sun.

Five

IN THREE OR FOUR DAYS THE RISE IN TEMPERATURE WAS perceptible; the yacht had more graceful motion in seas less ugly; perilous squalls were mostly of the past; and they added sail as the winds slackened. Within five or six days the warmth made it possible to wash comfortably, by stripping on deck and dropping a bucket over the stern. It was also possible to eat with ease, sleep less tortuously. Sleeping bags, pillows and clothes dried on deck in the sunlight; the chill and stench of the cabin diminished. Everything, in truth, became tolerable. Watches on the wheel were no longer so demanding, especially at night, under skies dense with stars, with waves lapping in phosphorescent lines from the bow; it was even possible, on quieter nights, to rope the wheel lightly for self-steering, and to sit and let an emptied mind fill with such peace as the unrolling Pacific offered. In this way Stephen often felt divertingly himself. Interesting, if not altogether curious, since he had always considered himself more social a being than most; he would never think to dismiss his publicly active and aggressive past as disguise. As an excuse, possibly, if Helen and Freud had it right, but never disguise. Yet much of himself seemed a tattering, peeling mask on a night watch; he became some primitive consciousness locked magically in flesh and bone; he could hear the beat of his heart along with sound of wind and sea, all rhythms one with the world. As if he were rediscovering the word peace as a lost hieroglyph in the language of men. Yet this personal truce was hardly purpose; he had almost to shake himself awake to regain sight of the voyage as something driven by the despairs of a larger world, a world elsewhere. So his new delight in privacy, given emphasis by the sweaty intimacy of the cabin below, seemed an illicit thing. A perverse satisfaction of the senses, yet one with no fire in the flesh. Anyway he resented intrusion, an end to the spell, as when Rex Stone climbed into the cockpit, long before he was due, to offer Stephen early relief on night watch. Stephen was never in haste to give over the wheel.

'What do you do up here at night?' Rex asked. 'Think?'

'Sometimes. Mostly I just go blank; I prefer that.'

'I talk,' Rex said.

'I see.'

'I talk like hell. You wouldn't believe it.'

'Try me.'

'First off I thought I was just talking to myself. Then I decided I must be talking to God. Funny. I didn't think I believed in the old bastard. I never seen any sign of him in the war. Or the peace, come to that. Under this bloody sky though, all those stars, you start believing in something. Maybe you got to, to stay right. You don't think I'm spooked?'

'Not at all. Not now.'

'Good. I don't want you to think I'm going off my nut. It seems we got the makings of that aboard already. I don't know what's been going on, and I'm buggered if I want to know. So long as we get there. You think we're still doing the right thing?'

'I like to think so.'

'Me too. I'll tell you one thing, I'll go bloody berkers if we're conned out of getting there. I mean into some tropical joy-ride instead. I'm no fool. There's only a couple of buggers aboard I trust. You and Peter. I don't listen. I just watch. I wouldn't of told you about my talking up here if I didn't trust you. You see that, don't you?'

'Of course. And I'm grateful.' And indeed Stephen seemed to be. Moved, at least.

'So what's the guts of our skipper, then?'

'He just wants a stable situation aboard before we move into the danger zone. He thinks our journalist friend might be on the edge of a breakdown, among other things.'

'What about that radio kid? He want to dump him too?'

'Possibly.'

'Well, I don't blame him there. He looks like another one of these protesters to me.'

'I thought we were all protesters here.'

'I'm talking about these buggers in the streets with banners.'

'I see little difference, technically.'

'You got to be bloody joking mate. I'm no fucking protester. I wouldn't be seen dead with those hairy bastards.'

This strained Stephen's patience. 'Then what,' he asked, 'are you here for?'

'To help you boys out.'

'I should think that makes you a protester of sorts. Even second hand.'

'Don't sell me that shit. Helping people's what it's all about. That's what we're all here for, isn't it? To help each other.'

It was hardly for Stephen to argue. 'I see,' he said, helpless.

'I reckoned there ought to be someone with you who knows what it's all about. Someone to give the French a real run for their money. Maybe even blood noses. Otherwise we're just shouting slogans in the streets, like those other moron bastards, until the French make us piss off. There's not one of you been in a real stoush before. You're all kids playing at it.'

'That's hardly fair. There's been damn little play so far.'

'We'll see,' Rex said. 'We'll see who gives it a go. I already got a fair idea. I just keep it to myself.'

'I think I told you we all need to take each other on trust.'

'Please yourself, mate. I take what I find, always have. I don't say I ever found bloody much. But that's the world.'

'So what do you talk about, to God or whoever, up here at night?'

'I tell him I haven't quit yet.'

'That's something.'

'I tell him I'm still doing my bloody best, I can't do more.'

'Fair enough too.'

'So don't hand me this stuff about being a protester again. I'm here to do a job. It might be the job God had for me all along. To fight anyone fucking up the world. Not piss around protesting. You see?'

Stephen tried to, though he was tiring now. Soon he surrendered the wheel to Rex, and groped down to his bunk below, to see what his new dreams might tell him. But before he slept he did see, with some surprise, that he liked Stone for his simplicity. Perhaps envied him; certainly trusted him. Elsewhere might have been different, but he was not elsewhere; distinctly not elsewhere. Neither he nor Stone. They were trapped together aboard this tiny boat bound towards trouble, some kind of trouble, even the biggest trouble possible, and there was comfort in his kind of man upon this ocean. And a relief to see something real at work among the trivia of a voyage, even if just a man in imagined conference with the cosmos while he held the wheel.

So Rapa, that unlikely landfall, now gave way to Rarotonga in what passed for cabin conversation over meals. No vague barren outpost now; a tangible tropical island ahead. Coral sand, warm lagoons, and frangipani. Peter knew it as a yachtsman's rest; Blair had glimpsed it from a cruise ship. Yet for all they could say, it still seemed to Stephen less real than Rapa, less real than the use his imagination made of the place; he could regret that loss. Rarotonga offered nothing to the imagination, Rapa everything. So his dreams now manufactured Rapa, compensation, consolation; at least he assumed the place to be Rapa. He was drifting, with unfamiliar companions, into quiet waters. Deep quiet waters with a windless, crystalline calm. Above were the gauntest of hills cut into cryptic shapes against a sky empty of all cloud. An angular place, rocky, razory, with little vegetation to offer softness or green to the eye. And silent; no birds sang across the water. There was a beach, though, a curve of dull-coloured sand with huts beyond, smoke rising, figures moving in the sunrise. Their craft drifted still closer, until the hills seemed almost to overhang them, with no evident power pushing them on; there was no wind, no motor. Now the brown figures ashore were fast gathering on the beach, each becoming distinct, standing separately, with no animation at all. They were looking, just looking. Statuesque, smooth, graceful. What was it in their eyes, though? Perplexity, or more? Then the boat was bumping, scraping, against land; there seemed some profound message in what the hull was saying, a gentle communication, or communion. Easy of understanding. An end to the ocean, all oceans. An end to the voyage, all voyages. An end to pain and peril, all pain and peril. That sense of an end was large enough. But for what beginning? Ropes were thrown, brown arms upraised; land lay like an open door ahead. And Stephen still searched the silence, and and strange eyes of the onlookers, for the truths which might be told there, as he waded shakily ashore, and fell. Was he embracing the shore? Possibly. But it had an explicitly and vivid fleshy feeling under his arms; a human flavour. It writhed like a suffering, living thing beneath him; or like a body in the precious torment and heat of love; and yet again he had sense of Jacqueline.

In daylight, with an albatross circling the crosstree, or a whale rising to starboard, it was Rarotonga, of course, which now lay somewhere beyond the brightening horizon, the slender and serene clouds. It was all good sailing. They often had the genoa up, or a full spinnaker tugging them towards a landfall. Even Peter was resigned to this new course, relaxed enough again; he often stripped naked and lay full length on the deck, drowsing, offering himself entirely to the sun when the demands of sail were few; or sprawled lankily on his bunk, guitar cradled, plucking tunes which he hummed and sang. Blair began to shave for the first time, even splashing on after-shave lotion liberally, when satisfied with his civilized face in a mirror; perhaps the radio told him all was well ashore, and prospering. Still more now, he appeared the only one with large concern for what was left behind. Natural, perhaps. He undeniably left more behind than anyone. Though it wasn't this, for the most part, which he talked about to Stephen as the days lengthened pleasingly, as they rocked toward the even more pleasing certainty of Rarotonga. He wanted intimacies, trying to revive the confidences they shared in student days, two decades and much of an ocean behind.

'This new marriage of yours,' Blair said. 'It's been all right?'

'Functional,' Stephen said, reluctant to talk at all. 'I mean it works, mostly, with no great damage done. What more can you ask?'

What more indeed? He would like to leave it at that. He would like simply to watch the passing water, feel the warming sun. That was all he and Blair should be sharing now. But that couldn't, wouldn't, be enough for Blair.

'An attractive girl, your wife,' Blair observed. 'Lively. I saw her on the stage once or twice. I'm not an utter philistine, you know; I still make the theatre now and then. She could act, all right. She must have loved you a lot to give that away, you lucky bastard.'

'She gave it away herself,' Stephen said quickly. 'Nothing to do with me.' That was the best face to put on it. The truth was the theatre had given Helen away. She had begun to make difficulty for directors; her talent, it seemed, wasn't sufficient to make her temperament acceptable, her erratic personal timetable, or her drinking. But that of course was not all that Stephen saw. He had also seen, indulgently, a vulnerable and childish creature who needed stability and feared rejection more than most. Given to tantrum and abundant bursts of self-pity, true, but also to moods of rare and refreshing sweetness. And that was something new. Stephen's life, as it lengthened after Jacqueline's death, had been desert enough. Yet this new union, casual at first, was more than oasis. He and Helen seemed to help each other. That warm sexuality in Helen's bed appeared to make most things possible. It certainly made for a child, something along with marriage to give Helen fresh grip on life. With stability the rest might vanish, the tantrums, the drinking, the despairs. So much for hope; a poor shrunken thing now. For at the worst Helen's version of their still rather meagre past was indistinguishable from the one Blair offered: he now heard often, too often, just how great her sacrifice had been; and silence was his only useful reply. Silence and evasion, lest unreason become flood. That was how things were now. Now? That, surely, was no longer now. Now was a yacht leaning into Pacific wind, and Blair beside him. There could never be a present tense more credible.

'I still say you're a lucky bastard,' Blair went on. 'She was bloody great up there on the stage. Vital. Funny and sad. Loving it all as much as the audience did.'

'Probably. Yes.'

'She must have been something pretty special to you,' Blair said, still probing. 'After your first time round, I mean.'

'Possibly.' He might have conceded the point altogether if pressed. Even in Helen's flashy drunken times, a gift of life seemed to shine; a gift he was often too slow to grasp. From fear of burned hands again? Jacqueline's death had left enough devastation for one man's lifetime.

'That first woman of yours. I never got the strength of her. Strange girl.'

'In a way.' He had first encountered Jacqueline about the time Blair began the drift out of his life. Blair met her once or twice then.

'Not that she wasn't attractive. I don't mean that.'

'No.'

'Bloody striking, in fact. That long black hair. And those eyes. I remember those big intense eyes, God knows why. I can still see them looking at me now. Not as if I talked to her a lot. She never had much to say to me. Deep waters there, I thought, too deep for me. Not quite of this world.'

'True. And she isn't now.'

'She probably never was your sort, old man. I hope you don't mind me saying. I mean I've never known anyone more of this world than you are. I don't know where you find the energy. Even I'm envious. You must have felt like calling quits sometime.'

'Indeed.' But Stephen stayed reticent.

'All those cases. All those causes. But then we all lust to get off the treadmill sometime. Why don't we? Perhaps we are now.'

'For a day or two,' Stephen conceded, and watched the flowing water.

'You can't say we didn't need this break. We were taking a hell of a hammering down there. All right for Peter, he's in his element. Ashore he's a fish out of water. We're not like that. There's a limit to what we can take.'

'Sure.' Though Stephen was frustrated again by the prospect he might never find it; how regain that ecstasy he first felt in high southern seas? And how explain it? It was entirely elusive now, unless in dream.

'Anyway,' Blair resumed, 'I must say I was surprised, a year or two later, when I heard you'd actually married the girl. What was her name again?'

'Jacqueline.' Curious how difficult he could still find it to pronounce so straightforward and familiar a name. Difficult? Painful.

'Surely not, I thought. Surely not her. But then I saw you somewhere together. You both looked all right, so I guessed you must have something going for you. Something I couldn't see, maybe in bed. At least I hoped so. And of course I heard the other news in the end. Word got around, the way these things do. Bloody terrible. Too late now to say I'm sorry, but I was, of course. I think I sent you a card, I was out of town for the funeral. If you don't mind me saying, I wasn't surprised, though. Not really. Some instinct at the beginning. I knew she wasn't right for you. But if I'd said, you wouldn't have listened.'

'Probably not.' Decidedly not, given Blair then.

'So there we are. We make our own beds, dig our own graves. Sorry; that wasn't very apt.'

'It's all right.'

'We certainly make our own bloody beds anyway. Take me. I ought to know; I've only made the one.'

And a comfortable one. Blair had married money, of course, as well as a more than presentable woman in a well-publicised social event. Probably not, to be fair, as a speculation; more likely he was embracing an inevitability along with his bride. Money had its own magnetism and Blair was already well on his way. Stephen saw with some relief that Blair was not talking about himself. Perhaps that had been the point, all else preliminary, of this hour in the sun; Blair's need to make account.

Mel Cross shuffled past them, white, shaky, now incredibly thin, and tried to find a place to make himself comfortable further forward on the deck. Neither Stephen nor Blair made comment; the man's appearance was sufficient commentary on his condition. His passing, though, left a pause until Blair collected himself again.

'Yes,' Blair said. 'It's still all a bloody mystery.'

Stephen was lost. 'What is?'

'The marriage bit. What people want. What people are.'

This was still obscure enough. 'What do you mean?' Stephen persisted.

'It isn't as if I haven't done my best.'

'In what way?'

'Every way. I don't mean just marriage.'

'I see.' Though Stephen didn't yet, couldn't.

'I know you don't care much for my kind of success. Probably don't approve at all.'

'It's been your life, Blair.' He doubted that Blair wanted judgment anyway. Sympathy, perhaps. Not judgment.

'Right. My life. All I've tried to do, would you believe, is keep myself interested. Otherwise I'm a dead man. And if keeping myself interested means having to prove I'm smarter, faster, than the next man, then that's the way it has to be. I don't know any other way. I often wish to God I did. You know what terrifies me most? More than death? Boredom. Bloody boredom. There are times when I risk everything I've got, throw every cent into the ring, just to stop myself losing interest. Just in case I get bored. Try that for laugh of the year.'

Stephen was silent.

'Come on. You must have an opinion. It's no joke. I just have to go on. And on. I could have quit with comfort years ago. But I don't have another game to play.'

'You've been talking politics.'

'Right. In case there's some other way to stay alive, kick boredom out the door. Besides, I like the idea I might have just been getting ready for something else all along. That make sense?'

'Of a sort.'

'A hell of a thing, if you think about it, to go running scared of boredom all your life. Building barricades. That's really my scene. The barricade business.'

Now he was asking for sympathy and possibly commanding some, with his perplexed face. Certainly Stephen couldn't be too short with him. 'I can imagine worse,' he offered.

'Can you? Maybe. On the other hand, if it's all been for something, perhaps it's for the good after all. I mean, like learning to run human affairs efficiently.'

'Or justly.'

'A just society is an efficient society. Don't misunderstand me there. It's just that it comes down to the old cash nexus in the end. I haven't forgotten my Marx. The economic base. The bread, man. If you've got the bread, you can do most things.'

'Like running a yacht to Mururoa.'

'Well,' Blair agreed, 'yes. But I was trying to talk generally. Take a big view.'

'We have a fairly big view at the moment, as I see it. Likely to become bigger.'

'You're in this for real, aren't you?'

'Well,' Stephen said, 'aren't you?'

'Of course I believe it's worth trying to see what commotion we can make. But I can't kid myself it's everything, not any more. It must be the day to day thing. The difficulties, the people, the weather. Lately I've had to look around and remind myself why the hell I'm out here. Then I see you. That helps.'

'So I seem to be some use.'

'And I don't just mean for my sense of security. It's someone real to talk to. You wouldn't believe some of the morons I mix with for their money. In some of those boardrooms I feel like a kindergarten teacher. As for things at home –'

Blair found it necessary to meditate for a moment.

'Yes?' Stephen prompted.

'I do my best, give her all she wants. Of course I've strayed, but never too far. Nothing like that. We've got a couple of reasonable kids. No complaint there. If they turn out to be dreamers, or rebels, that's the way the game goes. Right? With my money they can afford to be both. A Hawkins dynasty's not my bag anyway. Instant empire's more my scene. All for today. Tomorrow might be old square one again. No, it's nothing like that. It's just bloody baffling.'

It was even more so to Stephen. 'What is?'

'Ruth. My wife. The way she's gone.'

That left Stephen to contemplate the possibilities. He didn't find many. Suburban neurosis? Infidelity? A young lover?

'I've done my best,' Blair said with grievance. 'We have these kids, a big house, swimming pool, another house by the beach, this yacht, plenty of travel. I've never been one to neglect the family side of things, never. I try to keep everyone happy. I thought we had been. Until now. Now I learn it's all for nothing. Our lives are bad news, she announces, our lives are empty. Right, I tell her, speak for yourself. Get on with it. Do your own thing. Famous last words.' Blair at last appeared bitter. 'First off, it wasn't so bad. Social work. Meals on wheels, running round old age pensioners. Fine, worthy; no grumbles from me. Next it was art. Gallery openings. Sherry sipping. There are worse ways to spend a man's money. And she tells me it's good investment and brightens up the house. I don't have to understand, she says, just to look and let my vision flow where it will. Which means I flow towards a stiff whisky. Still no grumbles. But then, well, you name it, she's got it. Yoga. Transcendental meditation. Encounter groups. Vegetarianism. Organic foods. The whole bit. Suddenly my home's not my own. I have to go out to dinner if I want a steak. I can't bring an associate home for a drink because I might find my nearest and dearest freaked off in some trance. I can see her in the street soon with the Hare Krishna crew. Incense and bells. What the hell's going on, Steve, just what the hell is going on?'

Stephen shook his head. Despite Blair's dismay he was nearer laughter than consolation; his own problems appeared conventional. He managed, anyway, not to offer the cruelty of a smile.

'Strange times, Steve. Here we are, we should have it made, and what's happening? Everything topsy turvy suddenly. No one believing in it all any more. Or believing in anything. One thing I thought about this trip, it sometimes makes things seem simpler. Right?'

'At times,' Stephen agreed.

'Anyway it put some new juice into the home, before I left. When I announced the trip, Ruth was impressed, all right. The first time I'd got through to her in a year. Even the kids didn't take me for granted any more. It seemed I was cool after all, man. They even introduced me to friends. Their crazy cat of a Dad. The whole place was different.'

'Well, that's something,' Stephen suggested.

'True, Ruth wanted to have it that I was striking the first great blow for the age of Aquarius. And what, I asked her, in God's name is that. The coming, she tells me, of man's new Christ consciousness, the end of the cruel age of Pisces. The new thing, you see. If it keeps her happy, fine. Only I told her not to expect the full Christ bit. I mean the crucifixion. I'm just sailing the yacht to Mururoa to foul up the French, I said. But she had her answer to that too.'

'Oh?'

'Sure; all the answers. Pisces, in case it's news to you, was the age of man's crucifixion. Aquarius is the age of man's resurrection. No way I could win that one. Still, I can't complain. Things in bed looked up. There was certainly some Aquarian resurrection there.' Blair grinned now, boyishly, and slapped Stephen's shoulder. 'You get your share too? No complaints?'

'No.'

'So roll on Rarotonga. They tell me the girls are great. Rapa, that place sounded a drag to me. Old ruins. Old people. Ghosts. Next door to hell.' He produced a mock shiver. 'Give me the old palm trees and coral lagoons. And a few of those lusty island ladies swinging grass skirts. That's more our scene. Especially after what we've been through. The rest and recreation bit might do wonders for the boat. Four months is a long time off marital duty, right?'

'True,' he agreed, hoping Blair heard no relief in his tone. This turn in the conversation, though, put Blair's desire for change in course, and different landfall, in interestingly fresh perspective; the ocean was no test for Blair's virility, no substitute. To be fair, as he still rigorously tried to be with Blair, that was

66

probably only one factor; the rest wasn't altogether rationalization. But doubtless a factor, all the same. As much, say, as Mel Cross, who crept past them again, clinging fearfully to the rail, on his way back to his bunk.

'Poor bastard,' Blair said briefly. 'I should have known better.'

'Yes,' Stephen agreed.

'No telling how anyone will turn out. You get the feeling we're all watching each other?'

'Often,' Stephen said, and rose to take his afternoon spell on watch.

Six

AT MIDNIGHT STEPHEN WOKE, REFLEXIVELY NOW, NEEDING NO
call, to relieve Peter Lee. His dreams for once had been painless,
even peaceful, fragments and echoes of land left behind: places
rather than people, a ferny beach, a willow-hung stream, a bay
hugged by muscular headlands. Familiar, yet not quite within
memory's reach, pictures in a puzzle; but untroubling nevertheless. Likely explained by the fact that the yacht was almost
motionless; anyway dreams this time easy to lose as he dressed
lightly for the warm night, and climbed to the cockpit. Peter
was sitting comfortably, one casual hand on the wheel, his
face lit thinly by the glow of the compass, with the brilliant
sky behind.

'Light airs,' Peter observed. 'You just have to take what comes
now, and be grateful. A breeze now and then. Go with it. It
means we might sail twenty miles to make good two on the
course. Always better than nothing.'

'Impatient?' Stephen asked.

'I'm learning.'

'Learning?'

'Never a trip, friend, when I don't learn something.'

'About what?'

'Myself, mostly. If I listen to what the sea says.'

'So what's it telling you tonight?'

'To go with it. That we'll probably get there, in the end.'

'That's comforting anyway.'

'You sound an impatient man too.'

'True. Rarotonga wasn't my idea. But it makes some sense.'

'Not if the French put the balloon up before we get there.'
Peter's drawl was pleasantly slow, seldom emphatic.

'The balloon?'

'Above the atoll, friend. That's how they hoist the bomb for a detonation.'

Perhaps something fresh to feed his dreams. He took the wheel from Peter; the sails were slack, beginning to flap. 'A bit to port now,' Peter advised. And Stephen found the main filling slowly. Peter, however, made no move to go below. He sprawled back into a corner of the cockpit, took a pouch from a pocket, and made a thin cigarette. Stephen gave this act no attention until Peter lit the cigarette, drew on it slowly, and then held it out on offer.

'No thanks.'

'Come on. A reefer does things for a night like this.'

'Is that what it is?'

'If you've no objection, friend.'

'Of course not. It's just that I haven't smoked.' He had defended enough marijuana cases, often to police frustration, to know it wise to keep himself clean. Helen might sometimes smoke pot elsewhere with friends; he insisted on elsewhere, insisted on not knowing about it at all, the way things were. Or the way he was; not a square necessarily, but someone who didn't care to consider his work undone for the sake of an idiot possession charge. There were more than a few policemen who might crave such a charge. And an end to the irritation he provided.

'There's always a first time, friend. And we're a thousand long miles from the law.'

'Yes; I expect we are.' A thousand miles from such as he still had of his life. Certainly from his office, from Helen. And what was Helen doing now, at this hour of night? His imagination was reluctant to propose answer. He should care more, surely. He should care a great deal more.

69

'So come on. It won't bite. It does things for tension.'

He was holding the reefer tentatively, putting it cautiously to his lips.

'Take a deep draw,' Peter said, as mildly as he might supervise a sail change. 'Hold it down a while before letting it go. Then see how it feels.'

He felt nothing. Or a small prickling in the lungs, perhaps, before passing the reefer back to Peter. Nothing more.

'Give it time,' Peter said, drawing again himself. 'Don't expect too much first time off, friend. Here. Try again.'

Still nothing. Just the sea, the wheel in his hands, Peter friendly beside him, the glow of the diminishing butt as it moved between them. And the compass. They were still wandering way off course, following the breeze. Rarotonga? Remote. Mururoa? Remoter still. At least he could care about that, it seemed; his impatience still functioned, if not his imagination.

Peter said, 'When people ask what makes me a pacifist, you know what I tell them?'

'Go on.'

'I tell them the Pacific. I tell them the Pacific makes me a pacifist. And they think I'm joking, playing with words. Only I'm not, friend. I never joke about the Pacific. Something's got to be sacred, right? Everyone's got some secret, tender thing. And that's mine. Only it's not something I can keep inside me, or in a box. It's all here, friend, all around. All happening if you look.'

'I see.'

'Can you? Give it a try. Always a first time for that too. Just take it in slow, and see what it does. Same thing. It's a dirty world back there ashore. A sick dirty world. All that fighting and kicking, biting and scratching, grabbing and hating. Countries; people. Okay, so there's the loving and laughing too, the better bit. But after a while ashore it's the dirt that gets to me. It won't wash off my skin, friend, I can't rinse it out of my mouth. Until I'm out here again.'

It might have been the reefer talking, but it didn't seem irrelevant conversation. Not then, there.

And Peter, it appeared, was still talking. 'I like to think of one good clean place left. One pure place. So I'm all hung up on the Pacific like a woman who won't quite have me, friend, and that's why I'm here. On this boat. Anything to stop those sons of bitches pouring their poison into the place. What does this ocean mean to you?'

Stephen tried for honesty; truth appeared a steep hill to climb.

'Something,' he said finally, 'we have to get across. To do what we have to do.'

'No more?' There was a shade of disappointment in Peter's tone.

'Not much. No. An irritation, in a sense; there's too damn much of it. More than I counted on, I expect. I'm learning too, you see.'

'Sure. But it's dead to you, all the same.'

'Dead?' He had to consider that. Again a steep problem. Until his answer surprised him, as if an ambush had been sprung. 'Perhaps. Something like that. More a kind of death. Strange territory. Alien. Non-human. Nothingness.' He faltered, precision gone, and unable quite to find it again. Since he hadn't contemplated so vehement an answer, he had to discover just where it had taken him. And that was stranger still. 'Just bloody nothingness. One version of an after-life, I expect. We become like disembodied spirits out here, lingering on with memories of life left behind.'

A ferny beach. A willow-hung stream. A bay hugged by muscular headlands. Floating images which drifted back toward him, making sense after all. For, as if returned to dream, he knew them now. Places once shared with Jacqueline; places where they knew a short peace. And enough happiness to hurt him still. It may have been the largest happiness they had, that lazy honeymoon, before Jacqueline began her long and always perilous journey away from his side, his bed, his increasingly forlorn love. Love? Why shouldn't he confront the word? It still had sufficient truth to shock him. And leave him silent, shaken, beside Peter Lee with only an ocean as comfort.

'Right,' Peter said. 'So something's got through to you anyway, friend. Either the Pacific or that reefer. Or both. You all right?'

'Of course.'

'Just a touch to starboard now. That breeze is back again. If you're feeling queer at all, I'll take over. I never mind a double watch on a night like this.'

'I'm all right,' Stephen argued. 'I'm as fine as I could be. Great.'

He could hardly be more insistent.

'No dizziness, nausea?'

'Nothing. Everything's fine.'

'Some people go into a spin. If you find yourself flying too high, give me a call. Otherwise I'll get my sleep and give the night to you.' Peter made a huge, embracing gesture toward the ocean, the sky, before descending to the cabin. 'Here's the Pacific, friend, up for grabs. All yours.'

Then it was, in wholly stunning truth for Stephen. Surely there had never been a night more his. The ocean was an elegantly moulded mosaic, solid, shimmering. And the sky was a mystery of a million lights. The fragile breeze upon his bristled face gave him more than path upon the water. The compass was irrelevance; their course too. He had only to go where the ocean took him. And this freedom, if first frightening, soon become a shining door. He had only to let that light breeze ease it open to find himself nothing, everything; to find himself Stephen West, husband, father, lawyer, liberal, bewilderingly one with a landscape of light, a guest in most exquisite of gardens. Nothing, everything? A lover, merely. Necessary, for who else was there to cherish so vast a night? Without him, it all might cease. The breeze die; the intricate texture of the sea fracture and flatten; the stars sputter out, one by one, into cold and loveless dark. So Stephen West, then. Guardian, wheel in hand. Lover.

Love. Love, then. Surely the fittest of subjects for such a night.

There was no shame in confronting the word. Rather, relief. For who now was here to judge a man with lingering love for the dead, a love too cruel for the living? No man. Just mute ocean, indifferent stars, if he cared to look again. People once told him of his need to pull himself together; and perhaps he had, to their satisfaction. With his work, of course, and finally a fresh marriage. It had all been seen to be done. Yet he would most care now to imagine Helen tousled with passion, fondling flesh as fevered as her own, in some stranger's bed; or even their marital bed. That, perhaps, for preference. That, possibly, in compensation. For it left him even more free. Nothing now shocked on such a night. Let Helen arrange her solace in the dark within the space he left; he had his own.

He had, of course, sought others. After Jacqueline's death, a month or two after, he was visited by a well-meaning friend of hers. Not a friend to whom he ever felt especially close himself; he always saw this woman as someone in the shadows of life, too much like Jacqueline, and thus no real help to Jacqueline at her worst. A friend he might have preferred her to forget, and whom he certainly forgot after the funeral. But she came nevertheless, diffidently, into his house; and sat nervously, drink in hand, seemingly sensitive to his judgment, afraid of his hostility, as her conversation took a wandering course to the point. It appeared that this woman had lately gone to a sensitive of some kind, a medium. For her own purpose; she wanted a reading, advice on her life. This told, Stephen's disgust was doubtless as visible as his impatience with the woman. He did his best to hide it by fetching himself another and larger drink. Still more flustered, the woman went on to say things had gone wrong, the reading all awry. For what she received was not advice on her life but, according to this medium, a visit from a friend. A friend who had lately taken her own life. A friend who had things to say, messages to pass. A friend who, above all, hadn't wanted to hurt anyone, and was sorry now. Who else, this woman asked, could it be but Jacqueline?

That ended it. 'Get out,' Stephen shouted. 'Get the bloody hell out of here.' It seemed the reasonable thing for a man to say; and Stephen was eminently a reasonable man. And the confused woman went. He hoped never to know of her again. All things being equal, that might have been the case.

But all things were not equal, or equal to his capacity to control them. His drinking, for example. He was no longer using alcohol as a support. Alcohol was now using him, in still more ingenious experiments. He often woke cold on a couch, in a brightly-lit living room, with only a blank and hissing television set to tell him of yet another night passed. And yet another day at the office ahead. So there was his loneliness, then. And his indecisions. Whether he might, say, dispose of the household he had made for Jacqueline, and find himself a smaller place. Whether he might give up his practice, travel for a time, learn more of the world. Whether he might make his life afresh, and whether there was point. Even whether, or how, to rid himself of Jacqueline's clothes in the closet, where her scent still lingered; surely the simplest of things. But nothing was simple now, nothing small, and the pills his doctor fed him did nothing to make them less complex and large. They added more confusion than ever, given the alcohol too. There was certainly nothing on prescription to diminish his sense of failure. If he could fail one human being, what arrogance had he to suppose he could do anything for humans in number?

Soon there was more. At first he could only, and reasonably, suppose it was his drunkenness deceiving him again; his blackouts becoming more frequent and frightening. His partner's patience, in the office, was already under too great a test; friends had even ceased offering the inevitable dinner invitations, since he failed so often to arrive. If they came to sit awkwardly and soberly with him in the evenings, they offered the same message: He mustn't blame himself. They argued that he had done his best, only too obviously, through the most difficult years. Jacqueline, they said, had always been Jacqueline. A lost cause, they implied, if seldom quite putting it so indelicately. He might have replied: What the hell had that to do with love? If he didn't, it was because a question could never make for an adequate answer. That question: What the hell had a lost cause to do with love? As well ask why the entire race was a lost cause, so negligent and cruel a scenario of evolution, creatures conscious of pain and death; creatures whose most enthusiastic and single-minded activity was the creation of still more pain and death. As well ask why anyone, given that, should be worth the love and grief of another. And that was no question to be asked in academic inquiry. It was one to be lived, one to be survived.

So he tried that, teetering along the slender lifeline his work gave him. Until there was too much more to take. His drinking, those blackouts, made enough explanation for a time. Despite everything, after all, he was still a reasonable man, capable of rational inquiry, rationalization, in a world only too solid to his senses. There were the elements burning red on the electric stove when he arrived home late at night, having already eaten and with no intention of preparing further food. There was his alarm clock jangling when he couldn't recall having wound it; or failing to ring, stopping altogether, when he had. There was his crumpled bed when he had remembered, for once, to make it carefully. And there were Jacqueline's clothes, tossed carelessly from the closet, and her scent wholly announcing itself in their bedroom again. He could cope with some method, of course. He could remove the fuse from the electric stove. He could buy a new alarm clock, guaranteed against disorder. He could remake the bed. He could even hang Jacqueline's clothes carefully in the closet again. And then, those things done, find himself still another drink.

Finally, though, he found himself telephoning Jacqueline's friend. The one to whom, it seemed now, he had been so atrociously rude, when she merely meant well, within her vague lights. At first, his nerve beginning to fail, he only offered apology for his behaviour. Of course, she answered, she understood; he had been under strain, and she had been imposing unfairly. This left the conversation, rather, at a standstill; he found it quite impossible to persist. But she, with instinct, then saved the situation. So you want to know, she asked, about my medium? Is that it? It was, of course, and it wasn't. He desperately wanted to know, and as desperately didn't. Just say, she went on, I'll understand. He had never felt more a fool.

And no less a fool later when, a telephone number given, an appointment arranged anonymously, he discovered himself, far too sober, knocking on the door of an inconspicuous suburban house, as sanely set as any other around, with tidy shrubs, flower

75

beds, recently mown lawn; the commonplace made his mission all the more lunatic in the fading glow of a summer day; he had good reason to flee before his knock was answered, too quickly, by a slight grey little man, with a faintly mincing walk, and a mildly precise voice.

'Ah, yes,' he said, with no preliminary. 'I've been expecting you. And someone else has too, I think.' He led Stephen swiftly through the house, down a passage, and into a small room which he decorously styled his sanctuary. There, again with no pause, as soon as they sat, he began with the business of offering Stephen the woman he saw. A presence. Someone once close to Stephen, and still as close to him now. He described Jacqueline then, or some creditable likeness, in fine detail; he didn't even pause for Stephen's confirmation. But he did shake his head in bewilderment, or dismay. Seldom, he explained, did he ever encounter so powerful a personality. He was being bombarded with too much at once; she had too much to say. 'Please.' he said to his unseen presence. 'Please, please.' Then to Stephen, 'I'm sorry. It's really quite extraordinary. You must have patience.'

For the fraud to continue, Stephen imagined, for the lines in this farcical script to be recalled. He could not suppose otherwise. Jacqueline's description must have been won from her friend; he saw a plot furtively arranged for his consolation. He should have known better than to trust the woman. To have ever allowed himself this idiocy. Next would come the conventional messages, Jacqueline's happiness in the beyond. It was time to leave. He almost did.

But then, 'That's better,' the quaint little man said. 'Much better. She's slowing down now. She wants you to know she's been deeply troubled. Lost. For a long time. Hurt. Suffering.' The man looked up, seemingly surprised. 'I'm sorry; but that's what she's telling me. Did she take her own life?'

'Yes,' Stephen admitted with reluctance. Surely Jacqueline's friend, in this plot, had conveyed that crucial information? And if not? He was unwilling to think what that might mean.

'That explains it then. Explains what she's telling me. You see, she's saying she did it for you. To save you more hurt.

More damage to your life. Does that make sense to you?' This time he took Stephen's silence as confirmation. 'She's saying she meant it to save you. But she thinks it was wrong now, because it hasn't helped. That's why she's been so lost, wandering. Because of you; she's been trying to tell you. To say that it's too late now, too late, you must make the best of your life, with things as they are.' Another pause. 'Clothes. Does that make sense? She's trying to tell me something about clothes. Her clothes. I see. Yes. What she's saying is you must get rid of her clothes, her things, get them out of the house.'

That, true, was a small shock. Stephen had confided in no one about that problem, or about the clothes tossed crumpled on the floor, her scent again pervading the bedroom. But there was more.

'And she's saying you must find someone new. Someone to look after you this time, give you more support in your life. Someone to cook for you when you come home at night, someone to see that you keep reasonable hours. Someone to share your bed. She's been trying to tell you, she says. Do you understand? She wants you to understand not just for your sake. Hers too. Because she'll know no peace until you do. No rest. She's asking if you understand that. She'll know no peace until you do. No rest. Is that clear?'

'Fairly,' said Stephen, with a deep breath, his voice strange; the dim sanctuary had begun to suffocate.

'Because she loves you still, she says. Because your life is important. Because you have large things to do yet. You have to live.'

All conventional enough after all; a relief. It might be all downhill now, escape almost in sight, shrubs and flowers and mown summer grass.

'Now she's telling me something about a message,' the man said. 'A farewell message she left for you.'

'No,' Stephen said quickly. An even greater relief to contradict the man at last. For Jacqueline had left no suicide note, nothing written. Not that explanation was especially needed. The man was guessing now, and poorly.

'Oh.' A pause. 'I see. Yes. Yes.' He looked into his cupped

hands for a time, then looked up again at Stephen. 'She's saying now you didn't get it, didn't understand. And poems. She's also saying something about poems I don't understand. Did she write them? Did she write poems? Is that it?'

Again he was poorly prepared, if conspiracy were the case; or just a good actor, showing plausible bewilderment. Anyway he waited upon Stephen's confirmation.

'Yes,' Stephen agreed at length. 'She did.' Jacqueline's verse, with its cropped lines, jagged images, had some distinct and respectable critical reputation. There had been only the two small volumes in her lifetime. Otherwise she burned all that Stephen could not save. Towards the end she wrote little at all, perhaps at the limit of self-scrutiny; or because the act of utterance did nothing for the wounds of the world, much less her own. Stephen never quite knew.

'Wait.' The man held up his hand. A dramatic pause: over dramatic. 'She's shaking her head most vigorously. No, she's telling me now. No, not her poems. It seems I've misunderstood. She doesn't mean her own poems at all. I see. Yes. Now she's offering me the colour brown. Brown, quite distinctly. Yes. I think she may mean something in a brown book. Would there have been a brown book open somewhere in the house, perhaps on a desk, when she passed? Something you might not have noticed, brushed aside or put away?'

'No,' Stephen insisted. The truth anyway was that he had little memory of those first hours, first days, following his discovery of her cold and bloodless body on their reddened bed: the emptied bottles of pills, and the ruthlessly slashed wrists to make the act more certain. The truth was only the terror he knew; the reality was even more lacerating than his darkest expectation. For their life together had been rich in warnings and withered premonitions. A brown book? A book of even more remarkable hue, any book, might have eluded him in that daze of guilt and grief; most tangible things did. 'No,' Stephen repeated, if a shade more tentatively. 'There was no book. Not that I recall.'

He had to remind himself that it was all farce and fraud anyway. Absurd to answer seriously this mild little charlatan, or madman. What the hell was he doing here? Why hadn't he gone?

'Strange,' the man said. 'Most strange. She does seem quite insistent, quite angry about it. A book. Poems. Brown. And a desk. You did have a desk in the house?'

Another fair guess. 'Yes,' Stephen agreed.

The man shook his head. 'I must confess, I'm afraid, that she's not coming through so strongly now. Perhaps it's her anger affecting the communication, making it difficult. These moods do, you know. She seems as if she's being pulled away. Much fainter. She's still trying, rather urgently, to say the same things. As if she's afraid of being lost again. You must find peace, she's saying, you have important things to do. For her sake too. Her sake too. And that book; she's still trying to make you understand about that book, as if it's important. She seems in some distress now. Look, she's saying, look for it. Really quite desperately. She –'

Another pause, lengthening.

'I'm sorry,' the man said finally. 'So very sorry. I do appear to have lost her altogether. Most unusual, after such a strong beginning. As if she hasn't quite found her feet, having difficulty on the other side still. You must understand it isn't easy for some to communicate. Not easy for them or us to get these messages through. They want so anxiously for us to understand that they're there, still with us, and so often we misunderstand.'

'I expect we do,' Stephen said, tolerantly, as he stood. Whatever else the business had been, it was at least a capriciously convincing performance, worth all the five dollars he left behind, pushed swiftly into the man's hand before he walked briskly down the darkened path, smelling the grass and greenery, to his car. He opened a solid door, gripped a solid wheel, and took comfort in a substantial engine speeding him away from that confusingly conventional street.

Madness, of course. He should never have allowed himself the luxury. Luxury? At five dollars a time it was modestly priced consolation for most, if they chose; a long-distance telephone call might be more, with even less chance for lengthy intimacies. He was left chilled, for all his disbelief, on this mildest of summer evenings.

For home again he was aware most of the silence, the emptiness, the lack in his life. Drink in hand, fast more mellow with whisky warm in his stomach, he failed to telephone Jacqueline's friend, as he had promised he would, after the experience; he would prefer never to talk to the woman again, recall anything of the insanity of that hour in the house of a mincing little stranger who peddled his delusions to the gratefully deluded. Nevertheless, after a time, he was standing beside Jacqueline's desk, trying to recall what might have been there on the day of her death. For the desk had long been cleared of its usual clutter; he had been thorough in that respect, if few others. Any books once on the desk would have been shifted to the shelf behind. For the most part that shelf held verse, her favourite verse, volumes winnowed from her reading since adolescence. Not a large collection. Her own two volumes. A few 19th century writers. For the rest, mostly predictable names: Yeats, Eliot, Thomas, Lowell, Auden, Roethke, Plath. There was, of course, no brown book among them; or none announcing itself boldly as brown.

Another guess gone wrong; his relief was huge. He began to turn away, turn his back on the pointless enterprise altogether, when a name tugged at his eye. Not a colour; a name. And not Brown. Browning. His hand, all the same, appeared to be shaking distinctly as he removed the collected work of Elizabeth Barrett Browning from the shelf; he found some need to replenish his whisky glass, and did; he found equal need to sit down for a time, book and drink in hand, and did; he also found the silence of the house quite unnerving in its resonance. It was still some time, though, before he let himself put his drink aside and allowed the book to fall open, where it chose, on his lap. There was no note within, no marker, no need of one, since the falling pages knew their way: suddenly he had lines familiar to a million lovers, but now something as strange, freakish, as a summer flower rising through frost: 'How do I love you? Let me count the ways . . .'

Jacqueline, if it was her, and who else, had chosen to underline only the two last lines of the poem. Not merely to underline them; to encircle them too with thick black pencil so there should be no mistaking her meaning, and perhaps her despair. Yet the lines themselves could hardly be less ambiguous: 'I love you with the breath, smiles, tears, of all my life. And if God choose, I shall but love you better after death.'

It seemed all silence ceased. Time too. It might have been a minute or an hour later when he rose unsteadily, crossed the room, a dizzying distance, and inserted the book clumsily back in the vacant place on Jacqueline's shelf. He could not imagine himself having need of the book again; he knew the words.

He tried later to make himself understand, of course. Sanity said he must. For a month, two months, three months, he plundered bookshops and libraries in silent search of anything which might help his understanding; silent because, after all, who was there to tell? Jacqueline's odd woman friend? Never. When she rang him finally, impatient for news, he said simply that he had failed to see the medium; he had changed his mind; he hadn't patience with such maudlin nonsense. 'Oh,' she said, dismayed. 'I was so hoping . . . but if you feel like that, perhaps it's better.' 'Yes,' he agreed decisively, and ended the conversation. Which disposed of her, and probably of fraud too; in any case that hypothesis was no longer needed. There were others in abundance. Everything in the end was explicable. Everything could be answered to his satisfaction, if he wished; and he did so wish.

It was all of the mind, it seemed, of his subconscious, some ferment of the unexplored psyche. His experience was in no way more extraordinary than a thousand others. The poltergeist effect in his household, for example: the business of the stove, the bed, the alarm clock, the clothes on the floor. That was a product of psychokinesis, the action of the mind, in some manner still insufficiently understood, upon the physical world. The result, often, of a disturbed condition; in his own case, doubtless, his subconscious insisting upon the imperatives in his situation; his subconscious running amok among material things to tell his conscious mind something in the most dramatic way it could. As for that mild little medium, he was probably honest within his understanding, or misunderstanding, after all: merely a man who, unlike most, had found and then widened a slender channel to his own subconscious, and also in some way telepathically to the subconscious of those who sat with him; he had discovered and dramatized Jacqueline not in the beyond, but within Stephen; small wonder the poor man, at times, suffered confusion in searching out messages in that alcoholic murk. Easiest of all to explain was the message in the book; Stephen's subconscious had very likely noted the page, glimpsed the message, while he cleared Jacqueline's things from her desk; his conscious mind had been too clogged with grief to comprehend what he saw. The knowledge of that message had been waiting all along.

And the dead? They were, after all, safely dead. They did not wander lost, suffering, in some outer dark. If they had existence at all, messages to pass, it was within the minds of the living. That was no news.

Jacqueline was gone. He should never have doubted. Perhaps he never really had. If her flesh had emptied itself of spirit, while life bled away into their bed, it was simply to take up fresh residence within Stephen himself. That was easy to see. Only too easy.

For clarity was no longer difficult. That was the one undeniable miracle he found. His drinking diminished while he searched for satisfying answers; it became an irritant, obstructing his concentration. Black coffee was now more his need in the lonely nights at Jacqueline's desk while he read, took notes, considered clues to the condition of men in their perishable animal flesh.

In their office too his efficiency returned; he could carry his workload, even send his partner on holiday. His routine was regular; there was no further disturbance in his household. Jacqueline's clothes, of course, had been dispatched to charity; there was little of her left in the house, not even that lingering scent in the closet. All was orderly, more or less, with Stephen West offering a presentable and in no way haunted face to the visible world: lively lawyer, social activist, man of conscience, widower, and reasonably attractive and available male. He made few demands on women, expecting few in return; his energy largely went to his work. And that widened the more he went at it, the more he became known: causes knocked at his door, fell on his desk, pleaded on his phone. With Jacqueline no longer taxing his ingenuity, he had time to offer, and patience. Remarriage was possibly inevitable, even if it had to be Helen. At first she seemed willing enough to accept his life as he most needed to live it. They made, some said, an interestingly complementary match. Their child might have been inevitable too; another gap filled palpably.

A child might have made a difference to Jacqueline, their marriage, though he reasonably doubted that now. She had as many breakdowns as miscarriages through the years; she might never have been a fit mother, and a child another cross for Stephen to carry.

Not that there wasn't one still. When Jacqueline's poems were published again, posthumously in collected form, finding much attention, mention was always made in reviews and articles of her tragic finish. True, he felt almost no pang, and little embarrassment, since people no longer seemed to link her much with Stephen West, an unlikely partner for such a woman anyway; he had small or obscure place in the little legend of her life already bearing strange fruits and which might bear fruits still stranger in time. It could become altogether unreal to remember that he had nourished that plant at its most tender, in a hundred menial ways, even cherishing the task, offering love as compost, patience as shelter, while he dispensed drugs and drink, nursed her hysteria, salvaged her grubby manuscripts, tidied away the broken glass and smashed furniture, healed the wounds petulantly self-inflicted, and laundered her clothes clean of blood, vomit, wine, mud and even, yes, the spilled semen of other men.

A rare, fine and gentle spirit, the critics said, plainly haunted by the horrors of the world, the suffering of the flesh, the crippling of the spirit, with war, disease, violence; and who fetched abrasive and disturbing symbols from her psyche to say what most of mankind might prefer to leave unsaid. Stephen, in contrast, of course appeared a single-minded, altogether practical and pragmatic man, with a touching and unimaginative faith in his capacity, and the capacity of others like himself, to better the traumas and ills of man as they paraded with slogan and banner; and who failed to see first causes, the spiritual crisis of modern man, his rediscovery of evil and his new Godless fragility before the fact. (As Jacqueline, they said, so grievingly saw.)

How to explain to anyone, since he couldn't entirely to himself, that Jacqueline had been his first real cause, his impetus? It was a matter of doing what he could, how he could. His own thing. Even Jacqueline saw that, had understood. Her dismay, really, was that she was so often distraction. Anyway it was something not to be said to the young scholars with interest in Jacqueline, and theses to write, who on occasion sought information from Stephen; and who received so cold a welcome from Helen in the home. On one such occasion Stephen discovered, when reaching for them, that Jacqueline's books had vanished. Or been banished.

'I married you,' Helen explained later. 'Not her. It's time we understood each other.'

So it appeared. If not a turning point altogether, it passed for one. After that Helen's discontent began to demonstrate itself, at first mildly, then distinctly; impatience with his lengthy hours at the office, at meetings or elsewhere; impatience with his inadequacies as husband and father, even as provider. 'If you'd just settle for being a good lawyer,' she told him, 'we might be a damn sight better off. We might even buy a better house. One I could call my own. I've never felt this place was mine anyway. It was hers, yours and hers.' And again, 'I didn't give up my career to keep television company in the evenings.'

When there had been no question of her giving anything up; when the issue had been their child and such security as he could arrange. But if he was articulate, it was in the office, in court, or on a platform; not with Helen in the home. There, reason rebounded coldly in his face, after striking one frigid obstacle after another. She began, after announcing herself prisoner of his whims, his pride, his past, his reputation, his grotesque conceit, to search out other company, old friends;

she began, she said, to enjoy life again. He was able, genuinely, to say he was pleased. At least he was able, with less troubled conscience, to get on with his work, not only with the daily detail of the office, but also with the larger things which might make that detail tolerable. Which might make, in fact, life tolerable; his life. Without point, the point Jacqueline demonstrably failed to find, there was – what?

Well, perhaps Blair's telephone call to his office one Monday morning. This yacht searching for wind. This night, this ocean. This nothingness; this facsimile of death. He understood, at last, why more restless men sometimes found need to sail the sea alone, given the world. Not love of life, the challenge of living, which drove them; nor necessarily love of death. No. More the hope of making truce with their own ultimate anonymity, their extinction; a premature peace.

The afterglow of the reefer had gone. Ocean, night and stars all settled for saying no more than they could to a man tired at the wheel and frustrated again by sails gone limp. It was exactly two in the morning, and Rex Stone was rising to take his turn on watch.

'All right?' asked Rex cheerfully.

'Fine. I just hope you have more luck in finding something to sail with.' He left the wheel to Rex gratefully.

'Never mind,' Rex replied. 'I'll soldier on.'

'You do that.' This old man, anyway, was never less than real.

'I won't talk tonight,' Rex announced. 'I won't talk out loud.'

'No?'

'I'll whistle instead. The old salts reckon it sometimes works. To bring a breeze up, I mean.'

'Anything's worth a try.'

Anything? The question followed him down to his bunk. Anything? The answer seemed, after all, to be yes. Anything. This journey certainly, wherever it led.

So he found sleep while Rex, above, whistled bravely and altogether tunelessly for a breeze. And Stephen's sleep for once, that night, seemed dreamless.

Two, perhaps three nights later, risen at midnight again to take over from Peter, he was given something unexpected; a sensation he could never have foreseen. More than marijuana could offer this time. Much more.

All smell; a saturation of the sense. An entirely stunning thing after three weeks or more on barren sea. For it found instant and mellifluous echo in every other sense too. A smell with sight, sound, touch and taste. A warm green smell of soil and leaf, abundant growth and abundant decay, and queerly of human fires and fevers too. Of life, enough of it to leave any spirit singing.

'Land,' Peter announced, as if it were necessary to say. 'Rarotonga off to starboard.'

With morning, little said, they watched the spiky peaks, grey and blue with early haze, then coloured with sunlight, grow fast and tall above the sea. Soon they could even hear, and see, the surf beating white upon the coral crust of Rarotonga. Land, life? It shrank visibly to an island, this slight island. No mystery at all. An entirely, absurdly comprehensible thing.

Seven

TWO ANTIC DOLPHINS FOLLOWED THEM TOWARDS RAROTONGA'S shore, first weaving in their wake on the brilliant sea, and then swerving ahead, leaping, scattering spray before their bow. The coconut palms ahead grew higher: pale buildings began to obtrude from the dense greenery of the island. They reefed, and began lightly to motor into Avatiu boat harbour. The entrance was narrow, tricky with coral and tide, and Peter worked the wheel with caution as they left the ocean behind.

A last wave, a surge forward, and they were clear of coral. Flat water, rippling reflections, a throbbing engine; they could hear the calls from shore. And observe the gathering crowd there, cars pulling up, antique buses, people running to see. There were dozens of hands to grab and secure the ropes they threw as they moved into a mooring. There was singing; there were guitars; there were flowers.

For here they appeared to be heroes again, at least, and something more. One again; together. Barry, on his transmitter, had given the islanders warning of their arrival that morning. With the motor silenced, all was a confusion of island voices, and song. Girls climbed aboard, with the customs men, to garland them with flowers. Frangipani, tiare Maori, hibiscus, in leis and headlets; the girls were far from shy; they giggled with delight as they moved from man to man.

There was even a local politician, a plump smiling man, calling for quiet, until his face shone with the effort. When silence came, it seemed he had things to say. Rarotonga, he announced, welcomed all seafarers with peaceful purpose; and none more than the men of *Moana Nui*, the men of the yacht named for the great Pacific, who were so bravely offering themselves against those who would harm the inheritance of Tangaroa, mighty god of the sea. The children of Tangiia and Karika, those immortal ancestors who claimed Rarotonga from the Pacific in a century long gone, rejoiced to see such voyagers. The man might have made more of his theme, since he appeared merely to be finding its measure, had not applause intervened; and another song of welcome, with drums and dance. And if the tired men of *Moana Nui* had not begun to step ashore.

'My God,' said Blair, aside to Stephen, 'this is more like it. To think we mightn't have made this scene.'

Even Stephen, then, could hardly feel the loss of Rapa. Dream, all dream, perhaps the worst of the ocean too. His legs shaky on the land, he felt drunk with the heat, the colour, the sound. He might have fallen without brown arms in support. Mostly female he supposed, but his eyes stung too blindingly with sweat and sunlight to see. And the scent of the flowers was smothering. If only the shore would cease to sway.

There was an ancient ambulance waiting for Mel Cross. Mel was helped towards it, limper by the moment, fitted comfortably inside, and driven to hospital. The end of that, at least; it couldn't have been swifter, cleaner, for anyone's conscience.

The others? Rex Stone, ancient voyager, freshly grey-bearded old man of the sea, was every bristle the part, the sailor in port with tales to tell, something he hadn't known since the navy. He was among elderly islanders, instant friends, laughing, joking, gulping hugely from a brown bottle of beer pushed into his hands. Barry Purchase was borne away somewhere, among girls entirely entranced by his red hair, bright beard, and possibly his youth too. Only Peter Lee remained aboard, quietly and inconspicuously moving barefoot around the boat with method, making sure all was tidy, the moorings secure. He at least seemed not to have forgotten his role.

Nor Blair, in his way. Unmistakably skipper again. Having shaken hands with the politician and passed amiable conversation, done the diplomatic thing, he had moved on to another man, a European, a journalist obviously, with pen and notebook: a rather fat, jaded, and red-faced man in floral shirt. Stephen was near enough to notice the smell of the night's whisky. The man, it appeared, was some visiting antipodean writer, preparing a tourist piece on Rarotonga, who had happened along by chance, and now might have a scoop of sorts. No Mel Cross, probably; but Blair would doubtless make do.

'Tell me the truth now,' this journalist said aggressively. 'Have you buggers quit?'

'Far from it,' Blair said coolly. 'I think it's quite apparent that we're well on our way to Mururoa.'

'A bloody long way off your course.'

'For tactical reasons. Human ones too.'

'Trouble aboard, is there?' The journalist scented possibilities. Despite the whisky, he might be quick to the kill. 'You got some strife?'

'We're all in this together. A solid team. It just so happens that we had a man ill, as you might have seen; we couldn't risk him on our hands in the danger zone.'

'And that's all?'

'Enough, surely.'

'So otherwise you're a fine bunch of heroes.'

'I didn't say that.'

'I'm not quoting you; I'm not that stupid. To tell the truth, what I think is beside the bloody point. And you know what I think? That you're a shower of mad buggers on an ego trip.'

'I could find that offensive, if pushed. As it happens, I don't want to spoil the day. Or improve your nose. So don't push it.'

'I've got to get something out of you. Look, Hawkins, you're well enough known back home. For wildcat schemes, among other things. And there's some think this is another old load of Hawkins bullshit, that you're just up here to fuck around for the fun of it again. You don't really think you're going to fool the French, do you? Try telling me different.'

'I thought I had been.' Blair stayed impressively calm despite the heat, the still thicker crowd around. 'But please yourself.'

'All right. Let me try again then. Purpose. What's your real purpose? About three sentences would do. Even two. Or one, if you're short. Something fetching for the masses. I'll do the rest.'

'No doubt.'

'I'll take it down slowly. Even read it back slowly. Come on, now. Name your poison.'

'Try Strontium 90 for size.'

'All right, you want melodrama, I'll give you melodrama, with trimmings. But you know better than that.'

'Perhaps.'

'So what about something realistic?'

'I'm trying.'

'Purpose, then. Your purpose here.'

But Stephen had heard enough; his first delight in land was gone. He moved away, among people slapping his back again, people trying to shake his hand, while Blair began, in one sentence, or two or three, to elaborate on purpose.

Purpose? Before long there was larger cause to ask the question. It seemed to perish soon upon the pale sand and black soil of Rarotonga, under the swarming palms. That is, when land at last ceased to move beneath them, the hazy hills grew solid, and the crowd dispersed. Not that they were ever left to themselves; not that they were often with themselves. True, Peter got on with the business of refitting and replenishing the craft, usually with Stephen's help, and using every day as yet another chance to check that they had a safe ship for the danger zone. Blair, for the most part, appeared anxious enough about their needs, but was seldom visible when the work was done, supplies loaded or rigging renewed. If money were necessary, though, it surfaced without problem before Blair departed again; his problems seemed to be elsewhere. He had, certainly, a great number of telephone calls to make, with reliable communication ashore, and without Barry's grudging mediation on the boat's transmitter. Mainly business, perhaps, and to his wife; he also said he had rung newspaper editors. 'Just to put a stopper on that drunken quisling bastard who met us,' he explained. 'We've got to get our story straight before he does any dirt.'

'I didn't think our story could be straighter,' Peter observed mildly. 'That is, friend, if we're still going straight into the danger zone.'

'No one's going to make fools of us,' Blair insisted.

'That,' said Peter, again as mildly, 'depends on us.' There seemed to be a question left lingering in everything he said to Blair. 'It depends on us, friend, on what we do. Not on newspapers.'

'If we're made a laughing stock, it kills the value of what we're trying to do.'

'Let them say what they like, then,' Peter said lazily. 'The newspapers have their world. We have ours.'

That, naturally, was difficult for Blair to see. Peter's truth was most vivid on the ocean, in cockpit or cabin, as the yacht pitched in a swell, or heeled into mild wind. Blair was ashore again, a man of other and many affairs, newspapers and stock reports among them.

'So I think we should set a sailing time,' Peter added.

'Right,' Blair agreed, 'but there's no panic.'

Stephen's latest information from the transistor radio was that there was still no sign of the French nuclear fleet leaving Tahiti for the testing grounds. An Australian protest boat had problems in the Tasman sea and was turning back; the missing yacht had arrived in Samoa. They were still on their own, and would be, unless others put to sea as promised.

'We have the trades yet, friend. All the way. They'll set us back more than you know. We should be there when the French get there. And in their way.'

'Fair enough,' Blair said. 'But there's a problem or two yet.' He showed no desire to be specific. 'I'll get things sorted out.' And he left them, then, to get on with problems more precise around the boat.

91

Peter was the only one who slept aboard; he had no apparent inclination to leave his familiar bunk, or walk land for long. In any case someone should remain with the yacht, in case of tampering or pilfering. Blair and Stephen had the comfort of motionless beds in the ramshackle hotel nearby. Mel Cross remained in hospital, and then was flown home. Rex slept wherever his revels left him; he had reverted to shore leave, navy style, his boat mostly forgotten so long as there was land under his legs, a bar open, and willing mates around. Failing an open bar, there was often a bush-beer party around the island to be searched out, with ever more willing mates. If he called at the yacht, it was almost as if only to check that they hadn't sailed without him; his eyes were bright and never other than amiable, lit with alcohol, and his conversation confused and garrulous. Yet he hadn't quite forgotten their business. 'We'll show them,' he announced, offering fists to a mock opponent. 'We'll show the buggers. We'll show them all.' He might never have left the navy, or lost his youth in some suburb ashore, as he swaggered away with his friends.

Barry, on the other hand, altogether disappeared. His belongings remained aboard the boat, one reminder he was with them, but that was all. Last seen, he had been still enmeshed with flowers, among some equally colourful Rarotongan girls, on his way to a party around the other side of the island; he never returned. His transmitter was conspicuously quiet in the aft cabin. Anyway there was less use for it now, with efficient communication ashore. And there were, after all, no watches to be kept on the Rarotongan nights. He was hardly missed. Or, if missed, not needed.

In truth all they needed, soon, was a sailing time. That depended on Blair. Most of the local politicians and dignitaries, and Rarotonga had a spectacular number for so slight a population, had already been pleasantly cultivated by Blair; and possibly more than one or two women along the way. There was a limit to other sights: the island could be circled at moderate speed, in an aged hire car, in forty minutes. Stephen and Peter tried that for a couple of days, bathing at Muri lagoon, when they could do no more for the yacht.

'Something's getting at me, friend,' Peter announced, drying himself down. 'Something's giving me the message that our skipper's got this big new love affair going for him.'

'Oh?'

'With land. He still feels he's something ashore. And nothing out there. Or nothing much. None of us are anything much out there.'

'I wouldn't say that, exactly.' His companions, after all, were never less than substantial aboard the yacht; sometimes too sweatily so. 'I wouldn't say that at all.'

'I would. It's the beauty of the thing.'

'I see.'

'If you don't, friend, you will. Give yourself time.'

It seemed more threat than promise. But it was not the day to consider the problem, or feel the threat real, under the feathery shade of the ironwood trees by the lagoon. When they had used such sun and sea as they could, to pass time, they drove back to Avatiu boat harbour. There, Blair was waiting on the yacht, with cold cans of beer in the shaded cockpit, some islanders keeping him company.

'Well,' he announced, 'I think it might be cool to consider making a start again.'

Peter's relief, at least, was visible.

'Besides,' Blair went on 'our very good friends here are anxious to fix the date of our farewell party, give out the word, and get the feast ready. Rarotonga wants to do us proud, even if the French don't.'

That was no news. The only real news would be that the French nuclear fleet had made move from Papeete harbour. Not that they had to wait upon that. Still, there might have been more urgent cause to decide departure than the need to fix a party date. But who was to be ungrateful for small mercies? Not Stephen. Nor Peter, plainly. The islanders with Blair were presenting the warmest of smiles, their goodwill as real as Rarotonga had become through the hot days dragged out in the boat harbour. The handshakes had long ceased. There were just the inquisitive children, giggling, pointing, about *Moana Nui* now.

'Well,' Peter said. 'The sooner the better, friend. It doesn't take long to cook a pig.'

'There are ways of doing things here,' Blair answered, possibly expert now. 'Their ways. We're among friends here, allies. The best of friends.'

Again evident enough, too comfortably so in the case of Rex and Barry, both still lost somewhere ashore with bush-beer and girls respectively. The islanders were smiling in emphasis again as Blair passed around fresh cans of beer.

'You want to know the big word on Rarotonga?' Blair went on. 'Apopo. Tomorrow. You might say it's the equivalent of manana in Mexico. So let's fix it for apopo, then, and that should give us three or four days to get clear.'

'Fair enough,' Peter agreed, gratified by something definite at last; as definite, anyway, as Rarotonga could make it. He took a beer can from Blair and sat down, allowing himself to relax loosely.

'All right with you too, Steve?' Blair asked.

'Any sailing time's fine with me. So long as we do.'

'That's what I like to hear. We're all still making this scene together.' This was likely said for the Rarotongans, or to convince himself briefly, because later, taking Stephen aside, he had a rather different story. It concerned Barry.

'I might as well tell you,' Blair said. 'I've reached a dead end.'

'Finding him, you mean?' It seemed unlikely. The island wasn't that large.

'No. I'd sooner we lost the young bastard, the way things are. He not only buggered up Mel. He buggered up most of our chance to get the world press on our side as we go. Apart from downright defying me. He's bad news and might get worse. God knows what's ahead. I don't trust him.'

'He's been doing his best. The other was according to his lights.'

'Not mine. It was a bloody blackout.'

'So what's this dead end?'

'Finding someone else. Someone who can use that transmitter effectively. That way, we can drop him off, sweet farewell and bloody goodbye. I've been hunting the island. There's no one, or no one available. We could get someone flown in, but that might be a couple of weeks. I don't think we can take that.' Still, he looked at Stephen with some inquiry.

'No,' Stephen agreed firmly. 'We can't.'

'All right. So it looks like we're stuck with the bastard now. There's no one else. You better go find him, talk him back aboard. He speaks more your language than mine.'

'I thought you were the one who remembered your Marx.' Stephen didn't mean to needle.

'I'm not ashamed of my Party days.' Blair's answer was sharp.

'I wasn't saying that.'

'Part of my education; I've always argued that, and never cared who heard. Essential curriculum. You've got to understand the system to beat it. Freedom is the recognition of necessity, the old sport said. Well, I got my freedom; I recognized what I needed, and went out and got it.'

'For yourself.'

'It seems I didn't leave much behind anyway. Slave camps. A bloody butcher by name of Stalin. Hungary. Which didn't seem to be any future that worked for anyone. All I'm saying is these young bastards don't know anything. Don't want to understand. Too much of a drag. They want to rubbish the world without even knowing how the wheels turn. At least we did, I did. Right? And if we wanted our hands on the levers, it wasn't to grind the wheels to a halt. It was to get the wheels working for everyone, not just for a fortunate few. All right, then; a bad dream after all. But it wasn't meant for the worst. And if I turned out one of the fortunate few, that's my good luck in the lottery. Apart from which, I wouldn't have this yacht out here.'

It had been said before, of course. But it was easiest said in the calm of a Rarotongan boat harbour with sunset fading from the hills, and a guitar playing somewhere ashore. Nothing here quite insisted on relevance; nothing could ever be assertive in contradiction. But Blair, in the end, managed to regain the point. 'Will you find him?' he asked. 'For one thing that transmitter should be checked out, and a new routine established, before we sail. Communication is going to be crucial from now on. So far he hasn't been near it. It seems he couldn't care less.'

'I think he cares, all right,' Stephen said. 'Given the chance.'

'Well, go give him the chance. Get the bastard back here.'

Next day, then, Stephen hired a car again and drove around the island, stopping at villages and trading posts, asking after a red-bearded young *papaa* recently arrived on Rarotonga. Yes, most said obligingly, they had seen him round. Here, and there; last week, and this week. Mention of Barry could spring the largest of Rarotongan smiles. Not that it made things any easier to find him. But he did at last discover Barry, near nightfall, on the veranda of a house built high up a hillside, overlooking reef and lagoon, among fruiting citrus groves. In the last light the oranges seemed to produce their own illumination, glowing globes by the thousand upon the well tended trees, all as if decked for carnival.

Which was what Stephen appeared to have arrived upon, breathless after his climb. The veranda was all guitars and girls, with Barry still florally garlanded at the centre. 'Haere mai,' Barry said. 'Welcome to Raro. She's all tika here. All mai taki, man. You want a pad? You got one for the night if you want to stay. Company too. I wondered when someone else might turn up. You've been missing all the fun.'

'So it seems,' Stephen said.

'You just let the music get you, man. Go with it. They know where life's at.'

Stephen wasn't unwilling to believe it, given the scene and Barry's insistence. But it was not the moment to allow the possibility of being persuaded. There were, surely, things to be said.

'I didn't think I'd learn to take that old tamure,' Barry went on, 'but I got with the dance in the end. My knees seem double jointed now. The old body doesn't seem the same. It's all about life man. That dance. And love. The whole bit. You just go with what your body says. And that's the coolest thing you ever saw. The wildest too. Sit down. You look done in. A long cool drink's the story.'

Stephen was still sweating after his day of search, and that last climb.

'Steve's not as old as he looks,' Barry advised the girls around. 'He's not a bad cat. A good tane. It's just he's had his troubles too. Right, Steve? We all have. And this, man, is where you leave it all behind.'

Easy to see things getting out of hand here, too easy. The orange groves, the pale reef and darkening sea, the friendly bodies, the fresh frangipani, cool coconut milk splashing down his dry throat; and the guitars beginning their sound again. A hibiscus flower had found its way softly behind his left ear; the left, as he recalled, announced availability.

'Sorry, Barry,' he began, or tried to.

'Never be sorry here. It's all today, man. All happening.'

Nothing was going to be easy, then.

'I've got to talk to you,' Stephen persisted. 'Rather urgently.'

'Sure. I guessed you might.'

'About sailing.'

'I must be psychic. I guessed it.'

'Well, it seems it might be on at last.'

'Great,' Barry observed ambiguously, before he resumed his theme. 'You know those hippies at home? They're all to hell, man. They'll never have it made. They don't know where it's at. Up here is where. Look around. What do you see? The original hippies. The first flower people. They have a really cool proverb up here in the islands. You know it?'

'So tell me.'

'The palm tree shall grow, the coral spread, but man shall cease to be. So it's all on today, man. All happening. How does that grab you?'

'Interestingly,' Stephen conceded.

'It's grabbed me. Up here I see the whole bit again. Like I've been blind.'

An old story, often told, yet no less vivid freshly minted. Stephen, then, was patient.

'Well –' he tried again.

'You want to talk about sailing, right?'

'Firstly. Yes.'

'And bloody Blair Hawkins.'

'Not altogether. No.'

'It's all one to me, man.'

'The voyage isn't Blair's. I see it as a mutual thing. With mutual purpose anyway.' Stephen, though, found that definition an enormous effort. Any definition might have been. For one thing, the guitars were too loud. He had to speak above them, or through them. And through the flowers, their scent; and all that scented flesh. Solid words had a fight to be heard.

'Look, man,' Barry said, 'you mind if I tell you what I see?'

'Please.'

'I see a rich shit with a fancy yacht.'

'One way of looking at it,' Stephen allowed.

'For my money the only way, man. Or maybe I mean his money. For his money the only way.'

'I don't feel that's altogether reasonable; to hold what he is against him. It should be what he does. What he's doing now. Anyway,' Stephen persisted, 'I don't quite see where that leaves us.'

'I'll tell you where it's left me, man. As his crapped out office boy on that radio. Okay, so I bought that scene, I could even wear it a while. I tell you, I could almost play the stock market myself now. You wouldn't believe his short cuts. I think he's even got another takeover on out here. Before he left, he worked out little secret codes to get his story through, in case anyone risky was listening in. Nothing he didn't think of to keep the pot boiling. Sailing that yacht's not enough for him, man.'

'He does have his responsibilities back there. We all do.' Though these, if Stephen thought about it, were even more obscure now, more remote. He should have brought a photograph of Helen with him, at least; something to keep her features in mind as memory wandered and the immediate past became imprecise. True, he had written to her from Rarotonga, while he had this chance ashore. He had also talked to her by telephone, under some strain, obviously on her side too, with domestic trivia and reassurances travelling strangely through the rise and fall of the island's crackling communications system. A certain amount, of course, got through clearly. That he was all right; that she was all right. That he loved her; that she loved him. That he had to take care; that she must too. Possibly enough for her comfort, if not his own. For he felt relief, if honest, when the conversation ended; when he walked out into the blinding Pacific noon again, and found the ocean vast before him, beyond the untidy green foliage of the shore.

'His responsibilities I don't want to know about. I mean his irresponsibilities. Because that, man, is what it's all about. Doing people down to get what you want. Selling short to make a scare, then buying back in cheaper again. I know the scene. He makes it big again, and the others carry the can. For what? For Blair Hawkins. Number one. Every time. And you know what I think about this trip? I think it's for the same number one, the same Blair Hawkins. All the way.'

'I don't think that's fair,' Stephen observed, 'until he's given the chance to show what he can do. He hasn't had that chance, you must admit.'

'I admit only to being a free office boy for the bastard. For someone who stands for everything I'm protesting against. As much as that bomb; he's part of the scene that makes it. Know something else? I think he's got troubles back there too. Something that gets him in a sweat. I think he might have wanted to be out of town anyway while the dust settles around the old stamping ground. They don't set dogs on a hero.'

That was a new thought, and not one to be set aside. For Stephen, at least.

'Like I said,' Barry finished, 'I see a lot of things different here.'

That was plain. A female arm surrounded Barry's neck impatiently; there was something whispered in his ear. Barry was obliged, briefly, to whisper something back.

'I thought I saw a certain political commitment.' Stephen said, trying to summon some firmness to his voice. 'Tell me if I'm wrong. Or if you see that different now too.'

'Nothing's different. I'm just saying Hawkins' bag isn't my bag, not any more.'

'In any cause, you make strange allies. For the moment. All a business of the possible, as the saying goes. No one stays pure in any fight. And Blair makes this possible, surely. Impure, maybe –'

'What I said. A rich shit.'

Stephen felt despair among the fragrance. 'Don't make his money a disqualification; he may still be sincere. Or the stock market; I can see how you feel about that. But you're our link man. We want you back aboard. Peter and Rex too. Not just Blair.'

'You go tell him I'm playing the market myself now. My own. And I'm cleaning my stock out, right?'

That was it, then. Stephen had to work with the worst, see what he might shape. 'So you're quitting?'

A challenge, possibly, was all he had left.

'I didn't say that.'

'No? Try me again.'

'I'm no quitter, man. I'll wait along here a while. There could be another protest boat turning up.'

'A pure one?'

'Anything with sails. And without a fat cat running the scene. You reading me now?'

'I seem to be.'

'So tell Hawkins to get up himself with bells on, man. And my compliments.'

Stephen paused. 'About the transmitter,' he began.

'I'm sorry about that. I had a big love scene going there. Sweet. The best money could buy. I could almost talk to God on that one.'

'It doesn't tempt you now?'

'Not if I have to buy the rest. I can't find the soul bread.'

So Stephen, at last, was empty of argument. He had another drink in his hands. Go with it? He'd gone. Or Barry had.

'Tell you what, though,' Barry went on, 'I'll come down to the boat to say goodbye before you go.' He made that offer seem generous. 'I have to get my gear anyway. And I'll give you and Peter, maybe old Rex too, a rundown on the transmitter. The basic routine. Not Hawkins, though. Just keep him out of my hair. Once you get the style, learn to work the right frequencies, you should have something going for you out there. Maybe not so fast, if things get tricky, if you have to chase quick for contact. Or if the boat takes a beating, and the set needs repair. You'll just have to make the best of it.'

100

Not an unreasonable offer, with things as they were. Stephen wasn't without something salvaged when later, much later, he descended through the orange groves in the dark; he soon lost the sound of guitars, and fresh rhythms sounding from drumsticks on a kerosene can. The headlights of his car flashed over leaning coconut palms, bulky flamboyant trees, and dimly strolling villagers, on the narrow road back around Rarotonga. Another world? He knew for the first time and suddenly, stunningly, a desire for sea, for the uncomplicated kick of a fast craft beneath his feet on a pitching ocean; and nothing more, nothing at all. Perhaps it was Peter's knowledge he shared now. The beauty of the thing.

It wasn't, though, a desire quite yet to be served. There was Barry's promised instruction first, sitting with Peter and Stephen at the transmitter in the aft cabin; Blair was conveniently out of the way, and Rex still ashore. There was much to learn in too short a time, among those dials and knobs, intermittent lights and flickering needles. 'Too much magic,' Peter said succinctly. 'Too much magic, friend.' Between Peter and Stephen, though, it seemed some communication might still be managed with land after all, while out upon the Pacific. Given luck, that was, and patience.

Then Barry packed his kitbag and said goodbye. 'I wish I could say it was good while it lasted. But I can say good luck anyway. Haere, man, haere ra. Keep your cool. Don't spit till you see the whites of their eyes.'

Still brisk, he vanished from the voyage, shouldering his kitbag along the waterfront, finding his way back to the orange groves, the frangipani, and to whatever his body might yet have to tell him. It wasn't an ungraceful departure, or a saddening one.

That left them only to get free of the social function to celebrate their departure. For it appeared they were now a day from sailing.

He wished he had been warned. Perhaps he should have known.

A lane of sputtering light led them towards the function, the feast; lines of flares, and vastly unfurled banana fronds overhanging them as they walked. Then they were in a clearing, some village square perhaps, all rippling with even more brilliant light, with bulky trees shadowed around. There they stood, the men of *Moana Nui*, while drumbeats rose and women danced welcome. There were garlands again, ferny floral headlets, and a dozen guides to take them to places of honour at the centre of the affair: all confusion, brown bodies and flowers, dancing and drums, tables glutted with food, raw fish and coconut cream, baked breadfruit and taro, seaweed salads and pineapples, chicken and pork still steaming from the earth ovens, everything according to schedule, the good things of earth and ocean with the warmth of men and the wonder of women in the fleshy tumult of the dance they called the tamure.

All arranged, perhaps, as if they might never see its like again. That expectation would not have been unreasonable; they could hardly have seen its like before. True, there must have been the beat of the ocean upon the reef, somewhere beyond those solid trees, but it was not to be heard here among the human drumming. They might have been first to find such celebration of life, explorers in a new Pacific, offered now as compensation for never, with all human brevity a singing thing. What was it that Polynesian proverb said? The palm tree shall grow, the coral spread, but man shall cease to be. Stephen seemed to comprehend it now, and strangely felt no pang.

For this celebration would have no early ceasing. The drink was as heady as the dance. Whenever food was finished, there was more to come; whenever dancers dispersed, there were more to follow. They were never left alone. Rex, fast drunk again, was dragged off among friends. Even Peter, for the first time ashore, had his impatience mellowed by the night; he began to laugh, often, and banged the table in time with the drums. Blair appeared to find it most politic to move among the dignitaries at first, high chiefs and hangers-on; but before long he was in the evidently interesting company of a rather substantial woman, one of some dignity and stylish dress, perhaps a politician's daughter or a trader's woman, seemingly prosperous, with fine features and taunting smile. Clear, too, that she and Blair were no strangers; but if they were already familiar, that didn't diminish the intensity of their conversation. They were soon out of sight, beyond the crowd, the dancers. Soon Stephen too was losing sense of their departure: the drink, of course, the food, the wild sound, the human confusion. The whole bit, as Barry might say. Because the thought of *Moana Nui*, the main filling tomorrow, the ocean opening wide again, became grotesque. A fool's fancy. Worse: a nightmare of negation. Men were most real ashore, of the earth, of their familiar flesh.

That was what he was most discovering now, what the drums were telling him, and ranks of swinging thighs. Queer that he should have suffered so little lust in a month's celibacy; it couldn't be merely that it lacked direction. But there was no denying it now, no cause to deny it now.

For he and Peter, without preliminary, were gathered up with laughter, drawn in among the dancers, awkward at first on their legs, but persuaded, always with the wildest of laughter, to persist until they learned to loosen their limbs, jerk their knees to the drumbeat, their arms keeping rhythm, while their partners opposite rolled their thighs in fluently ritual invitation. Those partners came and went; there was always choice. The drums, beating faster, offered climax after climax. And no end to the night.

But there was, of course. There had to be. The palm tree might grow, the coral spread, but all human fever perished; it was just a transaction with time.

More exactly, it was a transaction under palms, upon sand and beside a lagoon, within arms as soft as any imagination might arrange. The drumming had grown faint in the distance; there was the sound of gentle water near. He hardly knew her face; he certainly did not know her name. They were still hot from the dance, and breathless, having mutually dragged themselves clear of the larger celebration in immodest haste; not that there was call for modesty. Or for anything more than need. Their sweat lost itself in the flowers crushed between them, all moisture mingling among spilled petals; if there were hesitation, unfamiliarity, it was not on her side at least. With no foreplay, or plea for it; that was past, within the dance; now was need alone, relief. She took his buttocks tight, the act hers alone, and held him still between her open legs, not even allowing him thrust; her flesh made fluid grip, drew him in and down, still deeper, until he was swiftly one with her swinging loins; loins and thighs which might never have left the dance, the thudding tamure, or hadn't. There were no words to whisper, faces to fondle; there was just delight while the flesh lasted, and relief when it gave. For it was all quick, savage, over soon; he was hardly taken within her, into that fervent rhythm, before sucked dry, all lust leaving him in jab after stinging jab, until he had nothing more to give, or be taken; until the wrecked flowers fell away from their parting bodies, only the scent left whole, a memory, a lingering apparition of the brief and loveless act.

Too brief. For then they were standing together, not even hand in hand, as casual as strangers met on any shore. He was not empty, it appeared, of some despair grown from the heat of his flesh; it gathered still more densely and numbly, a swift infection, as they walked off the sand, into the palms and shadows, towards the light again. It was not something to be understood. There should be no despair. Nor guilt; or none to do with his visible life, with Helen. There could hardly have been a purging less profound, or more a thing apart. Was it the coming loss of land again? Or, more, some last bizarre and extravagant gift from Jacqueline? Infidelity to the dead was absurd: no such thing. And yet there was. This lump in his mind seemed to tell him so, this blockage in his being.

He might more profitably ask himself why aboard *Moana Nui*, try to understand tomorrow, when he took his first watch on the Pacific again, with an eye on the compass to see they kept true course. For he was off course now. That was only and strangely too clear.

Even the sound of the drums, as they approached, had grown subdued. The dancers were mostly vanished, the last of the feast cleared.

104

Much better to ask himself tomorrow. For that would insist on arriving. The girl? When he looked around, she was gone. Not even thanks were necessary. There was only tomorrow left to embrace, if he wished, and what the ocean might tell him yet.

Peter was standing beside him. 'All right?' he asked.

'Sure,' Stephen said. 'Fine.'

'Me too, friend.'

Yet they appeared, for the first time, uncertain of each other. Might Peter too have mystery to wash from his skin, rinse from his mouth? Land was not the place to share.

'So let's go,' Peter said finally. 'The party's over.'

Eight

NOW THEY WERE FOUR WITH THE PACIFIC. ENOUGH. ENOUGH for comfort, certainly, and more space to spread themselves in the cabin. And enough to sail *Moana Nui*, with watches equally divided through day and night, and none on stand-by. The jagged heights of Rarotonga began to drop beyond the swell, soon the last green tips of the island too, as they found familiar footing on the moving deck. Stephen didn't deny relief in himself; he had no wish to deny it, or cause. It was evident elsewhere too. Blair, amicable, satisfyingly refreshed, appeared as optimistic as at their beginning; he uncorked another bottle of whisky to mark the day. This time though, more cautiously, he didn't toss the cork overboard with abandon; they had only so much liquor to see them through, and they might be a long time sighting friendly shore again. Peter, after moving lightly about the boat, pleased with a freshening wind, took the offered bottle with satisfaction; Stephen too.

But Rex refused. He'd had enough, he said, and a hell of a hangover now. He needed to dry out, have a sober day or two.

Yet he already seemed steady again to Stephen, later, sharing cockpit and sunset, with Blair asleep on his bunk and Peter cooking a meal below.

'Good while it lasted,' Rex said. 'But it never bloody lasts.'

'No.'

'A man wouldn't want it to. Not like that.'

'Probably not.'

'No,' Rex insisted. 'Too good to be bloody true.'

He appeared to be dismissing land from his system along with the liquor; perhaps an old trick of the navy too, a rationalization. Something to keep him safe, or sure, when other things were less so.

'You know something?' he went on. 'I even had myself a woman back there.'

Stephen managed surprise. 'You did?'

'A big brown bitch, she was. She knew a thing or two. You'd think she might of been past it. Not on your sweet fanny adams. Didn't do me any harm.'

'I expect not.'

'First time in years, I don't mind telling. The old marriage went dry a long time back. Like I said, nothing lasts. A man's got to take it. Get a grip on his life.'

Anyway Rex now had good grip on the wheel, his eyes ahead; he wasn't watching the sunset. The colour was vast across a cloudless sky as the day ebbed. There was nothing to disturb it, diminish it, unless the talk of men.

'I don't mind admitting,' Rex added, his day for admissions, 'there was a time when I couldn't get enough of it. A real young ram, I was. Funny to think now. Even deserted once, on account of some bint I'd sooner forget. She left me the pox. They dragged me back aboard and flogged me. That was back in the flogging days, before they had to sweeten things up to get sailors. A man had to take that too. On top of the pox.'

Stephen wished some way to offer sympathy. But Rex, after all wasn't looking for it. He just wanted a mate alongside to hear him out, help him pass a watch.

'It didn't do me no harm,' he argued, 'learning to take it. There was worse in the war.'

'I imagine there was,' Stephen said.

'They tied a man down. That's how they did it. So you

couldn't wriggle, they had a clear target. Then they stuffed something in your mouth so you wouldn't scream. That might unnerve the poor sod who had to do the job. I had something to say, though, before they stuffed my mouth. Just don't let me see the bastard, I said, just don't let me see who does it, I don't want to know who. Let it be anyone, everyone. I don't want a fucking murder on my hands. And leave me alone after, don't bring any doctor round to see I'm all right. I might strangle that bastard too. Just let me learn to swallow it down. So they did that. They stuffed something between my teeth, and got on with the job. Know something dead funny? It wasn't me who fainted. It was the poor mug doing it. He was new to the job, couldn't see it through. An officer had to take over to see I got it all. But they did leave me alone after, like I asked. I swallowed it down.'

'Swallowed what down, though?' Stephen asked.

'What people can bloody do to each other. Because I had to learn. You can't hand it out unless you can take it. I was just a bloody kid. A kid tied down with stuffing in his mouth and a bare back. You wouldn't know.'

'No,' Stephen agreed without difficulty.

'They were making me a man. That was the idea. They probably did. When I was collecting that bit of bronze at the palace, I had to think of something to keep my mind off things. So I thought of how I was then. Tied down that day. Only soon there wasn't much room for men in the world, not my kind. Not after the war. It's all long hair and fancy pants now, boys half way bloody fairies before they're born. You tell me what it's all about. I wouldn't know.'

'Most of us have the same problem,' Stephen suggested.

'It wasn't what I bloody fought for. I knew who I was fighting, that's all. The mugs and the shits. A man's always up against the mugs and the shits.'

'Oh?'

'You got a lot to learn. The only way to see the enemy. The shits do all the planning, make the rules. And the mugs do all the dirty work. I ought to know. I been a mug in my time.

The bugger who beat me was a mug too, only he was still learning the game, couldn't teach me how.'

'I see.'

'But when I look around I still wonder what I fought for. That bit of bronze won't tell me. And it isn't what I see anywhere. Maybe it would of been better to leave the world to Hitler after all, some shit who knows what discipline is all about.'

'Like flogging?'

'Well, I learned. Didn't I say that?'

True. Rex had indeed. And the sunset no longer flourished. Stars had begun to prick out their course eastward. Land was well gone now, already arranging itself as unreal in memory; the ocean had settled restless, real, around them again.

Now they were truly in the trades, with what that meant; the wind against them all the way. They tacked north, then tacked south in compensation; they could consider themselves fortunate to make twenty miles on course in a day instead of the hundred miles or more they made daily in southern latitudes. Sometimes it was less, much less. For huge calms could swallow them, leave them limp and lost on oily ocean under lifeless sky. Worse, their transistor radio was telling them that the French nuclear fleet had left Tahiti for the testing ground at Mururoa; the area had already been declared a danger zone, off limits to shipping and aircraft.

'That, friends,' said Peter, 'is just what had me scared. That's what Rarotonga did for us.'

Desperately, then, they began depleting fuel to motor out of calms, looking for patches of breeze, ruffled water, to carry them on. But they didn't find enough disturbance to be useful. Men were gathering at Mururoa, to celebrate the worst they could do to their world, and *Moana Nui* was still hundreds of miles short.

Even a sight of Tahiti, in mountainous silhouette to the north as they passed, gave no consolation. The island of love, the original Eden? A superfluity after Rarotonga; and now at best a painted whore for swarming tourists and legionnaires.

Those of *Moana Nui* might have been in the French Pacific at last but they were still only half the distance to Mururoa, that barren atoll of coral and sand upon which Western man had never spent dreams and fancies, or looked for love. Upon which he merely demonstrated the destruction he might work, the worst hate and fear could do, given half a chance; half a chance too much.

That, after all, was why they were upon the Pacific. For the most part they didn't miss that point, even at the most difficult, the most frustrating, when the hot timeless days of the tropics produced irritation with their sluggish craft, with themselves, their unwilling passivity; they idly cursed the calms, which remained indifferent to the most elegantly and ingeniously obscene expletive; the ocean was all hindrance now, always an enemy, never an ally. There were, again as if every element were mocking them, capriciously quiet electric storms by day and night in which the whole horizon was vastly lit, with the sky turned pale and trembling, the flat ocean flashing eerie blue. With no thunder, no rain, no wind. Parodies, ghosts of storms.

Between them Peter and Stephen managed to keep the transmitter functioning, if with difficulties, in the aft cabin, maintaining thin contact with the other side; they were able to tell those who wanted to hear that they were still on their way, still voyaging, making the best time they could, so that scientists for once might not have the Pacific as they wanted it, empty sea to saturate with radioactive fallout about Mururoa; this time there would be a yacht, with four exposed men, in the way of the military machinery there.

Still, Blair wasn't happy with communication. Their inefficient use of the transmitter, with Barry's casual expertise now lost to the yacht, meant large drain on the batteries; it meant they often had to keep short conversation with the shore. More, it seemed for some reason that the batteries weren't recharging as they should, after transmissions, from the diesel engine when Rex cut it in. There appeared to be a fault in the generator, though it was new when they left; there was no replacement aboard. An oversight on Blair's part, of course, but this didn't diminish his irritation with Peter and Stephen when they tried themselves at the transmitter. Communication from shore told them, anyway, that their messages were weaker. They were soon receiving more poorly too. Changes of frequency didn't help; nothing did. They had to hope that the generator lasted, while keeping communication to the sparest, to the point. Rex helpfully picked the generator apart, tinkered, put it together again; but the batteries remained only fitfully charged. Enough to give the diesel a kick, when they wished to motor instead of sail; but not much more. For safety their radio routine was cut to one contact a day.

This meant Blair was now short of information still significant in his life; he had less chance to hear of personal concerns, or pass on his own. 'My God,' he complained. 'I'm beginning not to know what's going on back there.'

'They still know we're out here, friend,' Peter said quietly. 'Still trying to make out. Maybe those up at Mururoa do too. What else is there to know?'

'Anything could be happening back there. Anything.'

'Like what?'

'Things in general. Our individual affairs. We all have them.'

'But you're thinking about yours.'

'Right. Why not?'

Blair was sweating, perhaps not merely because of the heat in the airless aft cabin as they sat, the three of them, around the frustrating transmitter. And attempted to explain, 'We all have things on the line back there.'

'I'm saying yours especially, friend,' Peter insisted.

'All right. Mine especially.'

'There are things on the line out here too. Different maybe, but still pretty special.'

Heat may have begun Blair's sweat, but anger made his face shine now. 'Look,' he said, 'there's a limit to what I can take.

'Sure, friend.'

'It's my fucking yacht.'

Which was, at least, making one issue plain.

'I wasn't saying different,' Peter observed.

But it didn't steady Blair. 'You two,' he argued loudly, including Stephen in his anger now, 'bugger around too much when you've got the chance on the air. Right, so you're working within limits. But you could try to be faster, get more things back and forward.'

'Your things.'

'Right. More of my things anyway. I've got something pretty big swinging at the moment.'

'There's something pretty big going to swing over Mururoa soon too, friend. Any day now. A big balloon.'

'I'm not forgetting that; don't twist what I say.'

'Blair,' Stephen intervened quietly, 'no one's twisting anything. Misunderstanding, perhaps. We shouldn't be at each other's throats now. Not over this.'

Blair breathed deeply, calmer. 'All I'm saying is you two bugger around. Repeat yourselves. Reel off figures twice over.'

'We repeat ourselves to avoid misunderstanding on the other side,' Stephen answered. 'More necessary now when we're not sure how we're getting through.'

'About our position, for example,' Peter added. 'Just where we are out here. More necessary now too. Safety, if anything goes wrong. And the weather; they try to tell us what they know of things out here. Important things, first things. If we have to tell it twice, or hear it twice, that's how it goes. We might have troubles, but I've never had a trip without them. No sweat, friend. This is small beer.'

'Not for me,' Blair said. 'I'm trying to swallow hard.'

'Try harder,' Peter suggested. 'We all might.'

'No harm in wondering how I stand out here,' Blair replied, gone to the defensive, 'or where I am.'

'I'm just going to take a shot with the sextant,' Peter finished. 'Then I'll tell you just where you are. Precisely where you are, friend. Okay?'

'Okay,' Blair agreed. 'So it damn well has to be.'

Sleep in the tropics was a restless, sweaty affair. And Stephen's dreams became vivid again. Dreams of land, mostly, which told him nothing here, nothing he didn't know, and helped not at all. Always a relief to go on watch at night, grow cool at the wheel, inhabit a larger and solid dream, one never less than articulate. For that was what the Pacific appeared to become, still well short of the danger zone, when the hugest of calms swallowed them. They had no hope of motoring out of this one; in any case they had already used too much fuel in the trades. They had to make the best of moonlight, stars, and utterly motionless water, shiny from the sky above, while serving out a watch; and hoping, whistling, praying, for a breeze. The earth itself could have come to a standstill, quitting its task in space; and the stars often seemed stationary in the sky, so slowly did time move at the wheel. Frequently the boat just drifted, circling. And the lights flecking the still water might have been some subterranean excrescence surfaced from transparent deeps. No shimmering delight; no longer. Life had become leaden on the ocean, if life at all.

He still shared a reefer or two with Peter, when they changed watches at midnight; not quite a habit yet, nor really offering to become one. Rather just a way of keeping human company, sharing themselves, with no more consequence than the comfort otherwise to be found below in Blair's whisky. For they did share themselves; they did seem one, at times, with each other while the yacht idled listless on the ocean. It wasn't indifference they found, whatever else. He began to talk of Jacqueline, Helen too, without such large inner hurt. Peter had a past too, some things he wasn't entirely unwilling to share. Love, for one, given too long and vainly. A wife gone, a child unseen. A woman he had failed or who had failed him. No matter whose failure when the loving and laughing were gone, he said, with only the biting and scratching left, then the grabbing and hating too. Stephen saw the ocean as something Peter put between himself and further pain. Difficult to say. As difficult as most things human were to say. Even if less so here, drifting outside the danger zone, with a thin reefer burning between their lives.

There could not be nights more substantial. With reefer finished, talk too, Peter would descend to find sleep in the sticky cabin, leaving the wheel to Stephen. That was no problem. Nor loneliness in the night.

The problem came, in truth, the night he discovered himself no longer alone, yet with Peter distinctly gone. That was what his eyes appeared to be telling him; it was nothing to be blinked away.

He had just noticed the faintest breeze cool on the side of his face too, something with promise for the first night in five. Nothing yet to fill a sail, push them on, and along a course again. But enough to waken him from the trance the night produced, and leave a tingle of expectation.

Jacqueline sat there. Not suddenly; she might already have been there some time, forward of the cockpit, made comfortable on a hatch, among rigging and coils of rope, without his noticing. Jacqueline, explicitly. Jacqueline, unmistakably, sitting as he had seen her so often on the seashore, rather childishly, her head hugged upon her knees. Jacqueline even to the long black hair falling untidily down her back. She wasn't looking back towards him. She was looking forward, somewhere ahead.

His senses sang; his mouth became a dry cavern in which tiny sounds, meant to be words, tinkled and died. It had to be madness or more. More? What more?

'Jacqueline,' he said at length.

She just sat there. She didn't look back.

Then, 'Jacqueline, darling.'

She had no response to endearment either. She still looked ahead.

'Why?' he asked. 'Why you?'

Not a realistic question. But nor did the night propose much realism now, with Jacqueline's presence, senses he could no longer trust. If the ocean could do this to reason, then how much more?

Then, 'Jacqueline, please. Please.'

Please what? He could not be sure. Please look at him, live again? Or please flee his palpable life?

But there was no purpose in a plea either; no result. She continued to sit, perhaps there forever, with eyes toward a remote horizon, something to be seen only by her.

114

He was too numb to leave the wheel and cockpit, and cross the deck to where she sat; too numb even to think of it.

'My God,' he said, still more loudly than before. 'Jacqueline. Darling. Say something.'

Her attitude there, immobile, quiet, appeared to argue that she had said it all; there was nothing more to say. And he had, once, thought that true. Even the students who came, with theses to write, thought it true; most did.

'Everything all right?' a voice asked presently.

It was Rex Stone beside him, his relief. Jacqueline? She was gone, if she had been.

'Thought I heard you talking up here,' Rex said. 'Don't tell me you're picking up the habit too.'

'I must be,' Stephen agreed, sanity evident at last.

'Hey,' Rex said, 'that's a fair sort of breeze. More bloody like it now.'

True. The breeze had risen unnoticed. They trimmed sail, and there was soon a distinct wake behind them, wavering on the moonlit sea. Perhaps Jacqueline behind too. He hoped to God so. By morning they were making course again, more or less, towards the danger zone. Or away from it, but that was Stephen's affair, his problem; his alone.

Blair appeared shrunken, often silent, since the business with the transmitter, since communication with shore began to falter. It left him lost between land and ocean, between worlds, belonging quite to neither.

He did confide to Stephen, 'I could be going up with a bang back there, while those bastards on Mururoa arrange theirs out here.'

'You were telling me you enjoyed a gamble.'

'When I'm around, in the flesh, to keep the odds short. Out here I never bloody know.'

'Let's concentrate on one thing at a time. This voyage, say.'

'You don't understand.'

'No?'

'I could be left without a shirt on my back. Anyway without this yacht.'

'I can't see angry shareholders climbing aboard to claim it. Not in the danger zone.'

'It's no bloody joke.'

'All right, then.'

'Things could be really serious back there. All bad news.'

'Here too.'

'Don't give me all that again,' Blair said bitterly. 'A waste of time talking to you now. I thought I could. You don't want to understand.'

'But I do,' Stephen insisted. 'I do, Blair.'

Nevertheless he left Stephen then, and went down below again to find rest, or more restlessness, on his bunk.

That afternoon they had even more difficulty with the transmitter, both sending and receiving. The faint human voices on the other side were growing yet further distant and it seemed they were just slenderly heard too. Peter and Stephen still shared the frustration at midnight, recalled it when they changed watches.

'I'd like to give the bloody thing away altogether now,' Peter said. 'We haven't got the magic.'

'Apparently not.'

'Best to forget it. Just an irritation aboard, so long as there's any hope of using it. A temptation.'

'True.'

'But I expect we'll go on indulging ourselves. Kidding ourselves we can communicate. Better this.' He passed the reefer.

Stephen was quiet for a time.

'So what, friend, is the wisdom for tonight?'

'Nothing special.'

'Try me.'

'I was probably thinking,' Stephen said, 'about someone I once met. A medium. So called.'

'A medium?' Peter was puzzled.

'A spiritualist of some persuasion. He was big on communication too. He thought he had the magic, even if it was all in his mind.'

116

'I see.'

'He saw himself as a kind of transmitter. Working a very special frequency, of course. Our troubles just happened to bring him to mind; he claimed to have his too.'

'Oh?'

'With the other side, he said, the dead trying to get through to the living. He told me they don't always know how. And we misunderstand.'

'Well, he's welcome to that freaky scene.'

'But that's it,' Stephen said. 'I don't see the difference.'

'We're not dead yet,' Peter insisted.

'I don't think,' Stephen explained, 'that that's what I was trying to say. Not exactly.'

'No?'

But what it was, exactly, now seemed lost. With the reefer, no doubt. 'Sorry,' he confessed, 'I've lost the point.'

'A hell of a story without a point.'

'Sometimes the best stories are. Too big a point can bring the shutters down, leaving the world outside. And us too tiny in the dark, trying to make our own light.'

'I think, friend, you might be copping out of the story.'

'All right. So perhaps the point was that he was under the impression that the dead don't think they're dead either.'

'No news,' Peter said. 'Nor do most of the living.'

'True.'

'So where does that leave us?'

'On this yacht, apparently.' Somewhat soothed, at least, and calmer.

'Then let's stick with it.'

'Of course,' Stephen agreed.

'And the hell with the transmitter. We know we're alive, don't we?'

'Most of the time. Yes.'

'So, friend, stick with that too.'

Some time later Peter absented himself from the night, the cockpit. Stephen didn't observe him depart, especially; but he was, on the other hand, at particular pains to observe the foredeck through the rest of his watch, and note no arrival of

117

anything which might propose itself as human there. A relief, in a way. A rebuke, in another.

'Jacqueline?' he asked, experimentally, towards the end.

Nothing. No answer. No one.

'Then the hell with you too,' he said finally.

It might be honesty of a sort. A painful sort, all the same.

At noon next day, while they tacked into a moderate wind, Peter braced himself on deck for a sun shot, then went down to consider his figures, and his chart.

Soon he announced, 'We're there.'

'Where?' asked Blair from his bunk.

'Two hundred miles from Mururoa. The edge of the danger zone. By my calculation we crossed into it twenty minutes ago.'

There was considerable silence then.

'I think, friends,' Peter added, 'it may call for some celebration.'

'By God it does,' Rex said. 'We bloody made it.'

Stephen was surprised by huge elation. More than forty days at sea had not left him stale at all. Even Blair's sourness was gone. They were shaking each other's hands, slapping backs, shouting. And Blair was breaking out champagne.

Then, as if mutually agreed, glasses in hand, they joined in the cockpit to consider the ocean around. The danger zone? Under the tropic sky the sea could not have looked less hazardous, more empty.

'Here's to it, friends,' Peter said, raising his glass ceremonially. 'To a long life in the danger zone.'

'To a long life anyway,' Rex echoed.

'To a long life anywhere,' Blair said.

'To life,' Stephen finished.

They drank.

To Stephen, in another place, another time, the champagne might have seemed too tart, rather off, perhaps travelled poorly. But it had tender disguise here; he held out his glass for more from Blair's bottle, and silently toasted the danger zone again, this time on his own account. Why? It wasn't necessary to know why. Sufficient to know that they were there, at last, inside the zone, living with all that danger might have to say. And who knew? Life at its limit could be worth more toast than one.

Nine

By NOON NEXT DAY, WITH USEFUL WIND, THEY HAD MADE GOOD another eighty miles towards the centre of the danger zone; and by the following morning, even with the wind failing, still another forty. They were less than eighty miles off Mururoa atoll, coasting in gently, and the ocean remained obstinately empty of menace, all shape and sign of other men. Their transistor radio, on which they were now more dependent, told them of no test due; in any case the men of Mururoa seldom gave precise forewarning. A test might be decided overnight. It all depended on the weather, the winds which should carry the fallout away.

So this quietest of seas could become unnerving. Uncanny; life stilled to the whisper of water along the hull as they kept course towards the atoll. They fell fast into silences where there had been jokes before: sentences unfinished, words left dangling. Still, they should have expected this, with any foresight; the danger zone was never meant to be a joke. It was just that it lacked visible substance. Yet if a countdown were to begin now, they had a large chance of being in the way of fallout from a nuclear detonation. The risk was real; and unreal too. They had to work at making themselves believe it. That might account for their silences now, their need to believe.

'If they've been eavesdropping on our frequencies,' Peter

observed, 'they'll know we're here, all right, and coming in fast.'

'And if they haven't?' Blair asked.

'Our bad luck, maybe.'

'A bomb exploded now just might leave us for dead.'

'Look, friend, we're just sailing. Sailing the Pacific. Four sane, grown men on a peaceful cruise. Not our problem that there happen to be some madmen, some stunted kids, playing with bombs over the other side of the horizon.'

'On the contrary. It's all our problem, why we're here.'

'But not something to think about,' Peter insisted.

'No?'

'Not until we have to. Otherwise we might go off our heads too. Let's stick with sailing. With what we know. The Pacific, friend. That wind's picking up. We could give the cheater a try.'

Blair refused distraction. 'Look,' he argued, 'I think the point of this voyage is to make problems for them on the atoll. Not literally to get a hot dose of radiation. That's not my bag.'

'Then you have a problem there. Your problem.'

'And my yacht.'

'I remember you saying, friend.'

'What I'm arguing is that we should let them know we're here, start making them worry. Then see what happens.'

'You want to parley with the French admiral? You could try on the radio. But what kind of deal could you make? There's no cut-price protest out here on the Pacific. No discount, no kickbacks. No deal at all.'

'I'm not saying that.' Blair became irritated. 'I said nothing about a deal.'

'While we're on the subject, friends,' Peter went on, 'I think we should agree among ourselves. And know where we stand. No deals with the sons of bitches; no deals at all. Right?'

'I never made a deal with no enemy in my life,' Rex said. 'Once, in the war, I tossed a German bugger overboard because I didn't like the sound of what he was saying. He was wanting some deal too, trying me on. So I'm not starting deals with any mugs and shits out here.'

'I should hope the question doesn't arise,' Stephen said. 'But if it does, then I agree. No deals or compromises.'

That left Blair. 'Fortunately,' he said, 'I have no quarrel with the three of you. As skipper, that is. And owner of the yacht.' His emphasis on this grew heavier daily. 'I think we know each other well enough now for a little trust to be shown.'

'Time to clear the air,' Peter said. 'About time, friend, seventy miles off the atoll. Or getting near sixty now.'

'And I'm merely saying that it's time to let the French know we're here. Break out our colours, if you like. If they're planning a test for tomorrow, say, our presence could very well make them cool it. That's why we're here. To stop tests, both in the short and long run. Right?' This time Blair looked at Stephen.

'Right,' Stephen agreed. But he hoped Blair wasn't going to use that agreement, in some way unseen, against Peter now.

'Too late,' Blair continued, 'if we start eating radioactive ash for breakfast. Right, so a little martyrdom mightn't hurt the cause. But I don't freak out on that. The idea doesn't turn any of us on. I don't want my name on any memorial, even carved in gold.'

Stephen could see it distinctly in printer's ink all the same, entirely perishable, in headlines and on newspaper billboards. Yet he still tried, often, to think more fairly of Blair. He did now, and didn't speak.

'So?' Peter said to Blair.

'We don't have any colours to break out. Literally, I mean. But we do have a radar reflector on board. And a bracket for it on the crosstree. I suggest we put it up now. They should pick us up fast, especially if they've got ships near, or planes out on pattern flights. When they know we're here, it's their problem. All theirs.'

'You mean the shit hits the fan.' Rex needed his own definition.

'Something like that. Yes.'

'All right,' Rex said, 'you're on for my money. Time something bloody happened here.'

'Stephen?'

'Yes. Fine.'

'Whatever you say, friend,' Peter said, 'They'll see how fast we're coming in.'

Rex went below to fetch the radar reflector from the hold. Then, to show age lost him no agility, he scrambled up the mast to fix the reflector in the bracket on the crosstree. With much satisfaction, as if it were some weapon aimed at the atoll. Half an hour later they had their first response. A gratifying sound, a perverse relief, after the waiting, the tension; an aircraft. There was, after all, a danger zone; it did have an existence.

Altogether undeniably. The plane flew in high and began to circle lower, and lower still, until it was only a hundred feet above them; and then almost brushing the sea on the port side. They could see French insignia on the fuselage; otherwise it was an anonymous grey military aircraft, with anonymous faces at the windows.

Rex, predictably, gave them the fingers with relish. 'Bugger off,' he shouted against the aircraft roar. 'Leave us alone. You mugs. You shits.' At least the pale faces at the passing windows had one unmistakable message to take from *Moana Nui*.

The others were quiet. The plane climbed away, its sound growing thin on the sea; the horizon was soon utterly without blemish again, and the sun even more warming.

'That's done it,' Blair said cheerfully. 'We're in business at last.' He seemed interested in their voyage again, in their enterprise on the ocean, as against his half-lost enterprises ashore. 'It's all on now. All on. I think we should be breaking out more champagne.'

Stephen suggested beer. He had never known his throat more dry.

The rest of the day was really anti-climax; it was merely a matter of closing with the atoll now. They were offered no obstruction, and the wind remained on their side. They still saw nothing. After the aircraft, the danger zone seemed to shrink into itself again, with secret to guard, something not to be given easily to aliens, strangers such as themselves. The day passed like any other, eating, sleeping, talking, taking watch; the difference now was that the horizon was more scrupulously observed.

At midnight, as usual, Stephen rose from his bunk to relieve Peter. 'Right,' Peter said. 'That does it, friend. That's it.'

'What is?'

'The voyage, for now. Time to heave to.'

'This soon?'

'We're about twenty-five miles off the atoll. I'm allowing for drift in the dark. Look over there. To starboard.'

Stephen looked. There was a distinct glow above the horizon, light which plainly had no commerce with moon or stars, rather with man and his purposes upon this ocean. And one purpose in particular. The most spectacular of all, if astute critical observers were to be believed; nuclear explosions seldom got less than rave reviews.

'Mururoa,' Peter said.

'Yes.'

'That's our baby, friend, that's our bag. The dreamy lights of old Mururoa. Now you know it's there. So make the most of your first look.'

Stephen needed no telling. Rarotonga announced itself with smell, warm, abundant. Mururoa had just chilly light to give a voyager, and perhaps a need for certainty about his covenant with the world, with himself. He might need longer to look at such light to see what it said. With no certainty at all beyond the truth that they were close to an unseen atoll, where other men had other business.

So he got on with helping Peter heave to. They backed the jib and adjusted the main until the yacht lay steady with helm lashed over to port. They could only drift to leeward now. That done, they relaxed with a reefer in the cockpit, and talked for a time.

'Only one scene now,' Peter observed. 'Sitting it out. Heaving to. Sailing back and forward. We can go in closer by day. Up to fifteen miles, maybe. No more. The sons of bitches wouldn't let us hassle about a mile or two if they wanted to arrest us for trespass in their national waters. Mightn't hurt to taunt them a bit, either. Just to see if they're going to keep their cool. They'll have to do something about us anyway, somewhere along the line. Unless they decide to forget us, pretend we're not here, let us take our chances when the balloon goes up. They'll have to decide now. Not us.'

'True.' The light above Mururoa had a strange trembling quality in the sky, coming and going; fading and flowing. A trick of the atmosphere, no doubt. Interesting nevertheless.

'It worry you?' Peter asked casually.

'What?' Stephen had been too distracted by the light above the atoll to comprehend the question.

'Being here now, friend. At last. It worry you?'

He tried to be truthful; he mostly was with Peter. 'Not much. Or perhaps I should say not yet.'

'You'll be all right.'

That was comfort.

'Probably old Rex too,' Peter added. 'I wouldn't want to know him ashore. Not my scene. Out here it's different, like most things. He's solid. With us wherever we go, whatever we do.'

'Funny. I feel that too. I did from the start.'

'Now we're here.'

'Yes.'

They both chose not to mention Blair. In the silence there was possibly the same speculation shared: how long, how far, would Blair last? *Moana Nui* might be durable enough. But Blair, for all his freshened interest, still seemed an inadequate prop, altogether too fragile, for any long protest upon the Pacific. Yet they would drift toward some answer, in the end. Speculation was profitless now. Stephen dismissed it painlessly, then, with the help of the reefer, looking back at the light in the sky. 'I hope we're all up to it,' he managed to say positively. 'However it's going to be. That's the odd thing, really. No one's ever done this before. Got this far. No guidelines. No precedents.'

'You lawyers like everything sewn up,' Peter suggested, 'with your freaky precedents.' He rose cheerfully. 'I'll tell you one scene you'll never sew up.'

'What?'

'This. The Pacific, friend. Like I said, a woman who'll never

125

quite have you. A really cold bitch. Precedents are for shore. Not for her. And no sweat, she's got her own thing going. Nothing's ever exactly the same out here, ever. Nothing.' Then Peter went down to the cabin and his bunk.

Stephen felt cool breeze on the side of his face. Superfluous now they were no longer sailing, but hove to, given to current. Nothing the same? Peter was wrong. One thing, at least, was exactly the same. Jacqueline sat once more on the forward hatch, long black hair untidy down her back, her head again childishly upon her knees. No difference at all in her appearance. Nor in the distant dreamy way she seemed to look out from the yacht. The only difference was that he could see where she was looking now. She was looking, just as he had been, at light in the sky above Mururoa.

'Do you,' Stephen began to ask, with difficulties, 'want to tell me something? Are you trying?'

Really no worse than Rex Stone talking aloud to himself, or to God, to pass a watch. And really no different either. To doubt that the Jacqueline he now observed was other than a creation of mind and memory, a vivid fiction of his subconscious, would be to doubt everything, believe nothing. He had no wish for that, not again; not even when he saw breeze flutter Jacqueline's hair while she sat there. He could admire the capacity of his subconscious to summon such authentic and delicate detail. Yet even that, in truth, was no more than might be found in dream. That was how it was, then, how it had to be. A dream of Jacqueline imposed upon his consciousness for some purpose. What purpose? Reasonable to ask.

'So why are you here?' he asked. 'Why have you come?'

This time he thought he saw the faintest of movements, a response, a slight turning of her face toward him. Not far. She remained largely in profile, if more distinctly, and still silent.

Then he could smell it. That scent, her scent. Jacqueline's. Something no longer secreted among her clothes, but flaunted insolently. There was now no sense to be trusted. Touch, taste, hearing? All were at risk.

He could only understand so far as he was given to understand. Surely there had to be a message from so elaborately

126

arranged a messenger? Unless Jacqueline herself was sufficient, an indecipherable scrawl from a hidden seething within himself. Something which might be decoded yet, with patience, a little sanity.

'Why?' he asked her, nevertheless. 'Why?'

She refused answer. Or his subconscious did. He was not to be confused again, deceived by death.

She was just sitting there. As if there were all the time in the world, and more, and no answers necessary. No questions either.

'Tell me,' he pleaded, though he should have preferred less fervour in his voice. 'Tell me what it's all about. This, I mean. You. For God's sake, say something.'

Again there appeared a faint response in her figure, a shiver of sorts. There was no message though, no meaning, to be taken from so slight a motion.

But there was, certainly, a limit to this kind of conversation, and to what all reason told him. He was at that limit, quite quickly, and then dizzily past it.

For he was distinctly saying, 'Darling Jacqueline.' And, 'You shouldn't have done it. There was no need. And not because of me. Nothing's the same any more. I could have gone on if you could.'

It appeared there was a large ache in his chest trying to escape as a sob. Then it did.

'I didn't even mind the other men,' he was continuing to tell her, for some reason. 'I knew why. I could understand. It was the way things were.'

After all, Jacqueline's promiscuity had been one fever among many, not always a frequent one, something which made her seek relief in unfamiliar flesh from familiar devils of her mind; devils Stephen had to share with her by day and night. At the worst, he never had to wonder who Jacqueline's current lover was; he had to wonder, if wonder was worth it, who wasn't. At the worst: there was also the best when, with infidelity spent, alien flesh failed, she turned once more to Stephen and comforts known, comforts gratefully taken and gratefully given; they were warm again and reckless, with enough

127

loving and laughing for Peter or any man to envy, a happiness she silvered with words for his delight, flashes of light upon a whirlpool. For even at its most careless, most abandoned, their love never had more than thin disguise as a gamble with time, with life, and at length a gamble lost with grief.

So that he should be saying now, 'I've missed you, darling. Had to start again. Another beginning. Another mess. But I tried with you. You shouldn't have gone.'

He no longer looked for response in that figure on the forward hatch; he no longer argued with the woman he saw, the scent he smelled, the reality or unreality, so long as she heard him out, or he heard himself.

He had to ask still, 'We did have something, after all, didn't we? That's all I need to know. That message, the one in the book. The one you left for me.' He paused, braced himself to finish. 'Love with all the breath, smiles, tears, even after death. You meant that, didn't you?'

An absurd echo in the night, that question, as absurd as reason.

Yet the figure, the counterfeit Jacqueline on the forward hatch, turned slowly, as if with effort, and looked full face at Stephen for the first time. She smiled gently, mockingly too.

'Of course,' he heard her say. 'Of course I meant that message, my darling fool.'

She was not there. Not there at all.

There was no further sob. He simply shuddered, once, and that too was over. He was left with the Pacific night and the pale glow of Mururoa on the sky. Yet that could hardly be taken as sign of sanity returning.

When Rex relieved him, later, he was more composed. On his bunk, for the rest of the night, he dreamed again of Rapa. Not lush and fleshy Rarotonga, an island known too well. But Rapa, unseen and unsung, austere and rocky, offering shelter with lumpy headlands to the tiny craft he was sailing – where? Well, to safety, plainly. A kind of safety. Still not a dream of which he could make sense; it always cheated him of adequate climax. He was grateful for morning light upon his face as it poured through the porthole above his bunk. And Blair saying,

'Let's see if breakfast tastes better at the centre of the danger zone.'

That day they sailed in closer, to within fifteen miles of the atoll, using the cheater. An excursion partly to taunt the French; but from curiosity too. Aircraft twice overflew them, circling low, as they cruised mild sea. 'At least we got them mugs baffled now,' Rex observed. 'And the shits on the island. None of the buggers know what to make of us, I reckon. Or what to bloody do.'

As for the four aboard, they could make what they liked of the sight through Blair's binoculars: a half dozen high radio towers, two large concrete buildings. Evidence of man only; the island itself was below the horizon. To see the average atoll, Peter explained, you had to be twelve miles or closer to its low-lying coral substance, and here that would be chancing arrest in national waters. They could observe at least that there was no balloon yet above the atoll, and thus no test imminent. So the reconaissance didn't leave them entirely without news. Another aircraft circled them in late afternoon, as they sailed out again, and hove to twenty-five miles from Mururoa; there was rising wind. They ate and slept without unease, after a day of some satisfactions.

At midnight, though, Stephen woke to a pitching yacht. As he climbed from his bunk, a lurch underfoot left him off balance, then crashing across the cabin. Stunned, still shaky, he got up to Peter in the cockpit. The wind had risen even more, the ocean all violence, with the jerking yacht seemingly about to buckle in protest against the restriction they imposed upon it. Impossible to get sure footing in the cockpit, or anywhere. 'We could always try running before this,' Peter said. 'No sweat, friend. Maybe in the morning.'

Meantime they had to ride it out rather than risk being blown into national waters, abandoning themselves as gift to Mururoa, and all the atoll meant; an end before they had begun.

'You can't say I didn't warn you, friend,' Peter said.

'No. I can't.'

'As if those sons of bitches weren't enough. Now she's got

to do her thing too. Trying to turn us off. We'll see. Nothing like the last laugh.'

Yet it was no night for laughing. Nor a night for reefers. Peter, though, shared Stephen's watch, then Rex's, finally Blair's, giving up sleep altogether for the safety of the yacht. In the morning Stephen woke to Peter shouting, 'A ship out there. A big one.'

They were soon together in the cockpit. The vessel was about half a mile away, also hove to, rising and falling with the storm. A large naval vessel indistinct beyond mist, grey gusts of rain.

'They haven't killed any time finding us,' Peter said. 'Not even in this.'

There was some silence, some indecision.

'What now?' Stephen asked.

'We get out of here. Fast, friends. We can run before this, no sweat. Agreed, skipper?'

'Agreed,' Blair said.

Not as if there could have been another answer anyway. Peter was observing ritual for Blair's comfort. Too clear who was commanding now.

'We want the storm jib and half the main, friends. See everything's well lashed down. You'll see how easy we slip them. We don't even have to try.'

But they did, of course. On that wild deck, in that vehement ocean. In minutes they were riding before the storm, the naval vessel lost in rain. And living with more familiar hazard, the vicious simplicities of the Pacific at its largest. In that turbulence the danger zone became an artificial thing, an irrelevance, a human vanity. They were back in the business of survival again.

The wind gusted to forty knots, fifty, sixty, finally seventy. There was no end to the shattering sea. Peter was never away from the wheel, though often with help, two to hold it hard. Even stripped of sail, with a warp slung astern to slow them down, they were running at eight or nine knots, they weren't sure where, but certainly somewhere east of Mururoa, in the Tuamotu archipelago, among reefs submerged, reefs spikily conspicuous, coral islets, swarms of atolls, a lethal lottery for navigators ever since Magellan first brushed with that maze; the sea stayed huge, with visibility small, little hope of sighting hazard. 'We could always, friends,' Peter said casually, 'try a refit in South America when we've wandered out of this.'

'It's the end,' Blair said. 'The bloody end.'

'It could be, friend, unless you help me hold the wheel.'

They were ants on a twig, and the twig in a torrent. Yet the rearing waves, those montonously seething seascapes, those desolate mountainsides, spray streaming back from their ridges, spray turned fast to tattering mist, never quite dumped them; never quite turned them over. Always miracle to be taken high, dizzily, then to surf down a divide, to begin again. Their days were a dense harvest of such miracles, with no sleep aboard, the cabin awash.

Yet there were only two days, though there seemed a dozen more, before the sea began to subside and the wind to drop.

'A hell of a way to slip the French navy,' Blair said. 'My God.'

'Like I told you,' Peter said. 'No sweat at all.'

The sky cleared enough for a sun shot, and Peter's reckoning had them two hundred miles east of Mururoa, out of the danger zone again. Rex made soup in the galley, their first hot food since the storm began, and passed steaming mugs up to the three in the cockpit.

'Know something?' Rex said. 'I chatted up God through that muck. And the old bugger saw us right.'

'I might even buy that,' Blair said. 'Someone was on our side. I don't even like to think about where we've been.'

'You should, friend,' Peter said. 'You should.'

'Oh?'

'You might know where you're going. Especially where we're going. If men aren't much, those freaks on Mururoa mightn't be much at all.'

'I think I'll try that one for size,' Stephen said. 'I've tried everything else.'

Because Peter, after the storm, was now more than sufficient on his side; someone neither more nor less than human, yet quiet in that commotion, that thundering water, steering a calm path through purgatory.

'Like I told you back on Raro,' Peter said. 'The beauty of the thing.'

There was no small beauty in this other thing either; this ally always visible at the wheel, through the worst, in the spray and rain. But it was not the time to say so, if ever he could.

'Yes,' Stephen said. 'I remember.'

That, and more.

So they tacked back towards Mururoa. The last frayed edge of the storm, as it passed, left only shreds of cloud in the brightest of skies. The danger zone grew around them again. Marvellously, it began to seem as serene a place as any upon the Pacific. As the sea flattened still more, with promise of idyll, their wake, now seen for miles astern, could have been something embellished with the most delicate of brushwork upon the waters of the danger zone.

Ten

THE CABIN DRIED OUT AGAIN; AND THEIR CLOTHES. THERE HAD
not been, for all the battering, any large damage to the yacht
itself. The only apparent casualty was the transmitter. It no
longer received at all, and this time possibly not because of
weakened batteries, but because of some hurt within the storm.
There were still lights flashing, needles flickering, but they heard
nothing on any frequency. They might assume they were
sending, if they wished, but it was a tossing of words into void:
there was never echo, never reply. 'This is the protest yacht
Moana Nui,' Peter and Stephen took turn in saying through the
microphone. 'This is protest yacht *Moana Nui* in mid Pacific.
Do you read me? We cannot read you. We are safe and heading
back into the danger zone. Safe and heading back into the
danger zone. *Moana Nui* calling. Do you read me?'

No way of telling. The other world was well gone. And Blair
angered, not only because of loss of his life ashore, but also
because they were left vulnerable within the zone. 'If we're out
of touch,' he said, 'it means the bastards can do anything to
us out here. Get away with anything. No one would ever know.
They could vaporize us and pretend we never
existed. Say we must have been lost at sea. Something like that.
Anything.'

Stephen had never seen Blair more dismayed, not even in storm.

'As for the scene back home,' Blair went on, 'I might as well assume it's all bad news. That I'm finished. Nothing, nothing at all. It's the not knowing that gives me a pain in the gut. Not knowing at all.'

The others were less unnerved. Stephen could imagine Helen's concern for his safety out here. But it was not an effort to be made long; there were other demands upon imagination. Peter had no dependents ashore he ever wished to contact. Rex seldom mentioned wife or children, unless as part of life on land he had been glad to quit again; his messages to his wife on the transmitter had been infrequent anyway, like hers to him, and he was indifferent to the prospect of long silence now. If anything, he appeared more cheerful.

'Only a lot of chatter on that bloody box anyway,' he announced. 'What we want now is some action. Not talk.'

Blair was slow bringing himself to make reply. His tone made it plain that he now often thought Rex an obtuse old fool. Another mistake. Perhaps not as large a mistake as Barry Purchase or Mel Cross, but near enough. 'If the world doesn't know we're protesting out here, then what's the point?' he asked. 'No point at all.'

Peter had nothing to say. Nor Stephen.

'Listen, sonny boy,' said Rex, indifferent now to Blair as skipper, another consequence of the storm, 'I don't know about you, but I'm out here to take on the mugs and shits at Mururoa. There was a lot in the war didn't get advertised either. Every day of the war. We just got on with the job.'

'You don't understand,' Blair said, with clear distaste for the argument.

'I understand all right. You want the whole bloody world to know about us. I'm telling you no bugger in the world can help us out here anyway. And most back there couldn't give a stuff about us. They got their little homes. Their little jobs. Their little gardens. It's just us out here. Us and those mugs and shits on the atoll.'

'I mean,' Blair said, even more patience on show, 'you don't seem to understand that we're not in a war out here.'

134

'Then,' Rex said, 'you go tell that to the French admiral. You'll make his day.'

Honours to Rex. Blair made irritable retreat to the cabin. Peter looked at Stephen. Stephen looked at Peter. There was nothing more said.

Wind came again and the next hundred miles back into the centre of the danger zone disappeared in a day. Thereafter, they encountered lighter airs, and made more erratic progress. Rex might see the French as enemy, the mugs and shits on the atoll, but the real battle seemed likely to be with boredom. For when they finally hove to again, some twenty miles off Mururoa, each tropic day lengthened as another unlovely and sweaty burden. They trimmed sail now and then, trying for greater efficiency in heaving to, less drift. The cabin stifled; they rigged awnings outside for shade and sleep. They swam, and sometimes looked for marine life, but the ocean here was dead, empty apart from a tattered French weather balloon, with miniature transmitter attached. No bait dropped astern brought up a fish. The Pacific was dingy under cloud, metallic under sun. And the Pacific went on, and the days. There was less conversation, and much of that heard before anyway; they had begun to know each other too well, too much. They were browned by sun, all but Blair bearded now, sea changed, well disguised as veteran voyagers. Land, life ashore, might have been fifty years behind; not fifty days.

Unsettled weather, unfavourable wind direction, probably delayed the testing. They could hardly claim it was their presence, not yet. The transistor radio, with tiny voices from the world beyond, told them that the French had restated their intention to proceed with their current nuclear test series despite all international opposition. The same remote voices added that the protest yacht *Moana Nui*, last heard from in the vicinity of Mururoa, was still believed to be in the danger zone, and possibly observing deliberate radio silence as a tactic. Concern, however, had been expressed through diplomatic channels about the safety of the four men known to be aboard the craft. The French, in reply, pleaded ignorance of any outside presence in the zone, repeating that mariners could now only proceed there at their own risk.

'See,' Blair said, 'that's just what I mean. The sods have got us sewn up. Easy meat. They know we're here, and they're not saying.'

For aircraft still overflew them, observed them, with some regularity. And one day a helicopter hovered noisily above the yacht, seeming just inches above the masthead. It stayed there for all of five minutes, its pilots observing what they could of *Moana Nui* and the four men beneath. Perhaps just curiosity; perhaps pity. For there were surely no secrets to be seen aboard. Anyway it was relief when the helicopter departed, and the air ceased to thud around them.

'Maybe something's up,' Peter observed.

'Like what?' Blair asked.

'Maybe like a start to the tests, friend.' Peter shrugged. 'They have to start sometime. Those cats on the atoll don't draw pay for nothing. Let's see.'

What they saw next was a ship. At first slight on the horizon, then shaping as minesweeper as it neared them, until about a mile away, and hove to upon a light sea.

'There, friends,' Peter said. 'How does that grab you? We've got big brother watching now.'

'Mugs,' Rex said. 'Shall we give them a run?'

'Not yet,' Peter said. 'No point. They're not coming closer. We'll just have to watch them too.'

The minesweeper was still there in the morning; no mistaking its purpose now. It was there for *Moana Nui*.

'Right,' Peter decided, 'so maybe a little run to remind ourselves we're sailors. And to see how those cats play it.'

Soon they were chasing downwind, with full sail, before the minesweeper had time to respond and get up power. It was good sailing. All pure pleasure, after the heaving to. The minesweeper quickly dropped from sight in their wake.

But not too long. Less than an hour later it rose stolid on the horizon, and began to gain. Peter decided to heave to again, and the minesweeper finally did too. This time, though, something less than a mile away.

136

The chase, or flight, had brought them closer to Mururoa than they had been in days, inside fifteen miles. And there were new things now to see. First a huge cruiser, cumbersome with tall towers and radar dishes, the *De Grasse*, flagship of the French nuclear force, standing off at a distance from the atoll. Second, more relevant, there was a large and strange elongated white object slowly rising above Mururoa; it was so sudden after days and weeks of anticipation that the mind had problem with perspectives their sight was given.

'Right,' Peter said. 'So there it is, friends. It's all happening. The freaks say it's all go now.'

They could listen to the sound of their own breathing. There wasn't much else to be heard, unless the slap of light sea on the hull of the static yacht.

'We don't matter a damn now,' Blair insisted on explaining again. 'Not if no one knows we're here. They'll just go ahead regardless. For God's sake, give that transmitter another try.'

So Peter did, and Stephen did. The transmitter clearly still didn't receive, though Peter tried a thump or two on its side to resurrect that magic, but they continued to send, in hope of getting information out. They sweated over the same message on frequency after frequency: 'This is protest yacht *Moana Nui* calling from the French nuclear test zone. *Moana Nui* calling. Can you read us? We cannot read you. Please pass on news that the balloon is now tethered above Mururoa with tests about to begin. Repeat. The balloon is now tethered above Mururoa with tests about to begin. We are still near the centre of the danger zone. Can you read us?'

There was a limit, though, to what the batteries could take. They had to end the experiment. For that was all it could be; an experiment to prove their existence upon the Pacific. Then they climbed from the aft cabin to ᴄ bserve the balloon.

Peter said, 'The bomb hangs in a cradle underneath.'

'All bad news to me,' Blair said. 'More to the point that this close we could be burned down to the waterline. If it's the big one. Just bloody cinders.'

'Depends on the wind, friend,' Peter answered. 'The wind up high. They like westerlies or south westerlies to take

137

fallout clear of the atoll. If it's a small bomb first, we could be all right this side of the island, the way I'm reading it.'

'Well,' Blair said. 'One relief.'

'That's not what I'm saying,' Peter went on.

'No?' Blair was surprised.

'I'm saying we should go round the other side of the island. In the path of the fallout, where it's heaviest.'

'You're putting me on.'

'No sweat, friend. We'd still be in international waters, within our rights as mariners.'

'For God's sake. Talk sense. You said in the path of the fallout.'

'You're reading me,' Peter agreed.

It was time for Stephen. 'Peter's right,' he said.

Blair was again amazed. 'You're not off your head too?'

'They mightn't have any problem with us this side of the island,' Stephen explained, though it was obvious. 'The other side of the island we mightn't be ineffectual. Anyway, Blair, you were the one who talked about making problems for them.'

'That was before.'

'Before what?'

'Before the transmitter packed it in. Before we got cut off from outside.'

'We may be sending, getting messages out. We don't know.'

'Right. We don't know any damn thing, not any more. We're on our own.'

'I thought we always had been.'

'I mean lost. As good as dead.'

'If you like,' Stephen agreed. 'But I thought we were talking about making an effective protest. I haven't come all this way for nothing. No one has. Tell me if I'm wrong.'

Blair eventually found himself without answer.

'Right,' he agreed wearily. 'But one condition. That the radar reflector goes up again as soon as we get around the other side of the island. So there's no mistake, they know we're there.'

'I think we plan to give them that idea, friend,' Peter said.

They waited until after nightfall, and showed no navigation lights; the lights of their guardian minesweeper, though, lay lazily on the sea. Aboard the yacht they heard French voices, feet on steel, radios playing. They made sail and, with good breeze, moved away quickly; finally they motored to a point in international waters on the other side of the island. There they hove to again; and Rex, given Blair's hasty instruction, fixed the radar reflector back on the crosstree. 'Right,' Blair said with relief. 'They'll know we're here. Just in case it's all on in the morning. If they're counting down to a test then –' He paused.

'Yes?' Stephen said.

'Well, they'll have to cool it, won't they'? Call it off.'

'Of course,' Stephen said. 'It's best to hope so.'

'Hope so? Don't put me on again. We should bloody know so.'

'All right, Blair. So we bloody know so.'

But Blair waited, all the same; they all waited. There were no lights but theirs on the ocean around. There was just Mururoa's glow in the sky again, perhaps more faintly. And, in the end, a limit to waiting. 'You three get sleep,' Peter suggested. 'Be fresh for morning. I'll keep watch till then.'

'A death watch doesn't turn me on,' Blair said. 'Nor being fresh for a firing squad.'

'Friend,' said Peter, 'we're guessing. They're guessing too. Everyone is. Right? Right. So leave that bit to them. We might have the sailing bit in the morning, our thing. Some interesting sailing too, if we have those cats mad. So get sleep, be fresh.'

Stephen, below, sought sleep with difficulty. He heard Blair restless on his bunk too. Only Rex appeared indifferent to tension; he snored loudly, with only a snuffle now and then disturbing his sleep.

When Stephen found his own, at last, it was deep and apparently dreamless. He woke to sunlight shifting across his face, and Peter calling, 'They're back. Big brother's back.'

They were soon four in the cockpit again. The minesweeper was pushing towards them, beginning to slow. 'See what they do first,' Peter decided, 'before we try a run. Rex, you stand by the diesel. Steve, Blair, you get forward for the genoa.'

But the minesweeper began veering away slightly, finally standing off a hundred yards or two, so they could read the name *La Bayonnaise* distinct upon its hull. Soon a voice with heavy French accent shouted through a hailer: '*Moana Nui*. Calling *Moana Nui*. We have a message for you.'

'A trick,' Rex argued. 'A bloody trick. The mugs will try and get aboard us. Take us over.'

Peter signalled that their call had been understood. Blair said to Stephen, 'You'd better fetch our loud hailer. In the locker at the end of my bunk. Lucky I remembered one.'

Stephen descended to the cabin and found the hailer with no problem. While there, though, he remembered something else. Something he had preferred to forget until now, this first explicit confrontation. Rex Stone's gun.

No reason to disbelieve Rex's announcement that he would use it, if the yacht were boarded. And no little reason to suppose he might. So Stephen pushed a hand around and then under the mattress on Rex's bunk, and with relief found something solid. The gun and clips of ammunition were thickly parcelled in waterproof material, but it was impossible to mistake the object within. Stephen shoved the thing fast, as if tainting him, into his own kitbag; he could find some better place to hide it later. No time now, with the men above waiting on the hailer.

Peter grabbed it as soon as Stephen climbed from the cabin. He used the hailer to say: '*La Bayonnaise*. Calling *La Bayonnaise*. We read you. We understand. Please give us your message.'

There was reply: 'We wish to make formal delivery. Do you read us, *Moana Nui*? We are obliged to make formal delivery of our message.'

Already there was an inflatable rubber dinghy, with outboard motor, being launched over the side of the minesweeper. Several men were swaying down a rope ladder.

'What I told you,' Rex said. 'A mug trick. They'll be all over us.'

But Peter was replying: '*La Bayonnaise*. Calling *La Bayonnaise*. We will accept your message from two men only. Do

140

you read us? Two men only. An officer and a seaman. The officer with the message is not to come aboard. Do you read us? Is that understood?'

It appeared to be, after some pause aboard the minesweeper. For there were two men only in the rubber dinghy as it bounced across the swell to *Moana Nui*. The officer passed a brown envelope up to Blair without making attempt to board. Then the dinghy stood off a little way, waiting on answer, while the four on *Moana Nui* read the message. It was straightforward and impersonal enough after all. For it said merely that an area within stated radius of Mururoa atoll had been declared dangerous to mariners until further notice. There was no specific warning otherwise to *Moana Nui*.

'So tell them,' Rex suggested, 'to go get stuffed. We make the running out here.'

'I'll look after this, if you don't mind,' Blair said sharply. 'The skipper does have a function on some occasions.'

That point could still be casually taken. Blair fetched pen and paper from the cabin and braced himself in the cockpit to compose a reply. Straightforward too. It thanked the commander of *La Bayonnaise* for advice received, but observed that on the best legal advice *Moana Nui* was within its rights to remain in its present situation on international waters; there was legal advice available aboard *Moana Nui* should there be need for further discussion.

Apparently not. When the rubber dinghy returned to the minesweeper, nothing more was heard on a hailer, though they waited for a time.

'Right,' Peter announced, 'so let's see if we're still good for sailing, friends.'

They sailed, but not seriously, back and forward for much of the rest of the day, staying on the same side of the island, the minesweeper never out of sight. Towards evening, when they hove to twenty miles off the atoll, the minesweeper approached close; they heard the hailer again, informing them of another message, this time directly from the French admiral. The rubber dinghy made another journey, and the same now tired-looking officer passed up a second brown envelope.

141

Inside was a cable: 'From the Admiral commanding nuclear test force: to Moana Nui. B.T. You are still in the danger area defined in the notice to mariners you received this morning. Stop. You are requested to keep out of the said area or at least sail immediately and join position 15 (fifteen) nautical miles west (270) of the island of Tureia where I will ensure your safety against nuclear effects. Stop. Should you remain in your present situation I cannot accept responsibility for ill effects from nuclear testing. Stop. The tests are about to begin at earliest favourable opportunity. B.T.'

This one could not have been more specific.

'So the old shit wants us to please bugger off,' Rex said. 'No news to me.'

'What now?' Blair ignored Rex. He looked at Peter, then Stephen.

'You tell them,' Peter said, 'that we're staying, right? You tell them this is our scene right here.'

'You too, Steve?' Blair asked.

'Of course,' Stephen said. 'Why not?'

Blair appeared to be looking for some answer. So it was left to Peter to take up the hailer and say: 'Calling *La Bayonnaise*. Convey our compliments to the admiral and tell him we have nothing further to say. Repeat. Nothing further to say. We insist on our right to remain here in international waters. Can you read us, *La Bayonnaise*? Can you read us?'

'I wish to hell someone else could,' Blair said. 'Anyone else. Anyone else out there.'

'Forget it,' Stephen suggested.

'Forget what?' Blair was puzzled.

'Anyone else. There's no one, Blair, no one there. They've shut down the office and all gone home.'

'And you think that's funny?'

'No,' Stephen said. 'Sad, mostly. But you can take your choice.'

'All right for you.'

'That's where you're wrong.'

'Oh? So tell me.'

'Nothing's all right for me. That's why I'm here.'

142

Blair said, 'I should have had you figured. Should have seen through you in the first place.'

'Probably. But you did ask me along.'

'My mistake. All you crusaders, you're mostly sicker than the world you crusade about.'

'That wouldn't surprise me either.'

'Oh?'

'If we know the sickness, you see, that numbness in the gut, the mind. The problem is with people who don't know all their own symptoms, maybe different ones.'

'Meaning me, I take it?'

'No, Blair. Meaning me too.'

'You lawyers. You always know how to slip an argument.'

'Are we arguing?' Stephen asked. 'So let's quit. The morale of your yacht. Important just now.'

'If I still have a yacht.'

'So go talk to Peter. Explain that you're skipper.'

'Funny bastard. That's a nice line in cool humour you're peddling there.'

'I'm trying, Blair,' Stephen sighed. 'Just trying. That's all. I thought we all were.'

So now Blair and he were truly strangers among strangers, less than friends among friends. Stephen wished for regret, and failed to find it. If a truce came it was because one had to come, aboard a yacht; the need to talk more temperately was just another ritual of survival.

Dinner that evening was quiet in the cabin. Afterwards, they carried their coffee out into the cockpit, the four, and watched the lights of the minesweeper, still close, as the vessel rose and fell in the light sea off Mururoa atoll. Before long there was a moon, and stars spread thick across the sky. The wind was westerly, veering slightly to the south. Perfect testing weather, Peter observed. Otherwise the evening was delight.

There was no test in the morning. There were, though, two minesweepers now, neither of them *La Bayonnaise*, their companion of the day before; fresh vessels with a fresh duty. Not long after first light they both got up power and began slowly

143

to circle *Moana Nui* with something of menace in that movement. Not too far off stood the flagship *De Grasse*, presumably with the admiral aboard; the two minesweepers were doubtless acting under instruction from the flagship, which itself stood off to observe.

'Just the way it always is,' Rex said. 'The shits sit up there in comfort and let the poor mugs down here do the dirty work.'

Work? Sport; that was what the business of the minesweepers fast became. The sport of driving *Moana Nui* out of the danger zone. The admiral and his advisers might come up with tactics more ingenious, given time. But for now their scheme had some simple attraction. The two minesweepers travelled in swifter and swifter circle around *Moana Nui*, making large waves in their wake; at the centre of this commotion the yacht began to roll heavily, sickeningly, with things crashing about in the cabin. Like storm, as cruel as any survived, but this time entirely manufactured by men; the four aboard had to take tight grip on the yacht, wherever something to grip presented itself. Not pure hell perhaps, but near enough.

'I never,' said Rex with awe, 'saw us taking on the whole fucking fleet. All the shits and mugs at once. Never.'

Peter unlashed the wheel and clung to it as the yacht tipped violently sideways, shuddering, almost overturning. 'Get the diesel going,' he called to Rex. 'We might try motoring away from these cats.'

The diesel, despite weakened batteries, began soon to drum under Rex's hand; *Moana Nui* now had its own power, though it still swung helpless, jerked in every possible direction by the clashing wakes of the minesweepers, like the men aboard too.

But there was more to come. No hasty improvization, this tactic. There had to be coup de grace; they should have seen, and now they did. First one minesweeper, then the other, would pull out of its peripheral course, and charge through the seething circle of water directly at *Moana Nui*. On collision course, unmistakably; and then at the last possible moment veering away. At times they came so close to the yacht that those aboard seemed able to reach out and touch a grey naval hull, if they wished. All splendid seamanship of a kind, or stuntsmanship, not least on Peter's part too. He was still as cool-eyed as in any crisis, and worked the wheel with method, often with swift jerks, precisely timed, when likely impact rose high and grey from the sea again, the sharpest of steel bows seeming about to slice *Moana Nui* apart.

'We can't last in this,' Blair shouted. 'It's not on. Never.'

'No sweat, friend.'

'Can't you see? Here they come again.'

'So close your eyes.'

It might, true, be only a question of time before they rammed *Moana Nui* deliberately; this might be cat and helpless mouse. Yet they also might hold off for a while, to see if the men on *Moana Nui* were bruised enough in the danger zone, enough to quit. No telling. Nor telling whether the minesweepers might ram *Moana Nui* by accident anyway. More likely than not, in the confusion of this wild water.

Peter, though, was just waiting for the gap to appear. This came with one circling minesweeper behind *Moana Nui*, while the other arranged itself to starboard for still another mock charge. Peter gave the wheel to port, and with diesel gunned they stuttered forward, through the swollen waves, and crashed out towards open water. The minesweepers altered course, both trying to head off *Moana Nui* and the gap shrank to less than a hundred yards between the two vessels as Peter hurtled through. Behind them, then, the minesweepers had problem evading collision with each other. And those on *Moana Nui* had a bonus of laughter as their own adrenalin dispersed. The *De Grasse* rose ahead then, vast in the water, encased against nuclear hurt, top-heavy antennae, radar dishes, something more of another and alien world.

'Where the hell you going?' Blair said. 'You're going dead towards it.'

'Right on,' Peter said.

'You mad?'

'Thinking, friend. Just thinking.'

'So share the secret.'

'Those other cats won't try to turn us off too near the flagship. If big boss got hit, the admiral might lose his cool. Even sack a skipper. And repairs to *De Grasse* might mean tests delayed. All bad news.'

'So where,' Blair asked, 'do you find the time to think that one out?'

'I'm at the wheel, friend,' Peter answered. He seemed not to have understood the question.

The violence ceased. They puttered in the shade made by the flagship in quieter waters. Above, sailors by the hundred were at the rail, gazing down. Some waved, perhaps friendly, a casual salute. The minesweepers plunging behind then, as Peter promised, gave up their hunt; they slowed, stood off from their flagship.

Soon a hailer sounded from *De Grasse*: 'The admiral conveys his compliments on the seamanship of *Moana Nui*. Repeat. The admiral conveys his compliments. He asks you to see that it is now pointless persisting here. Repeat. It is now pointless persisting here. He requests that you give your word to leave the danger zone immediately. Repeat. Give your word to leave the danger zone immediately.'

'We can't take too much more,' Blair said. 'How do we answer?'

He was giving all decision to Peter now.

'We say nothing, friend. Nothing. No promises, no deals. Remember? We do a fast fade. Give them the chance to think we're copping out. They probably won't block us. They're not to know we aren't.'

'What about tomorrow?'

'We finish today first, friend. Tomorrow we sail back in again.'

'But the risk. You mean the same thing again?'

'They might have postponed one test already. Because of us. That's worth the risk.'

'That's not quite what I meant.'

'Maybe not. But it's why we're here, right?'

'But no one knows,' Blair protested. 'No one knows about us, what we're doing out here.'

'We know, friend. We know.'

'All the same –'

'So try the transmitter again,' Peter said wearily, 'if you have to. But first get some sailing done before these cats think again.'

146

When they tacked away, there was some ragged cheering, ironic or well-meant or both, from the decks of *De Grasse*. But they didn't hear those human cries long; they were soon more intimate with sound of wind and sea, while flagship and minesweepers diminished on the horizon.

Stephen, at Blair's request, then lowered himself into the aft cabin, sat before the transmitter, and attempted to tell anyone on the other side, anyone listening, that *Moana Nui* was being harassed by naval vessels in international waters; also that the crew remained well, if shaken. He tried again and again.

'Ask for help,' Blair insisted. 'Ask for help too.'

'Whose?' Stephen asked. 'Whose help?'

Blair was unable to say.

That evening, with the yacht resting again twenty five miles off Mururoa, Stephen tried to tune the transistor radio to international news of relevance. There was a great deal of static. Also some loud French voices, obviously close, burying other communication on the bands he tried. Eventually, though, he found a bulletin which told that there was increasing concern expressed about the welfare of the men on *Moana Nui*; that radio men in several parts of the Pacific were still trying for contact; that nothing had been heard of the yacht since it entered the danger zone; that the French continued to deny all knowledge of *Moana Nui* and its men.

'My God,' Blair said. 'So that's it, that's done it. We no longer exist.'

The bulletin raced on with news of other affairs in the world; other places. For it seemed there were other affairs, other places.

'So switch it off,' Peter said.

Stephen didn't need telling again. Blair didn't object, nor Rex.

'Time to give all radios away for tonight,' Peter observed.

No one argued that either. Nor would have even with the energy. The silence was as limp as they were.

'All a waste,' Blair announced at length. 'A tragic bloody waste.'

'What is?' Stephen asked, but it was a cue rather than a question; he knew the answer.

'All this. All we've gone through. All we're going through. A waste.'

'Because no one knows about it?' Another cue.

'They don't, do they?' He seemed concerned that Stephen might suggest otherwise; his tone was tense. 'If no one knows we exist, what was that all about today? Nothing. Just more waste.'

Stephen waited upon Peter's objection, but it wasn't coming, not after so eroding a day; he saw then that he would have to contrive fresh choreography for the argument, something on his own account. If only to end it again.

'Nothing,' he insisted, 'is ever wasted. Nothing decent, nothing worthwhile, nothing human.'

And before Blair could answer he went quickly up on deck, to sit under a neutral sky, and to try to make himself believe it, for it sometimes seemed he could.

They took short watches that evening, so that each could get at least some sleep. Peter's idea was that at three a.m., three or four hours before the likely time of any test, they would fix the radar reflector to the crosstree again and cruise towards Mururoa. Dawn should find them well within a risk area for fallout; the French would understand that they still had a problem, that the protest wasn't finished yet. If a test was on the way, an hourly countdown would have already begun.

So Stephen found sleep difficult. Not fear, not really; his mouth was dry with anticipation, as if from some impending and long delayed sexual encounter; his entire body was sounding alerts. But with sufficient whisky he finally persuaded it into restful shape; and eventually, briefly, slept. He was then, it appeared, in some huge courtroom, with spectators far removed, and the magistrate or judge even further away, almost indistinguishable in the distance; he was quite alone, in the echoing space at the centre of the court, pleading a case. The nature of the case was obscure to him, but it evidently concerned the words of a poem, written out in large capital letters on

148

a blackboard. The poem, this exhibit, was clearly one of Jacqueline's – those terse lines could belong to no one else – but not one he could recall reading before. What was at issue, then? Not obscenity anyway; there was no four-letter word apparent, nor frank or perverse sexual reference. The metallic words made for sounds, images, which eluded him. He had to listen to himself talk before he understood the nature of the case he was presenting. The issue, it seemed, was clarity; the lines were ambiguous; the poem, he heard himself argue, was unfinished and therefore not as Jacqueline would have wished it known and read. There was tautology, for example, and confused metaphor; and plainly the poem still lacked a last line, perhaps a last stanza, anyway some adequate summation. What then was the point? Obviously that he, as her husband, had the right and perhaps duty to pay the poem some attention; and attempt what repair he could. Was that, he asked the court, so unreasonable a thing? The question was, of course, rhetorical; and the others in the court, whoever they were, were too remote for him to detect response upon their faces. Should not he, as husband, have the right to finish that which his wife had begun? Again the court withheld response. When he sat down, his plea finished, he understood that judgement would likewise be withheld. Unless he could come up with something of his own. And that was impossible, utterly impossible; he was fuming at the injustice of the thing, and the unreason.

There was a hand on his shoulder; he opened his eyes and looked into the faintly lamplit face of a stranger whose name he knew as Peter Lee. This stranger was saying, 'It's time, friend. We're sailing back in again.'

Eleven

AT FOUR, AN HOUR AFTER THEY BEGAN THE JOURNEY BACK INTO
the centre of the zone, they saw the light of a large vessel
approaching, then the light of another. Seen fast on radar,
Moana Nui was to be attended by minesweepers again. The
two vessels must have been standing well off Mururoa, to
appear so soon, and perhaps not just to intercept *Moana Nui*
should it return; perhaps a test was due above the atoll, with
wind direction favourable.

'We can do without navigation lights now,' Peter instructed.
'And the radar reflector too. No point advertising ourselves
now, friends, more than we have to. They got the message.
Now let them find us.'

But they had hardly begun a tack at an oblique angle to the
approaching minesweepers when they heard aircraft. One, then
two and possibly three, circling, sweeping above them in the
dark, red lights blinking.

'Nervous about something tonight,' Peter said. 'All the cats
are out to play.'

'Perhaps we've gone far enough,' Blair suggested.

'I think, friend, they're trying to tell us that. So what are
you trying to tell me?'

'I'm wondering what you want.'

'More wind, friend. To shake them off before daylight. You

want yesterday over again?'

'No,' Blair conceded.

'So it has to be hit and run. The only scene left. Into the centre of the zone, when they're likely to be testing, then wide again fast before they can box us in. Sure they can follow. But it doesn't have to be easy for them.'

'Or us.'

'Right. But then again, friend, I wasn't saying it would.'

'We can only play it this way so long. There has to be an end.'

'So what's the news?'

'They can't quit; they've got too much invested in these tests.'

'You're not saying we should?'

'Not exactly. No.'

'So tune me in. What are you saying?'

Blair appeared to have difficulty deciding.

Stephen suggested, 'We have something invested ourselves, Blair.'

'Don't sell me all that again.'

'I'm not selling anything. I'm saying.'

'I've got more invested in this than anyone. Even this yacht, if you haven't noticed lately. I'm trying to suggest we're all reasonable men. And –'

A pause. 'Yes?' Stephen prompted.

'And, well, there is a limit. There has to be.'

'Now?'

'Well, not right now, perhaps.'

'Then when? When do we begin being reasonable?' Stephen was genuinely interested in knowing; it was not a rhetorical question, nor an academic one.

'When we've made our point. Arguably we've done that. Not that anyone knows yet. The sooner they do, the better. We already have a good story to tell when we get back.'

'We might even have a better one.'

'And we mightn't be around to have anything to say. Anyway it's all going to cool fast if people think we're just lost at sea. No mileage in that, just another lost yacht in the Pacific. By the time we get back we might be a dead bore. Only half believed. The way things are, we're still news.'

'The way things are, we've done nothing.'

'We've made our point.'

'Nothing,' Stephen insisted.

'So speak for yourself.'

'We think we might have delayed a test. But we're not even sure of that.'

'Never a realistic prospect anyway.'

'But worth trying. And trying again. One less test, one less bomb. We stay in their way as long as we can. Make the best of our advantage while we've got one.'

'We're talking different languages.'

'Probably,' Stephen agreed.

'We have no advantage. This yacht, four men. As last resort the crazy gang on the atoll can forget us.'

The French, though, were demonstrably not forgetting them. Premature daylight seemed to burst about the yacht; lines of flares, on small parachutes, were drifting down from the aircraft above. Until the yacht was entirely visible, in blue magnesium glow, to aircraft and minesweepers; they were animals suddenly in a hunter's spotlight. With the yacht seen, placed, fixed, the aircraft dropped only occasional lines of flares until the minesweepers were close enough to use their searchlights on *Moana Nui*'s sails. No escape at all now.

'So heave to,' Peter decided. 'We don't want those sons of bitches any closer.'

They began to drift, in the unnerving illumination. The aircraft departed and the minesweepers, also heaving to, watched them from each side.

That was how first light found them. The searchlights were extinguished; the men on the minesweepers now observed them through binoculars. A dull cloudy morning, the wind still westerly, tending south. Peter, casual on the deck, eased the backed jib, hoping to make inconspicuous movement towards the atoll without objection from the minesweepers. Stephen, breakfasting in the cabin, was tempted by the transistor radio again, to see if they existed. There was one news item of interest. A report from unofficial French sources in Tahiti said the first nuclear test at Mururoa was expected within forty-eight hours; the same sources said the protest vessel *Moana Nui* was believed to have left the danger zone, in response to French request, and was now heading home.

Rex, usually indifferent to the words of the world, began to rage, 'The buggers think we've quit. They think we've run for cover.'

'All the more imperative,' Blair said calmly, 'that we get back and put the real story on the line.'

'What story is that?' Stephen asked.

'That we aren't chicken. That we did our best, with those bastards harassing hell out of us. They have a right to know, out there, that we didn't quit.'

'Not yet we haven't,' Peter observed ambiguously.

Blair looked up.

'No sweat in quitting just to go back and say we didn't quit, friend,' Peter said. 'No sweat at all, right?'

'It makes sense, though,' Blair argued.

'It makes more sense to keep those cats out there jumpy. More sense to me.'

'There has to be an end, though.'

'Sure. We all have one coming, along the line. You. Me. All of us. Singly, slow or fast. Or maybe all together, one quick big bang, the coolest you ever saw.'

Outside the sea was rising, and the wind.

Not long afterwards they heard the sound, and there was no confusing it with thunder, not near Mururoa: a long low roar, rumbling, distinct above the wind, the creak of sail and flap of pennant. Unlike thunder, it took some time to subside; and there was no lightning to follow, nor other illumination, as they watched on the deck, waiting. Altogether too cloudy a day. There was just the slow shock of sound across the water, reverberation they felt in their flesh, to tell them that the French had just finished the first detonation of the test series. Large or small? Impossible to tell. None had heard sound quite like it before.

Blair was first to find words. 'Just what I warned you,' he

announced. 'They've gone ahead regardless. They don't care whether we're here, not any more.'

'With respect friend,' Peter answered, 'use your eyes. You might see some cats out there who think we're safe in their care. And look now.'

There was some agitation apparent on the minesweepers. Signal flags were run up, and hailers were sounding across the water. It appeared *Moana Nui* was being told, urgently, to proceed north for safety.

'The way I reckon it,' Peter said, 'is we're still about twenty miles off, and probably too far north already.'

'Too far north?' Blair said.

'To be at risk in the fallout area.'

'Thank God for that then. But why tell us to move out further?'

'Can't be too careful. For our good, friend, their reputation. Things go wrong.'

There was sweat again on Blair's face. Yet a mild enough morning. 'So what now?'

'We put out all sail. Rex, Steve, let's have more of the main. Quick.'

'So you think it's safer to go north too,' Blair said.

'I didn't say that.'

'No?'

'The hell we're going north. We're sailing in. Towards the atoll.'

'You're out of your mind.'

'I've never been more in my mind, friend, listening to what it tells me. Right now I'm getting this message we're here to say no. And when we stop saying no, and say yes to those bomb-mad sons of bitches, we've quit. Quit just like they say.'

'You haven't consulted anyone else,' Blair protested.

'Sure I'll consult. Steve?'

'We sail in.' Words had never been cleaner. The trivia of the voyage washed away, fine dust, from his skin. His life, anyway, now admitted no alternative; only that utterance could give it shape. 'Of course we sail in.'

'Don't tell me you're mad too,' Blair said.

154

'Rex?' Peter went on.

'We sail in.'

'You would,' Blair said, 'you poor bloody old fool.'

Stephen was unable to look at Blair.

Because Blair was now saying 'Does the skipper get a hearing, the owner of this yacht?'

'Sure. Let's hear it, friend.'

'All pointless risk. We're done our best.' Blair paused. 'So maybe it wasn't good enough. They tested after all. No use prolonging the agony. Crying over spilt milk. Only it's not milk in there. It's fallout.'

'If we go north,' Stephen began.

'The only sane thing to do,' Blair interrupted.

'If we go north, they'll know we intend looking after ourselves. That we're no real risk, not serious at all, just a bunch of play-boys. And get on with it.'

'Nothing to fight in there,' Blair insisted. 'Just poisoned air. Poisoned water. We're too late.'

'Are we sailing in or bloody not?' Rex asked.

'We're waiting,' Peter answered, 'on the skipper's opinion.'

'Decision,' Blair said. 'The skipper's decision.'

'Opinion,' Peter persisted, 'and his vote. My guess is it's something like three votes to one.'

'So that's how it is,' Blair said bitterly.

'Right,' Peter agreed. 'You can always check the figures.'

'I suppose you'd consider mutiny too strong a word for this situation.'

'Probably, friend,' Peter said. 'Now you mention it. But we're still happy to have you along.'

'Steve?'

Stephen was now obliged to look at Blair, the appeal in his eyes.

'Don't you have any more to say?'

'Not really.' He had said it all; three words were enough. But it seemed he must say more now, for someone's sake. 'Only that we took a unanimous vote at the beginning. When we put this boat to sea, to sail international waters. Here; off the atoll. That's the proposition now. Nothing more.'

155

'But there's a bomb just gone off.'

'Perhaps. But an irrelevance.' For he had begun to see, at last, what Peter meant before the voyage began.

'You're all out of your minds then. All too long at sea. I should have known.'

'You should, friend.' Peter's tone was mild.

'If you don't bloody like the way it is,' Rex said to Blair, 'you can put the dinghy over the side and bugger off to the French. They'll see you right.'

Blair made no reply. He stayed sullen in the cockpit while the other three put out more sail, and took the yacht towards Mururoa. With growing wind, they sliced fast through the swell, clear of the minesweepers, away from the fluttering signal flags and men with binoculars.

As before, they were swift to put distance between themselves and the navy: one mile, then two. Perhaps the French skippers were waiting on instruction from their flagship; perhaps unwilling to proceed further into the danger zone themselves; or perhaps they were reluctant to believe what they saw, and were waiting upon *Moana Nui* to tack about towards safer sea. But the yacht, meantime, was closing with Mururoa; soon there was no mistaking its ultimate course. The minesweepers had to move, and did.

With chase begun, *Moana Nui* seemed still to be gathering natural pace, sails filled firm, slashing through wave, skimming through trough. Yet it wasn't long before the minesweepers began to gain, to rise grey behind them, finally to draw abreast. There were fresh signal flags out for the crew of *Moana Nui*; they insisted on danger. So, evidently, did the men on the decks of both minesweepers shouting fragments of English across the water.

And *Moana Nui* still sailed unchecked towards the atoll. Sailed peacefully, with Peter at the wheel.

'It's all go now,' he shouted. 'All on. Here they come. Hold tight, friends.'

First one minesweeper swung across their bow, pulling away a few hundred yards, then closing to fifty on their starboard side; they could see the captain now, among his officers, gesticulating vehemently, pointing north. Soon the minesweeper was only twenty yards off, close enough to see flecks of rust on its hull.

'Go back,' they heard the agitated captain calling now, in the plainest English. 'You must go back. Go north.'

'So tell them, Steve,' said Peter from the wheel.

With hailer, Stephen shouted back: 'We advise that we are within our legal right on international waters. We also advise you should not be manoeuvring your ship so close to a sailing vessel.' Then he repeated the message, for all the difference it made. The minesweeper still edged closer to *Moana Nui* and the captain, if anything, appeared to be appealing to the clouded sky for advice, or judgement. Then he was flourishing a fist. The bow of the minesweeper was now almost level with the stern of *Moana Nui*, ten yards or nearer. Rising and falling large and grey, chopping up and down, a giant knife at work with meticulous method; it now shut off wind from their sails.

'They'll kill us,' Blair said. 'Kill us all.'

'Cool it,' said Peter.

'Call it off. Tell them.'

'No way, friend. No way. Just another scare.'

'Not any more,' Blair said. 'You've blown it.'

'So go below. Don't look.'

'Can't you see –'

But they all saw, then; and heard. Apparently committed to collision, the minesweeper rammed *Moana Nui* – at first lightly, with grating sound, and finally, rising on a wave, with crunching of timber and metal; then, though its engines were now reversed full astern, it struck yet again. This time the two vessels rose and fell together with the ocean. Rigging snapped and stranded around them; the back stays were gone; a section of gunwale fell away; more screeching metal, more groaning wood; the runner on the jib sheet track buckled; it seemed the splintering yacht was being torn in two.

Yet it wasn't. They were still afloat, if limply, when the minesweeper parted from them, an apologetic lover, penitent rapist, and fell astern. Stephen had the wheel in his hands now, while Peter and Rex pulled down sail before the mast gave, with no support from stays. Blair was beside Stephen in the cockpit, still too dazed to help.

'That's done it,' he said finally. 'You blew it. You all blew it. The bitter bloody end. Lucky we're alive. Couldn't you dumb bastards see it coming?'

'See what?'

'See they had to do what they did. For our own good.'

'For theirs. If you're not going to help, hold the wheel while I go forward.' He left Blair and recrimination behind in the cockpit.

Occupied with repair, after pulling down sail, and determining the damage, plainly enough to stop them for a time, perhaps altogether, they were not watching for fresh activity from the minesweepers. Not that it could have made much difference; there were rubber dinghies around the yacht as it rolled lifeless in the sea, and then black-suited frogmen, commandos, spilling over their side, over their deck, with truncheons in hand and knives strapped to their side.

Rex, as soon as he saw, made a move for the cabin, and doubtless his gun. 'No,' Stephen said quietly, grabbing him back. 'You won't find it. Anyway there's too many.'

Blair was pushed from the wheel without protest.

'I still say they're mug pirates,' Rex announced, and in emphasis punched the nearest Frenchman. He managed two more punches before other commandos, efficient with truncheons, beat him down to the deck. When Stephen tried to push between, to stop the attack, his arms were taken from and he was held in hammerlock; Peter too was pinioned. They were as helpless as *Moana Nui* now.

In that way they waited on the arrival of the French captain, in the last of the rubber dinghies; he nodded to the commandos to release *Moana Nui*'s crew. Rex, bruising badly about the face, was lifted up from the deck, quieter now; he also bled from a cut lip.

'I regret that you made this action necessary,' the captain said, in more than adequate English. 'But I have been under orders to stop you, to the best of my ability. Unfortunately you made things difficult.'

158

'You rammed us, 'Blair said. 'You rammed us quite deliberately.'

'An incident. An accident of the sea.'

'You could have killed us.'

'You are the skipper, sir?'

'I am,' Blair insisted.

'Then I must ask you again to comply with my admiral's request to leave the danger zone immediately.'

'Like this? You're joking.'

'I do not see the damage as so great.'

'Look around then.'

'Should you not comply with this reasonable request, I shall be obliged to tow you some distance from Mururoa.'

'And leave us to rot? I warn you. People are going to know about this. The world is.'

This did not appear greatly to disconcert the captain as he found his way through the lines in his script. 'I have my orders,' he said. 'Should it be necessary, I am authorized to arrest you for violation of French national waters.'

'We're well outside national waters.'

'That, sir, is your word against mine, I regret to say.'

'The hell it is. I'll sue you. I'll take you to the World Court.'

With hazard past, Blair was convincing as skipper again. Impossible, while he revelled in the confrontation, to imagine him as the man of dismay less than an hour before. The captain might have the lines, but Blair was stealing the scene; something truly his scene whether in office or boardroom, or on the deck of a yacht.

'We have,' said the captain,' 'only your safety at heart. Surely that has been clear. We wish you no harm.'

'So you rammed us. And then your bully boys took us over. You're joking again.'

'This morning a nuclear device was exploded over Mururoa.'

'Large or small?'

'I regret that I am not permitted to discuss this subject. I can only say that should you have gone closer to the atoll, your crew could have been in great danger.'

'We're not fools. We know the risk around here.'

'Then you have my admiration, sir, my most deep respect. Some might think you foolish. Personally I do not, as seaman too. Nevertheless I must insist that you leave this area at once.'

'Impossible. There's too much damage done. I've told you that. Tell him exactly, Peter.'

'The bobstay fitting's damaged and taking water,' Peter said. 'The bumkin too. All the stays are strained or slack. The mast head fitting looks sick to me. There's rigging to replace. We might just be able to sail downwind, in very light airs, with the mast holding. But I wouldn't like our chances, friend. As for motoring, no way. We've got damn all diesel fuel left.'

'So I suggest you get on to your admiral,' Blair said, 'and tell him we insist on repair. And that we're here until he comes across with help. Understand?'

'Naturally,' said the captain. 'I think you will find the admiral a reasonable man. While I consult, my men shall remain aboard, of course, with orders to restrain you. Please do not attempt anything unpleasant or unwise.'

'We'll stick with those wise, pleasant bombs of yours,' Peter said.

The captain did not smile or even seem to understand. He returned to his minesweeper, and within half an hour arrived with the news that the admiral had offered repairs to *Moana Nui* if it were towed into Mururoa lagoon.

'Right,' Blair said. 'We accept on certain conditions.'

'Conditions?' The captain might have to consult a new script.

'We need fresh food and water. We also want to communicate word of our circumstances to the outside. To tell people just what's happened to us, what you've done.'

'I do not think, sir, that you are in a position here to state conditions. I think the admiral might possibly consider the sending of a message to your families, assuring them of your safety. But no more. You have an hour to accept or reject his offer. He, of course, has a condition of his own.'

'So?'

'You must give your word that once repairs to your craft are completed, you undertake to leave at once the vicinity of Mururoa atoll, and the danger zone as defined for mariners.'

'I don't think your admiral is in a position to state conditions either. At the moment we can't leave here even if we want to. We're not seaworthy.'

The Frenchman shrugged. 'It would not be impossible for us to tow you to some other, distant island to keep you there under arrest, for violation of our national waters, until testing at Mururoa is finished.'

'And that's it?'

'I think it is clear, sir.'

So the four of *Moana Nui* gathered on the foredeck, out of hearing of the French, to consider the admiral's offer. 'Not unreasonable,' Blair argued. 'Anyway where's the choice? We can't go anywhere. It's accept, or nothing.'

'I say nothing's better,' Rex urged. 'Sit here. Wait it out. If the mugs try to tow us away, cut the line. Or jump overboard.'

'Not on. For starters we're getting low on food and water. For another they could confine us closely so we couldn't get away with anything of the sort. Steve? Peter?'

'I'm with Rex,' Stephen decided. 'Even if it isn't practical. Make nothing easy for them.'

Blair grew irritated. 'Peter?'

'Right, so it's time for the skipper's decision, friend.'

'Oh?' Blair looked bewildered.

'Someone has to deal with those cats. I say the skipper. Naturally. His job.'

'I see. So I'm left to carry the can.'

'You wanted to earlier, friend. If you want a vote after all, I'll abstain.'

'You're not making it easy for me.'

'That's the hell of it, friend. The skipper's day is never done.'

All the same, Blair went soon to the French captain with unconditional acceptance of the admiral's offer. He did repeat as request, no longer as demand, desire to communicate with the outside world. One minesweeper remained with them the rest of the day. They made such repairs as they could, caulking fittings which took water, putting up the spinnaker halyard as temporary backstay to the mast. Otherwise they waited while

161

the yacht rocked useless in the swell. Next morning a tugboat arrived to take them in tow for Mururoa.

'That gun,' Rex said quietly to Stephen.

'What about it?'

'I wondered where you hid it.'

'Never mind.'

'I wish to God I had it. They'd never have got us so easy.'

'Probably not. Nothing would have been easy. For us, either.'

'Sometimes I think you're on my side. Other times I never bloody know. You didn't throw it overboard?'

'No.'

'Good. We might need it yet.'

'It's not a war,' Stephen argued.

'Something I might expect the skipper to say; not you. Not now. The mugs bloody near kill us, then beat us up, and you still say there's no war. What bloody world do you bloody live in?'

'This bloody one,' Stephen insisted, though he sometimes wondered now.

Twelve

THE SWELL DIMINISHED AS THEY WERE DRAWN INTO THE LEE OF
Mururoa. There were straggling coconut palms now, queerly
and greenly vivid to their sight after so long at sea, above pale
coral sand; and that shore, apparently at first intact, began to
shuffle itself into small coral islets as they approached. Islets
around the large lagoon into which the tug led them. Then they
were within Mururoa, encircled by land, or such of it as any
atoll could thinly offer; the turquoise lagoon was textured with
the underwater growth of coral at transparent depth. It was all
too serene. The shore was unblackened, the sea without blemish.
It could have been any tropical lagoon. Only those great
concrete bunkers, on islets north and south, told them otherwise. Like the helicopter, circling above, observing their progress.

Then more. Perhaps ten miles across the lagoon was a port of
surprising size: a half dozen large vessels, including *De Grasse*,
among smaller craft, tugs, minesweepers, barges, landing craft.
Two aircraft above were circling to land. Ashore were cars
and trucks travelling substantial roads, thatched native-style
huts and more considerable buildings among the palms, even
sunny beaches, men at leisure with sailboats, speedboats, and
water-skis.

Unreal? Hardly; that implied some relation to reality. This

163

had none after that shock of sound across the water, then the ramming and boarding of the boat. It was an unconvincing dream into which they were drifting, helpless; an absurdly imperfect fantasy. There was no brutality, no menace, no evil. It should all have been other.

And the French insisted on friendliness, waving from ship-board, clicking cameras, as *Moana Nui* was berthed beside a repair ship, against a steel pontoon. Could such smiling men in so agreeable a place spawn storms of fire, dragons of death? Stephen was at pains to convince himself as the yacht came to rest. Technically they may have been captive within this make-shift empire, but it was perilously like a homecoming, after the weeks at sea; they were citizens returned to the country of man.

His confusion took time to subside.

'It isn't so bad at all,' Blair announced, after a time. 'They're doing the decent thing.'

For a crowd of carpenters, painters, welders, and mechanics was soon busy on *Moana Nui*; broken fittings were detached and borne away into the repair ship; officers were discussing details with Peter; it was clear that no need of the yacht would be neglected. The admiral had even instructed that they be pro-vided with fifty gallons of diesel fuel, for safety, so they could motor much of the way back to Rarotonga if they chose.

Cameras still clicked. But it was soon clear that the photo-graphers were now official, on duty; that the repair of *Moana Nui* might have value as a French public relations enterprise.

No escape; even here. Blair was called upon to pose and smile, several times, among the activity on his yacht. When Stephen offered doubt, Blair answered, 'Keep your cool. No harm in a few photographs. People still know why we're here.'

'They might begin to wonder.'

'Don't be so bloody uptight. You always were a rigid bastard.'

'We don't know how they'll use those photographs.'

'Right. So maybe they'll prove we exist after all. Someone needs to know. Otherwise where's the point?'

Possibly elsewhere now, though there was no defining just where. Rex, true, gave no more than scowls to the garrulous

Frenchmen around him; he had no part in the handshaking. And Peter was severely businesslike among the repair work.

But there was more to come; an officer arrived by motor boat and asked for Blair. 'The admiral conveys his compliments, Mr Hawkins, and welcomes you to Mururoa,' this messenger said. 'He should like you and your crew to join him at lunch today, if possible.'

Blair nudged Stephen and said sidelong, 'We ought to make that scene. The old sport's likely to turn it on; he has so far.' To the officer he added formally, 'I think we should find that possible. Of course.'

'Then his launch will be sent for you at 1200 hours.' The officer made a move to leave.

'Tell me,' Blair went on, 'has the admiral been informed of our desire for some communication with the outside world?'

'He has,' said the officer.

'And?'

'He is not unwilling to do so. But not until you have departed from the area of Mururoa. I think you will find him a man of fair mind.'

'So long as we get out of his way?'

'If that is how you wish to interpret it.'

'What about food and water?'

'That,' said the officer, 'is a more difficult issue. And best discussed with the admiral.'

'Difficult? What's so damn difficult about it if he can invite us to lunch? I can pay good money for anything we take on.'

'That is not the issue.'

Stephen said to Blair, 'Surely it's clear. Hunger and thirst are more likely to drive us out of the danger zone than any harassment they can arrange. They're only interested in making us seaworthy so we can get the hell out of it.'

'You make them sound utter bastards.'

'Not at all. I'm sure most of them are kindly, agreeable, humane men. So long as we leave them alone to get on with their thing. There were supposed to be some kindly, well-meaning men in charge of extermination camps once too. They just had their job to do, of course; their thing.'

165

'You're being extreme again.'

'Marginally, perhaps. Or perhaps not so marginally. Those others thought they were tidying up the human race a bit; these ones are giving us a chance to tidy the race away altogether. Maybe there is some fine moral difference to be pondered upon. I don't think it's worth pondering, though.'

Blair stopped listening. He turned to the officer. 'Tell the admiral we shall be delighted to accept his invitation at 1200 hours.' The bemused officer left.

'You go,' Stephen told Blair. 'I'm not kinky for French admirals.'

'You're not only uptight,' Blair said. 'You're unreasonable too. At least we might get some real food for once.'

But the others, so it turned out, were equally unreasonable in preferring the mildewed rice and canned meat left in *Moana Nui*'s hold. Rex refused to lunch with any mug or shit enemy; his bruises were still distinct. Peter, cool to the proposition too, anyway didn't want to leave the yacht in French hands entirely, lest they cut corners in their haste to repair and be rid of it.

'For God's sake,' Blair said, 'I can't go alone. He's invited us all. No point in giving needless offence.'

'I thought we were here to give offence, friend,' Peter proposed. 'But tell me if I got it wrong.'

Blair looked at Stephen with plea. 'Steve, think again. I might need someone else if negotiations get tricky.'

'What negotiations, friend?' Peter said. 'You interest me more and more.'

'I'm still trying to get some message out,' Blair explained. 'And trying to persuade them we need food and water.'

'So cool it now. You really think they want to advertise that they rammed us? And to help us stick around?'

'It's worth trying,' Blair insisted.

'Sure. So is Christianity. You may even find the admiral a gentleman and a scholar, friend.'

Blair said, 'Steve, I'd still like you along.'

'I've never noticed you needing someone to hold your hand. In these situations.'

'I need some moral support. That was why I wanted you here in the first place. Remember?'

Indeed; but Stephen still hesitated.

'You'd better make that scene after all, friend,' Peter suggested. 'This negotiation bit doesn't turn me on.'

'I say bugger them all,' Rex Stone announced. And wandered off.

'All right,' Stephen sighed. 'So I'll do my best, whatever that is.'

At twelve the admiral's launch arrived, and sped them across the lagoon: Stephen and Blair were greeted on a concrete jetty, remote from other activity in the harbour, by French officers in light shirts and pale tropical trousers, all eminently cordial and urbane men who inquired about their health, the condition of their yacht, the length of their voyage. Then they were walked across a sward of sand to some large thatched huts set under coconut palms. Here another group of officers waited, with some civilian scientists, the admiral at their centre: he too was coolly dressed, with dark glasses, and a khaki baseball cap set casually back on his greying head. He warmly and firmly shook their hands.

'I daresay we have many things to say to each other,' he observed. 'But first I suggest we relax together as men of the sea should.'

Orderlies brought drinks. Tall, iced, with slices of lemon. And a taste which evoked other luxuries lost elsewhere, now almost forgotten. And there were distinctly comfortable chairs set in shade. Altogether too tempting a situation; even the earth underfoot was ceasing to sway. Again the cameramen were dogging them, and now it was much less difficult to see why. Stephen could already read the disarming captions beneath protest voyagers relaxing with the admiral in the comfort of his Mururoa headquarters. Disarming? Off *Moana Nui* they were in truth disarmed; only with land underfoot were they lost. Stephen wished himself back aboard, well clear of the place. But Blair apparently felt no disorientation.

And he was visibly flattered when the admiral said, 'I under-

167

stand that you are a man of some substance, and much reputation, in your own way, Mr Hawkins. Is that not so?'

'If that's what rumour tells you,' Blair agreed, 'I'm in no position to deny it.'

'Not rumour, Mr Hawkins. Our intelligence service is obliged to take an interest in those who in turn take too great an interest in our activity here. As you do. Naturally this information may be of use to me also. Certainly it makes me curious. For I still wonder why a man such as yourself should embark on so uncomfortable and futile an enterprise as this one.' The admiral looked into his glass, possibly for an insect, and then held it up to the light. 'Do you see yourself as serving humanity, perhaps?'

'Perhaps,' Blair said easily. 'In a sense.'

'And what called you to such service, if I may ask?'

'Call it conscience, if you like.'

'Conscience. Yes. Interesting. I have, you know, in the past seen surgeons working over my wounded; I have never been one to shut myself away from the consequences of what I must order. I have seen them take my men apart like beasts in a butcher's shop. And nowhere, strangely, can they find and repair this thing called conscience. It is not to be found.'

'Which suggests,' Stephen offered, 'that men might be more.'

'On the contrary. It suggests that they are no more. Merely more ingenious about the business of being beasts so they can get on with using the world as they will. Mr West, I understand you to be a lawyer, not so? Perhaps there is a legal definition of conscience at hand. Something to convince me.'

'Not really,' Stephen said. 'I just see that you're getting on with using the world as you will. And someone has to say no.'

'And that is all?'

'More or less.'

'Disappointing. Yes. The need of men for the fantasy of legality I find as interesting as their need for the fantasy of conscience. For both are adjustable, flexible to the needs of the beast.'

'But you're talking about war,' Blair insisted.

'Mr Hawkins, Mr West,' the admiral said, wearily, 'there is no peace. Another fantasy. To seek peace in man's world is

168

as profitless as seeking conscience in his carcass. There is only war, with many different names. And many different ways of playing the game. Apart from war itself, of course, honest and undisguised.' He sighed. 'Sad. I expect some little wisdom from men who sail here as servants of humanity. I see you merely as men, after all, men as fallible as we are, and as bewildered.' The admiral was in search of his insect again; presently he found it with his finger, and flicked it away. 'And who, might I ask, serves humanity best, does it the greater favour? The man who calls upon conscience as substitute for sense, who thinks it sufficient to say no to unpleasant knowledge. Or other men, such as ourselves here, who make it their business daily, not as holiday, to live with the largest and most demanding of all truth, that man now has the power to make of himself mere dust in the universe, and his world so much drifting debris? We demonstrate that possible destiny, is that not so? We make men think the unthinkable. Thus, we truly serve. Men no longer have their old fear of eternal hellfire. The loss is theirs. Consider the finest thought, the greatest art, the most profound imagination, expended on the assumption of hellfire. We now do our best to heal that loss in their lives. We provide the hellfire again – not out there, or down there, or in some eternally mysterious beyond, but here upon earth, before their eyes, so none can avoid the sight. What greater service to offer mankind?'

He smiled then, and went on, 'Also, my castaway friends, where would your supposed consciences be without us? You may think you are necessary; I argue that we are even more so. Consider. Without us you do not even begin to exist here. Without us you would have no challenge, no voyage, no adventure.'

Stephen was quiet. He watched the civilian scientists. They seldom smiled. Men with a job to do; they allowed the admiral his humours. A chilly if perplexed tolerance distinguished their faces. After lunch, of course, they would be back at their business.

'Interesting,' Blair said to the admiral.

'So I should prefer,' the admiral said, 'to think I am providing you with adventure, at least. I envy you the adventure, of course, even if I officially lack sympathy for your other aims. I too, as a much younger man, sailed with joy about these islands. But this world was simpler, then. There were no bombs here.'

'And no fallout,' Stephen said, his eyes shifting from the scientists at last.

'Something much exaggerated. But if the human race needs such fear and phobia we shall again, of course, do our best to oblige. Nevertheless, see how we live here. Look for yourselves. I frequently swim in this lagoon, even the day after a test.'

'So long as the wind blows the right way, Stephen suggested.

The admiral affected surprise for a moment. Then he laughed. 'True. But then who cares to sea-bathe in unpleasant wind?'

'And you wouldn't claim you eat the fish and shellfish too?'

'There is no such need. We are amply supplied, as you shall soon observe, with the finest foods of France.'

Tempting to point up the evasion, but useless too. Such an encounter was plainly designed to dissolve into pleasantries. Their drinks were replenished, and the photographers still hovered.

'Say your piece and then let's get out,' Stephen quietly told Blair.

'Lunch yet,' Blair replied. 'Our bonus. One thing at a time, old sport. The name of this game's diplomacy.' He was soon even more mellow with the tall iced drinks, laughing at the admiral's anecdotes.

Then, true, there was lunch. As they rose from their chairs and drifted towards the laden table, Blair said, 'Who'd have damn well thought, at the beginning, we'd finish here?'

'Finish?' Stephen asked.

'Well, find ourselves here. Right in the corridors of nuclear power. Dead in the centre of the scene. And look at that lunch. That food.'

Food anyway, real food, prepared with care to be eaten with pleasure, was no small distraction. The heaps of warm French bread with crisp crust, for example. Weeks since they had seen any bread at all. And the glossy salads, the glistening artichoke heads set on silver trays; they had forgotten food could be fresh and green, and not tugged stale from a can. And the finely sliced hams, the chicken in garlic and herbs, the prawns tenderly fried. Not least the bottles of chilled fine wine arranged the length of their luncheon table.

The admiral appeared to take satisfaction in their appetite; the photographers were busy again. There were, while they ate, one or two toasts of neutral colouring. The admiral's officers sat to his left; the civilian scientists to his right. Stephen tried, with increasing effort of will, to see these men across the table as enemy, just as Rex Stone might: the mugs and the shits. Who then were the mugs, and who the shits? The answer made no problem at all. Surprising. Not if the shits were there to make the rules and plans, and the mugs do the dirty work. The mugs were the affable men of rank on the admiral's left; the world's new shits were the silent ones, the indulgently smiling men, who sat on his right. And the admiral himself? There, perhaps, was the pity. An elegant and eloquent mug, but a mug all the same.

'I understand,' the admiral said, as food vanished and bottles emptied, 'that there are some things you have to ask of me. Please proceed, by all means.'

He might have considered them sufficiently weakened then. And the photographers seemed largely to have finished their work.

'We'd like some message sent out concerning our presence and safety here,' Blair said. 'Also we'd like the opportunity to stock up on food and water, as mariners in need.'

'We are both, I think, reasonable men, Mr Hawkins. Your task, as you see it, is to make difficulty for me. My task is to see that you do not make further difficulty for me. Is that clear? I am given to understand that repairs to your craft will be complete this evening. Very well, then. Tomorrow morning I shall provide you with an escort out of the lagoon and the French national waters into which you have trespassed. The moment I have word that you are clearly leaving the danger zone, I shall order a bulletin released on your condition and recent presence here. If you now give me your word to leave, as a man of honour and substance, I shall make that a guarantee.'

'No problem about that,' Blair said genially. 'We've done our dash. Made our point.'

'Of course,' the admiral smiled.

'And the food and water?'

'I should not like to place temptation in your way, Mr Hawkins. The temptation, I mean, to remain here a little longer. I am informed that your supplies are sufficient for a return home by way of Rarotonga if you proceed there immediately. I have to advise you solemnly that any other course now would be perilous in the extreme with tests begun.'

'You mean you're going to blow the big one now, a hydrogen bomb?'

'That is something I cannot discuss. But you are welcome, of course, to place your own interpretation upon my statement. That need be no affair of mine.'

'So you are.'

'I am in a position neither to confirm nor deny. Besides, as you must know, I am in the hands of my scientist friends in this respect.'

The men to his right did not blink, did not smile, did not even look up from their plates and glasses. They just had their job to do, as complex, as tiny and vast, as anything man might devise. And the admiral after all, was merely stating a fact. They were familiar with facts.

'All right,' Blair said. 'You've made it very clear.'

'I think I have made it clear only that you must leave urgently, Mr Hawkins. We cannot any longer be responsible for your safety here.'

'We never asked for that.'

'Naturally not, and you have my respect. All the same, we are not barbarian either. We have done our best to save you from hurt. That is no longer the case. This game we have played is over. You have had your say, and we must have ours. Also we cannot waste favourable weather any longer. So you must leave. Let there be no mistake.'

There was certainly no mistaking the admiral's hardened voice now; the public relations part was finished, the real business begun and finishing briskly. Stephen felt more and more distant from their dialogue: the heat perhaps, the wine, the rich food after weeks of austere diet. It all left him dizzy, less able to concentrate. His gaze wandered past the official French faces around the table, beyond the shady palms, to the hard afternoon light on the coral shore and the lagoon with a nuclear fleet at anchor. There could hardly have been a scene of more substance.

Until, that is, he observed someone sitting by the shore. A female form, ignored and alone, utterly unmoving and perhaps immovable. A woman with knees drawn up under her chin, and black hair falling down her back.

Not here, not now; surely to God not.

She did not flee, though he closed his eyes for clarity, and swiftly passed a hand across them. But his eyes alone did not make the problem. She remained there when he looked again.

'You must understand,' the admiral was saying, remotely, 'that the danger zone now means what it says.'

'We never supposed different,' Blair answered, even further away.

She had been easy to dismiss as a thing of the night, a fancy of the sea, a ploy of loneliness and its fevers. Not as something of day, and land; and company. She should not be there at all, looking across the lagoon like some fixture on this ambiguous shore. But Jacqueline was. Jacqueline? It was, of course, not Jacqueline. It was himself: this cruel imitation, this caricature, this jest, had to be his own creation. Not that the knowledge helped at all. For he rose shaky to his feet, his legs not yet in command of land, as he might in a court with a case still insufficiently made, nothing proven at all, groped to remove a chair from his way, made some excuse or none to the others present, and lurched toward the shore.

To an impossibly empty shore. A shore which swayed gently in his sight, perhaps, but in no other way extraordinary; just a place where solids met sea. Blocks of coral, patches of sand, scanty tufts of green growth. A stump of a palm which imagination might have sculpted to his need. And nothing more. His stomach was first to protest; it heaved. And then, out of sight of the admiral's table, it heaved again and erupted painfully, bruisingly, seemingly without end, until his lean body was empty of alien sustenance.

Until he was calm, or again in a state which passed for it.

When he returned toward the party under the palms, it was apparent that leavetaking had begun; the admiral was shaking Blair's hand warmly enough, other officers too, while the scientists drifted away. Then Blair talked at length to someone, possibly a public relations man, or journalist, who scratched down what he said in a notebook. Stephen stood at a distance, until last words were spoken, and then joined Blair on his way back to the jetty.

'What in hell happened to you?' Blair said with irritation. 'You copped out of that scene fast. I didn't think the old boy was saying anything so unreasonable.'

'Probably not.'

'Nothing to get uptight about. Or make a stiff-necked protest like that. Luckily, he didn't take offence; he chose to assume you were unwell.'

'Perhaps I was.' Indeed; more so than he could say. Sooner or later he might have to say, if only to reassure himself of one reality. Not two, or even more. He felt dizzy again.

'You could have fooled me. You looked fine until that moment. Right up with the play. What happened then? You just stood up and shot off. As if you'd seen a bloody ghost.'

'Or something like that,' Stephen agreed.

On the way back to the yacht in the admiral's launch, Blair became a degree more solicitous. 'You're all right now?' he asked.

'Perfectly,' Stephen answered, since he might yet have to be.

174

Thirteen

MOST REPAIRS WERE COMPLETE BY NIGHTFALL. THE LAST OF THE rigging was replaced under the floodlights of the repair vessel. Then the French naval tradesmen left, and the yacht was put under guard for the night; the four aboard were forbidden to leave.

'A shakedown sail in the morning might be the story,' Peter said. 'To get everything tight.'

'No way,' Blair said.

'Oh?'

'They want us out first thing.'

'What's the hurry?'

'They're not saying. No threat. Just cards on the table, face down.'

'So what happened to the big negotiation bit? Where's this fresh food and water?'

'They wouldn't play.' Blair shrugged. 'They checked us out quietly. They say we have enough to get back to Raro if we leave now.'

'Then they are anxious cats.'

'They agreed to a message, though, just as soon as it's clear we're leaving.'

'So I hope the admiral's food was fine, friend.'

'What do you mean by that?'

'Just it seems about all you got.'

'That's unfair. The message was something.'

'Sure. So we'll all listen fairly to the news about our regrettable accident off Mururoa in their national waters. If we hear anything at all.'

'We will,' Blair said. 'The admiral gave his word.'

'Right. Just like I told you. A scholar and a gentleman.' Peter, for once irritable, wiped his oily hands with a rag. His face twitched, his eyes were tired; he had taken the strain of the day aboard the yacht. 'So that's it. Cool it, kids, and home to mother.'

Rex, listening with confusion, then asked, 'What's bloody up? Is it all finished?'

No one appeared quite ready to say. In the end Stephen answered, 'Nothing's finished. It's just that we seem to be.'

'We did our best,' Blair suggested. 'No one could argue that.'

'No one's trying,' Peter said.

'So the mugs got us beat,' Rex said. 'The shits really won.'

'It's never been a matter of winners and losers,' Blair insisted.

'No? Then tell us the tale, skipper.'

'Technically we couldn't win. That's never been on. Our triumph had to be a moral one.'

'You mean that's the consolation prize?'

'If that's how you must see it.'

'I'd like to take this place apart. And those buggers out there one by one.'

'That's unreasonable,' Blair said.

'Only losers have to be reasonable.'

'So start learning.'

'When I'm good and ready. I don't feel like no loser yet.'

'If you want to make a kamikaze charge with a crowbar,' Blair said, 'be my guest. There are probably ten thousand Frenchmen out there. Just leave me out of it.'

'I just might of done that. Put up some real kind of fight. If only –' Rex looked toward Stephen, then despaired of what he most wished to say. 'Never mind. The hell with it all.' He left the cabin to sit out on deck.

The night outside was noisy with cranes working, chains

rattling, other mechanical sounds. Rex's departure left silence enough for them to be aware of activity around them in the harbour, probably with the nuclear fleet about to move into test positions again.

'So what was he on about, Steve?' Blair asked.

Stephen was slow to say.

'Come on. The old goat was on about something.'

'I think he was on about his gun,' Stephen said. 'He had one, you see.'

'You're joking.'

'He might have used it, anyway made some pretty impressive gestures with it, given a chance. I thought that chance too big a risk. So I stole it, hid it.'

'Thank God for that, then. You should have said.'

'No point. There was no trouble. No hurt pride.'

'There could have been big trouble if he'd found it again.'

'Well, he didn't.'

'So where is it now?'

'I don't see it's necessary for anyone else to know.'

'And I think it is. Knowing it's aboard leaves me damn uneasy, with the French still around.'

'All right. So it's down in the bilges, under my bunk. Safe.'

'He could still find it there if he was keen. A logical place. Let's have a look at it anyway. I'll take charge of it. Find a safer place. Until we're clear of the French anyway. Then he can have his toy back.'

Stephen retrieved the gun in its waterproof cover from under his bunk. Blair unwrapped it with interest and care. A large black Luger of most functional design.

'He's looked after it well,' Blair observed.

'Well, you never know, do you?' Stephen said. 'It's still likely to be good for another war.'

'We might have had one all right, or something damn near, if he'd started flourishing this around. I'm tempted to put the thing overboard now. Still, it's only another day or two. And I must admit it's a collector's piece. He'll get it back.'

Blair then wrapped the pistol up with its clips of ammunition again, and left the lamplight of the cabin for the murk of the forward hold. A minute later he returned with the gun gone. 'Safe now,' he announced. 'He'd have to take the yacht apart.'

'He just might do that too,' Stephen suggested.

But any jest fell flat; the entire day was deflating, with the business of the gun a last weak hiss of energy aboard, an untidy and nonsensical postscript. What, Stephen wondered, did they share as purpose now? Survival on the long seaways home: that, merely. That, alone. So they soon went listless to their bunk; even Rex, who came quietly back down to the cabin when the lamp was extinguished. The yacht, upon lagoon waters, was strangely without motion in the night. And the sounds of the harbour, human voices confused and close, made the dark unfamiliar too. Nevertheless, they slept. Stephen too, in the end. For he had begun to dread what dreams might tell him now.

That night they told him nothing, still worse.

They were woken before five next morning by a naval officer more brusque than most. 'The admiral's good compliments,' he said in awkward English. 'He wishes you leave now, this hour.'

'It can't be too soon for me,' Rex told him. 'So piss off fast.'

The officer nodded stiffly, not quite understanding, but went quickly all the same.

They weren't long leaving. Before sunrise they were already sailing across the lagoon towards the channel, a minesweeper following behind. Peter saw no fault in the French repair work; the yacht was solid again, ready to offer to the ocean. 'At least we should make it home,' he said, as if that were consolation. 'No sweat at all, friends. None.'

There was no reply, not even relief expressed. Blair, though, looked toward open sea and possibly distant landfall.

Mururoa lagoon, at first still and grey, began to tint and flood with the shifting colours of sunrise, the coral in the transparent water below echoing every hue; no small glory there. And there was yet more to the morning. When they had cleared the channel, and were out on the open Pacific with the deck beginning to move vigorously beneath them again, they looked back, soon, for a last sight of the atoll they were leaving; and were given, instead, first sight of a long balloon rising above the horizon.

'The sons of bitches,' Peter said, 'just love to rub the salt in.'

True that the balloon seemed a rebuke, a last snub, with their course to the west and safety. The minesweeper still rolled in their wake.

'Obvious they couldn't wait to get us out,' Stephen agreed.

'What do you think, friend? Tomorrow?'

'Probably. And a big one. The big one. The last one was possibly just a triggering device. The weather seems with them.'

'The hell with it,' Peter said, looking away.

Stephen looked away too.

Their course continued west.

So they sailed most of the rest of the day in silence, falling into familiar routines, no speech necessary. The balloon, that long pale bullet in the sky, soon shrank, soon slipped below the horizon astern. At some time in mid-afternoon the minesweeper drew up alongside them, flying flags of farewell; and the skipper, through a hailer, called bon voyage. Then the minesweeper turned back toward Mururoa, other duty; it too was fast gone. The entire Pacific, so far as they could see, was theirs; and dead. Not even a wandering seabird contested their claim.

It seemed still to be agreed that anything they might have to say was better left unsaid. Even Blair took no issue with the silence.

Nightfall found them fifty miles or more from Mururoa, still running west on a favourable wind; at this pace the next day should see them altogether out of the danger zone. But they already seemed well beyond most peril, and possibly were.

There was the same quiet in the cabin after dark. At seven Stephen tried, and failed, to find a news bulletin on the transistor radio.

'Never mind,' Blair said. 'Probably too soon. No reason why the old boy shouldn't keep his word. They've got nothing to lose now.'

179

Blair lay comfortable on his bunk. Rex stood outside at the wheel. Peter made calculations on the chart table, and filled the day's log. Stephen tried, now and then, to read a book; it appeared he might have forgotten how. Everything again seemed to be as it was; as it should be, perhaps, with all tension remote. They had become men upon a mere Pacific cruise. Why wish more?

Their enterprise in these seas began to seem forlorn and futile, an extravagant fantasy, the more Stephen thought about it. So he tried not to think about it. The human world would have its way; he had to learn not to care.

His imagination ran forward to their return. To landfall, homecoming. The wharfside crowd, the wives and friends. The greetings and reunions. The moist eyes, possibly, and then the dismissive laughter. And home and office again. Sanity of a sort; a commonplace life to live, to shape, with some cunning and craft, fresh rituals for survival. He might even survive long enough to wonder why he had tried another, why he had tried at all, given the madness of men. He had never felt more tired, though his watches that day had been as easy as any.

Towards eight he experimented with the transistor radio again; and this time was more successful. A news bulletin, coming through loud at last, told them that the protest yacht *Moana Nui* had been reported safe and was on its way home. An official French statement, just released in Papeete and Paris, said the boat had been involved in an accidental collision with a naval vessel off Mururoa ('At least they didn't say in national waters,' Blair observed with premature satisfaction) and had been given repair facilities at French headquarters on the atoll ('Fair enough,' Blair added). The four men still aboard were unhurt and healthy. Members of the crew were entertained, while on Mururoa, at a lunch arranged by the admiral in charge of the French nuclear force. Photographs had been released to the international press showing the yacht under repair, and crewmen relaxing in the company of the admiral. The skipper of *Moana Nui*, Mr Blair Hawkins, had expressed his appreciation of the kindness and consideration shown by the French; the yacht was said likely to make landfall at Rarotonga, on its way home, within a week. Asked if this year's nuclear tests were still proceeding as planned, a French spokesman said he was unable to comment.

And that was all. All? It could not be less. The voyage, their survival in the danger zone, shrivelled on the arid airwaves.

Quiet in the cabin was well ended.

'So that's it,' Stephen said to Blair. 'Satisfied now? All you wanted. Our message to the world.'

'All sweetness and light,' Peter said. 'A really cool scene. A picnic at Mururoa. Champagne with the admiral.'

'There was no champagne,' Blair said. 'Just a little white wine.'

'And that grieves you, friend?'

'I thought,' Blair observed to Peter, 'you weren't worried about what the outside said.'

'No,' Peter agreed. 'But you just got me interested, friend. Now I'm really wild for what they say.'

'Be reasonable. Of course the French are bound to put the best possible face on it.'

'With our help?'

'I didn't expect a little ordinary courtesy to be used like that.'

'Then you're a fool, Blair,' Stephen heard himself saying. 'A bloody arrogant fool.'

Blunt enough, and final; but the silence afterwards was brief.

'Look,' Blair said, 'We've done our best, haven't we? More than millions have done. At least we didn't just sit this one out bitching at home. Did we?'

'No,' Stephen agreed. 'But for all the difference I begin to wonder.'

'I'm tempted,' Peter said wearily, 'to put this yacht about and see how much more sweetness and light we can still find for ourselves around friendly old Mururoa. Why not?'

'Food and water,' Blair said with haste. 'That's a good reason why not.' He was sweating perceptibly now, with the heat in the cabin, and other things. 'Nothing more we can do back there anyway. Nothing. We did the best we could. Now it's time to get back and tell people the whole truth. Tell the whole damn world the truth about what it's like out here, how it's been.'

181

'If anyone still cares,' Peter said, his voice still tired; his face too. The voyage, then the days in the danger zone, had left him visibly older, even more weathered and wrinkled. He no longer had will or energy to argue with Blair; he shook his head. 'Never mind,' he finished. 'Never mind, friends. It's only the one life, short and sweet or long and sour, soon over either way. Forget it.'

Relief was distinct on Blair's face. 'For a moment, then,' he confessed, 'I thought you were serious.'

Quiet appeared about to return to the cabin. And acceptance of it.

'If Peter wasn't serious,' Stephen said suddenly, 'then he should have been.' Blair began looking at Stephen with surprise, perhaps his risen voice, and then Peter too, with fresh interest in those tired eyes. Stephen could understand Peter's exhaustion; he shared it. Possibly Corporal Schmidt, if that had been his name, had known it too, weary of purpose with only insanity to be seen. 'I don't think we should quit,' he continued to say. 'Not until we have to. Not until there's a finish.'

'What in hell's got into you now?' Blair demanded.

Difficult to explain even if he wished. True, however, that he appeared to be talking to more than two in the cabin now; there appeared to be three, and the third was Jacqueline. She was both there and not there, technically, which didn't mean her presence was any less literal. He was beyond surprise, beyond pain, beyond lethargy, beyond most things. He was even thinking, irrelevantly, that the light purple caftan gown she appeared to be wearing now was the one in which he found her that day of her death; the only visible difference was that his mind had laundered all bloodstain away. She sat beside Peter as if this were natural. And nodded approval as if participant in the conversation all along. He had the sensation, then, that this immaculately imagined Jacqueline was willing the words he uttered.

'We had a job to do out here,' he argued. 'Let's sail back in again.'

'Talk sense,' Blair said.

'I am,' Stephen answered. With some conviction, it seemed.

182

Some conviction? More and more.

'We've done all we could. Made the moral point. Embarrassed a military machine. Never been a real hope in hell we could do more. Never. Not four men on a yacht. We thought we might have been delaying a test, but they just went ahead anyway.'

'And we've obligingly left them to it.'

'The hell we have. We've just reached the material limit of our capacity to stick it out. Maybe you can invent more food and water. I can't.'

'So we go on half rations. That gives us an extra week at sea. No sweat.'

'Your mind's wandering, Steve.'

Indeed possible. But Peter, at least, was roused now. 'You give your word to the admiral?' he asked Blair. 'Was that the big deal?'

'He gave his word,' Blair said evasively, 'that he'd put news of us out when we left the area. He also kept his word, I might add.'

'I said was there a deal.' Peter was grim to the point.

'Not exactly, no.'

'Inexactly, then, friend.'

'I just said there was no problem, since we had to leave anyway.'

'It smells like a deal to me. A really sweet one. You sold out to those sons of bitches for that crap we just heard on the radio, right?'

'People know we're still alive now, at least.'

'It sounds more like you did your best to leave us for dead, friend.'

'There's no more we can do,' Blair protested. 'Just the same again.'

'So it's still better than nothing,' Stephen said.

'Next time we mightn't get off so lightly.'

'You mean no picnic under the palms, friend?' Peter asked. 'Not even just a little white wine?'

'Come on, Blair,' Stephen said. 'The real reason.'

'Speaking personally, I've had enough. We all have, if we're honest.'

183

'So you're bored. That it? You're bored again. And it's scaring the hell out of you.'

'Right,' Blair agreed. 'So I'm bored. Who wouldn't be? Sailing out, sailing back in again. Day after day. There's no future in that any more.'

'So you'll clip the newspapers, put the toy boat away, and find the next game.'

Perhaps cruelty was necessary now. Stephen didn't know, no longer cared.

'I just want to get home. Not unnatural, is it? I've been out of touch too long. I don't know if I still exist back there; God knows. And this has begun to go on forever. I can't do it. Nor can you, if you'll see sense.'

'If you're copping out,' Stephen said, 'you only have to say so. Not explain.'

'Beyond a certain point,' Blair pronounced, 'all protest is counter-productive. Turning in on itself. Feeding on itself.'

'I see.'

'We're well beyond that point now. It's become pure self indulgence. You can't think of anything better to do with your life.'

Blair, of course, had a point there of sorts.

'Nor could you, as I understood it,' Stephen observed. 'Earlier on.'

'Well, I can now. Right? I can think of a hell of a lot more to do with my life than roll around this bloody ocean until the next thing happens. Another bomb, another storm, and then more again. Where's the point any more? Where?'

'We're only talking about another week,' Stephen said. 'Peter seems willing. So am I. What's a week?'

'Seven days,' Blair said. 'Seven days too many.'

'If things are bad at home, you learn about it a little later. That's all. Me, I'd sooner not know at all.'

'That's your problem. I'm saying no.'

'Then that,' Stephen replied, 'is really too bad, Blair.'

'What are you saying?'

'Just that I think Peter and I are going to take this yacht about, and sail back in again. Provided of course that I can persuade Rex too, and that shouldn't be too hard. I might even promise his gun back this time.'

'I'm telling you no. Warning you too.'

'Sure,' Peter said. 'So sue us all, friend.'

'We could really be in trouble now. The biggest. You know what's going on back at the atoll.'

'That,' Stephen said, 'could just be the point, Blair. Try it for size anyway. The new antidote for boredom in the giant-size packet. It might even get you out of the barricade business.'

'We've pushed our luck. And my patience. So I'm saying no. And no again. Steve, see reason, for God's sake, before this goes any further.'

But Stephen imagined himself already seeing reason with some clarity for his own purpose, if not for God's sake, or Blair's. Purpose shaped, perhaps, as Jacqueline; there had to be some message, surely, in that presence. She was rather less substantial now. But still approving.

Yet he could say, 'I'm sorry, Blair. I really am. But the first thing is to see what Rex says.'

'The bloody old warmonger. You know what he'll say.'

'Probably. But he was your choice, as I recall.'

'Sure. You all were, for what that matters now. We've been out here too long.'

'Probably,' Stephen agreed, and climbed to the cockpit to talk to Rex. That wasn't a problem. Rex may have been predictable, but he was also reliable, more to the point in any danger zone.

'Too bloody right I'm on,' Rex said. 'I been moping up here on the wheel because we let those mugs and shits have it all their own way after all. Half rations? Bloody hell. In a lifeboat your problems start when you're down to no rations at all.'

Stephen felt a large surge of affection for Rex then. And if that offended his sense of fitness, so much the worse for his sense of fitness. He could trust the man.

When he descended to the cabin, he was aware of one difference. Jacqueline was no longer a presence; he was on his own, and a fool ever to dream otherwise. Or on his own, now, with Peter and Rex, more than enough human substance.

'Charming,' Blair said. 'So our friendly neighbourhood liberal and our quota pacifist make common cause with our militarist mate. As near a fascist as makes no difference. What would you say, Steve?'

'Just that the vote is three to one again.'

'So surprise, surprise.'

'And we're taking the yacht about. Sailing back in again. Since you brought us out here, Blair, you're welcome to tag along too.'

'Thanks for nothing. Is jumping overboard my other choice?'

'No. Pretending we're still in this together. I'm serious, Blair. We're sailing back in. The sooner the better. Peter?' Peter rose from his bunk. Stephen, strangely, had found himself in command. He saw no reason to resist the proposition.

'You're going to regret this,' Blair promised.

'Anything's possible.'

'I mean it. You'll be sorry. I'll make a very special point of seeing you are. To think we were friends once, Steve. Remember?'

An implausible plea. That friendship, if it had been, belonged to another existence, another Stephen West, a shadowy Stephen West in an existence of shadows. This yacht and this ocean, these men, were palpable. The danger zone too, as if he had never lived elsewhere. Anything elsewhere, behind or beyond, was wishful thinking, feverish human fancy; a mortal conceit.

'So what does that mean?' he asked Blair.

'That I'm not going to let you get away with it.'

'I see,' Stephen said coolly. 'So try.'

It was like a flick in the face. Blair began to rage then. And roar.

'You creep,' he said. 'You cruddy high-minded little creep. Always have been, always were. You're nothing, nothing, never have been and you know it. Your whole pathetic life is just an excuse for amounting to nothing. All your scruffy causes, the lot. So now you got the death wish written all over you. Like that sad bloody bitch of a wife you had. Only she had the guts to be honest, not drag others along too. I'd like to wipe some

186

of that bloody virtue off your face just to see what smells so much underneath.'

Then, perhaps a roll of the yacht, some part of the cabin seemed to collide with Stephen's face, stunningly, blindingly; it turned out to be Blair's fist. He replied in kind. Then he was battering Blair's head on the edge of a bunk with ugly satisfaction, and Peter was pulling them apart.

'Time to cool it, friends,' Peter said finally, 'if we've got this yacht to sail.'

'Right,' Stephen agreed, and without pause climbed back to the cockpit, with Peter following close behind.

Fourteen

STEPHEN TOOK THE WHEEL AS THE YACHT TURNED ABOUT, WITH a tack toward the centre of the danger zone again, toward Mururoa. Rex and Peter were on the swaying deck, trimming the newly close hauled sail.

'Leave the radar reflector up?' Rex asked.

'From shore they should pick us up between twenty-five and thirty miles,' Peter observed. 'Planes? We haven't heard much pattern flying at night, so they shouldn't pick us up too soon. A ship, maybe twelve miles. They shouldn't have any this far out.'

'So leave it up,' Stephen said.

The yacht swung, surged into its new course, lively; all life. And an intoxicant. At the wheel, as he took the craft closer to the wind, Stephen seemed never to have inhabited himself so lucidly before, never with flesh and spirit in such duet; the sensation, the reality, surpassed even that first luminous night upon the Pacific. True that he wanted to live then. Still true that he wanted to live now. But no longer with despair as gregarious mistress, promiscuous seducer, disguised as reason. That was not life as man was most meant to live it; that was not life as he was living it now. Never. So the hell with despair in that bland dress; the hell with reason too if that refusal were necessary. There was freedom, after all, at life's limit, where it

188

became just legible, the faintest of frontiers. Because now he was brushing something else, tasting something more; unfamiliar. Joy, no less. At first as a larrikin companion. Then as something fluid, crystalline, pure upon a parched throat; water welling from a high mountain spring. Joy? In wind on his face, in spray on his flesh, in moonlight scattered on the sea. Not something to surrender.

He had forgotten Blair, doubtless still surly down in the cabin. Blair, most things, had become irrelevance. All but this yacht, this course.

'We'll take short watches through the night,' he announced. 'And if we lose the wind, we'll motor. How far off in the morning, Peter?'

'Between thirty and forty, maybe,' Peter estimated. 'Better than that if we motor.'

'So we'll motor after midnight; we've got the fuel.'

'More than enough, friend,' Peter agreed. 'Gift of the admiral, to get us home. If only that cat knew.'

'We shall have to hope he does.' Stephen hesitated. 'That test could be on in the morning,' he felt bound to add.

'I'm reading you, friend.'

'Rex? You understand too?'

'If you mean about those buggers blowing their bomb. Of course I do.'

'Well? Haven't either of you more to say?'

Peter shrugged. 'What more, friend? You said it all just now. It could be all on. Right. So we're sailing back in. Right. Is there anything more?'

Perhaps not; a pause.

Then, 'Yes,' Stephen said finally. 'One thing more. Hope. The hope they'll pick us up in time. That we'll be a flicker on some radar screen. An inexplicable little ghost. Enough to tell them that something, someone, is in their way again. That something, someone, might always be in their way until they quit. At least enough to make them stop this time, call it off, if they can. Not much to hope.'

'Right. So we'll hope.'

'And pray,' Rex said. 'I like to keep my hand in.'

189

'Why not?' Peter said. 'A little of everything, friend, goes a long way.'

Such as their silence then. Perhaps Rex and Peter shared his exhilaration. Or perhaps they already knew that men were most free, most alive, when life meant least; it may have been no news to them at all. They remained on deck with him in the warm night, sitting forward of the cockpit, on the cabin roof.

'You should both try some sleep,' Stephen suggested.

'Not tonight,' Rex said. 'I'll stick around.'

'Peter?'

'I'm here when you want me, friend. You're all right now?'

'Never better,' he answered, since truth couldn't hurt; nothing could.

That, though, was where joy ended. For Blair was no longer an irrelevance; he was climbing up from the cabin.

'Put her about,' he said.

'Like hell,' Stephen answered. 'This tack's fine.'

'We're putting about.'

'Not now,' Stephen insisted. 'We're sailing back in. Or did I forget to tell you?'

'You're sailing nowhere.'

That appeared possible too. Blair, he saw, held the Luger in his hand.

'Put that away,' Stephen said, 'Don't play silly buggers.'

'I'm not playing; you'd better believe it.'

Stephen might have to.

'Overstating your case again,' he answered. 'A hell of a way to cope with boredom, Blair.'

'Just taking charge of my own boat,' Blair explained. 'Quite reasonable. I have the right.'

'Think about it again,' Stephen suggested. 'You can't force three of us home with a gun. Not all that way. You have to get sleep sometime.'

'I'll think the rest out when I have to. We'll finish tonight first. I want the boat running west again. So turn her about.'

'I'm still prepared to listen to any considered objection.'

'I'm not arguing. I've had a gutful. I'm telling you.'

'With that?'

'Right on. With this.'

He was perhaps three feet away, braced against the side of the cockpit, and the Luger remained remarkably steady.

'The only argument I've got left,' Blair added. 'The best in the business.'

'Still pretty weak,' Stephen said. 'I think you should consider just where it leaves you when I say no. Because that's what I'm saying. No.'

'You don't think I'm for real?'

'I don't doubt you think you are. And guns don't turn me on. They go off by accident in the best of hands.'

'I'm for real, Steve. Try me and see.'

'But I am. I am trying you, Blair.'

Blair then seemed to weaken slightly. 'It can't have come to this.'

'Apparently. Yes.'

'You really think I can back out now?'

'And do you really think I can?'

'Of course.'

'That's why we're sailing back in again. To show we won't, or can't. The same thing.'

'One of us has to back out. One of us is going to. Logical. And since it can't be me, it has to be you. Right?'

Plain, though, that Blair didn't know what to do, having come this far. Possibly always the way, and mostly for Blair a winning way; he could only go on. And on. The yacht lifted on a wave, subsided into a trough, and rose again on its way toward Mururoa. There was a small distinct sound as Blair pulled back the safety catch on the Luger.

'Believe me now?'

On and on; Stephen's throat was dry.

'As much as I believe in whatever hangs under that balloon. Of course.'

'So don't push me. Just get back from the wheel then. Let me take it.'

Perhaps Blair was weakening after all, but Stephen was never to find out. Nor Blair, for that matter. For he made the slightest of moves toward Stephen, still with the gun pointed, and that action called down Peter lightly from behind; he leapt, trying to take Blair around the neck, and only part succeeding. As the two fell together to the floor of the cockpit, in front of the wheel, Stephen grabbed out for the gun, but failed to get a grip. The two others rolled over together, kicking noisily. Then the gun exploded. Peter fell away limp. Blair rose with the gun.

Stephen knelt to Peter. He also said, 'Get it, Rex. Get that bloody thing off him.'

But reliable Rex needed no telling. He chopped the gun from Blair's hand, then used its butt to hit Blair into a corner of the cockpit. 'We ought to shoot you straight off,' he shouted. 'Like any fucking deserter.'

Stephen, meanwhile, groped across Peter's long and bony body in the dark, searching for his wound; only a bubbling sound came from his mouth. The wound, at length, turned out to be an opening in Peter's chest through which blood was now rising in considerable quantity. Stephen's hands came away sticky. The bubbling sound in Peter's mouth stopped. Stephen then tried to find Peter's pulse, but there was no pulse to find. 'He's dead,' he admitted finally.

The yacht had jibed, was drifting, jib aback.

'You shot our mate.' Rex raged at a bruised Blair in the distance. 'You killed our mate. You ought to be buying it too.'

Stephen tried to command detail again. The yacht, directionless, rose and shuddered sidelong in the waves.

'Get this old bastard off me, Steve,' Blair pleaded. 'It was an accident. Just an accident. You both saw that.'

Rex struck him with the butt again.

'He's dead,' Stephen said, as if repetition might yet make truth acceptable.

Blair was saying to him, 'He shouldn't have jumped me. I thought he was pacifist anyway.'

Rex was saying to him, 'What you reckon? Shall I shoot the bugger now, or just throw him into the drink?'

Everything else was saying to him, Peter is dead, dead.

The Pacific had never been more empty.

To make death credible, then, he took the slack weight of

Peter's body in his arms, his balance at risk on the capricious yacht, and lurchingly carried it from the cockpit to rest it on the foredeck among coils of rope. He had only ever managed the one body before, Jacqueline's, and then strangers took charge. Here death was all his thing; no doctors, police, or undertakers to call; he could hardly have a greater intimacy. Yet where to begin?

For the world was tugging him away with some apparent urgency. Rex. Blair. The yacht. And more.

To Rex he said, then, 'Just don't let him get that gun again.'

To Blair he said, 'You'd better get below and stay there.'

That left him free to give himself to the yacht and the ocean, if he could. And it seemed, after all, that he might.

'We'll forget sailing now,' he told Rex. 'We'll motor in. Get the diesel running.'

'We're still going east?'

'Of course,' he answered, surprised Rex might think otherwise. 'You're my boy.'

'The only direction we've got anyway.'

'Come again.'

'I mean if we went west, we wouldn't know where to to find Rarotonga anyway. Or any other island out here. With Peter gone needles in haystacks would be easier. Or thistledown in high wind. Queer, really.'

'How?'

'Because the danger zone's the only place where we have a hope in hell. Certainly of being found. The danger zone's suddenly the only safe place we know.'

But Rex had no interest in the paradox. 'What about that bugger down below?' he asked.

'Just make sure he stays there.'

'I'll shoot him if he shows his head,' Rex pomised.

'That shouldn't be necessary,' Stephen said, without great conviction.

'Well, I won't tell him twice anyway.'

Minutes later, sails stowed, diesel thumping, they were motoring toward Mururoa. East. The only direction they knew, the only direction their navigator had left them.

Rex was beside him the entire night. They shared the wheel. Blair made only the one attempt to surface from the cabin. After that, they locked him down there; sometimes they heard him shouting, but his silences soon lengthened. The racket of the diesel killed most other sound anyway. Rex and Stephen had to talk loudly to be heard above it, if they spoke at all. For a time Peter, in his way, was more eloquent than either, dead on the foredeck, a silvered shape in the moonlight. Otherwise there was just ocean, more ocean, ocean without end.

At some time around five in the morning, and perhaps not too late, they thought to hoist the radar reflector on the spinnaker halyard, higher than the bracket on the crosstree; it might mean they were picked up a few miles sooner, depending on the efficiency and sophistication of others on this ocean. They could have been sixteen miles or sixty from Mururoa; no way of knowing. The diesel, though, gave a steady seven knots, the most it could give, with perhaps no more than a knot lost against the current. A guess might give them less than forty miles from the atoll, wherever it lay. Certainly they had to be well back within the inner danger zone now. One late seen hazard of the approaching day was the possibility that they might overshoot the security of the danger zone, passing too far north or south of Mururoa, and into entirely landless ocean, with nothing to find at all unless themselves diminishing in the distances of the Pacific, shrinking into infinity. But that risk, if real, was just one among many. Without accurate navigation they might also finish their voyage, and possibly their lives, on some all too substantial reef; or anywhere at all.

By five thirty they were distinctly voyaging towards day: pale light ahead, spreading, washing slowly up from impeccably clean horizon. The yacht under their feet lifted sharply from the dark. Peter's body at rest on the foredeck briefly seemed an offering, a sacrifice, to the peaceful advance of light. But then the light, perversely, was at some pains to demonstrate the colour of blood everywhere, along the deck, in the cockpit, and staining Stephen's shirt.

They warmed themselves with the whisky Rex had grabbed before Blair was shut below.

'Yes,' Stephen said. 'That's better.' Rex looked strange to him in the growing grey light. Strange? A stranger. An unkempt old man with bloodshot eyes, shaggily bearded, in an oily singlet, with a gun piratically wedged in his belt. Yet no stranger. Friend now; and ally against all the day might tell them. 'We'll have to do something about Peter,' he added.

'I know the routine,' Rex said. 'I seen enough burials at sea.'

'Good.' Which wasn't quite what he meant to say. No matter.

'It's what we do with the other bastard that worries me. The one below.'

'We leave him there,' Stephen said. 'At least for now. He can't do any more damage.'

'So he gets away with it.'

'He usually does.'

'It's not right.'

'Nothing brings Peter back. We'll just have to say we lost him overboard. The simplest story. Otherwise there'll be no end to the business when we're back. The inquiries, the inquest, even a trial. Anything we tried to do out here would be forgotten.'

'It's still not right.'

'Of course not. Few things are. That just might be why we're here. It's more than the bomb; that's only the part we can see. A symptom. One symptom. But one that suggests the illness might be fatal if left to run its course. Unless man himself is the illness, a terminal malfunction in the evolutionary system, something it can't profit us to believe. Not if we have to make the best of things.'

Rex took the last point, at least. 'Of course we have to make the bloody best of it,' he said.

'So, who knows, people like ourselves might just be some sort of antibody, a purely biological phenomenon, as the species develops a defence against the illness. Or life, all life. Not just a race with time. With eternity.'

'You've lost me there,' Rex said. 'I just know the world's all fucked up.'

'Which possibly is all you need to know. Perhaps biology does the rest. Or the life force. Or some universal mind. Even God, if you like. Take your pick. Anyway we're here. Pass the whisky.'

'You think they've seen us on radar yet?'

'We shall have to hope so. Or think so until we know otherwise.'

It was near six, near sunrise. They could hear the reflector banging about on the halyard above.

'And if they don't?'

'We may have to console ourselves with the thought that life isn't everything; or our lives in particular. That whatever happens to us may be necessary in some larger scheme of things. Not a very fetching faith, perhaps. But the only one I have at hand.'

'You're not talking about God, then?'

'No. Much as I should like to.'

'What, then?'

'Probably the need to live, then die, without too much regret. That's all. A modest ambition. Not an impossible one. God would only get in the way. Make for some intolerable aspiration. Or make for nothing at all. We could sit and wait for him to deliver the goods. Something he may well have done at the beginning. Only he hasn't had the heart to come back and look, to see his damaged goods, the mess we've made like children. A creative imagination so fertile is bound to discard its less satisfying experiments. All the more reason, then, to suppose we're on our own.'

'You sound like a man trying to bloody convince himself,' Rex observed, with surprising pertinence.

Stephen took fresh grip on the bottle, his brain beginning to thud, and tipped more whisky into his mouth. It didn't diminish the new chill in his flesh; a familiar chill. Or that scent. Her scent.

'Possibly. Yes. Also like a man searching for safety in a danger zone. I try to believe in what I see, feel, smell, hear and taste. No more. That's safety. Land as against sea. Life as against death. The known as against the unknown.'

For what he needed now, more than anything in his life, was the knowledge that Jacqueline had no measurable existence

196

on the foredeck; that she was not sitting there, still purple gowned as on the day of her death, beside Peter's body; that it was merely his mind in fever again, some sickness of the sea. And whisky.

'Rex,' he said. 'Look forward. Tell me what you see.'

'The usual,' Rex answered. 'With Peter there. It's hard to see past him.'

'That's all?'

'That's all.'

Case proven. But Jacqueline evidently refused to agree. His mind even arranged that she should turn slowly, as he spoke, to consider him with large intense eyes. And say quietly, as if it were the drumming diesel which had no existence, 'It's all right. I'm with you. You'll be all right. Understand that.'

She was no longer there.

He understood nothing then.

For it was suddenly six. Suddenly and seemingly sunrise. But it was not sunrise, not the sun at all which filled the sky silently with moving bands of brilliant colour, first pale yellow, then deep yellow, yellow turning to red; one shade following another fast as the extravagant central source of light grew in ungainly form, and then slowly shrank into something orange red, grossly churning, and began to spread outward again.

Abundant beyond the largest expectation. And almost dead ahead. So Stephen found no words for the wonder.

'That's it,' was all he could say. 'Too late. We blew it.'

Rex was quiet, as paralysed.

Blair was banging and shouting something below.

'We've gone far enough,' Stephen decided. 'Let's get the hell out. Turn about.'

Rex swung the wheel. The boat rolled sideways to the fountain of incandescence climbing the eastern sky, the red reflections crawling toward them across the sea. As they motored away the sound overtook them, banging, battering. It came from above and below, a storm all around, a wind of noise, an eruption of energy clamouring against them, trying to grab *Moana Nui* and shake it from the sea; there were smaller concussions like rifle shots beside their ears.

Given the speed of sound, Stephen estimated they might be some thirty miles off the atoll; it was just three minutes past six. He looked back. That dazing brightness was gone; there was now just a tall cloud rising, spreading wide towards its top, finding soon emphatic and familiar shape. The magic mushroom of Mururoa, with guaranteed high, one which left all other hallucinogens for dead.

Blair was still shouting below.

'So let him out,' Stephen said, taking the wheel from Rex. 'Nothing more he can do. Nothing we can.'

It seemed the true sun had risen, rather meagrely, and altogether unobserved.

There was, though, one more thing to come. Just one more.

Though the day at first promised fine, the sky clouded over as they left the atoll in their wake. A high fog appeared to be forming. Then a light rain, the lightest of rain, began to fall.

Later that day, stitched professionally into a torn sail by Rex, Peter was buried at sea. Rex had some faintly remembered words of formal Christian ceremony to speak over the lumpy canvas bag before they last gave Peter to the Pacific, cool lover to cold mistress, with almost no sound at all. The bag rolled over in their wake for a while, slow to sink. Less formally Rex added, 'Even if life's all a load of bullshit, no one can say the poor bugger didn't give it a go.'

They heard the ocean then, the wind in the main.

'So roll on the age of Aquarius,' Stephen muttered. 'Roll on the resurrection, friend.'

The wind took his words away.

'What's that?' Rex asked.

'Nothing,' Stephen answered. 'Nothing at all, friend.'

Man, then. Men. Let the palm tree grow. Let the coral spread. Man might never cease to be.

Fifteen

STORM THEN PULLED THEM OUT OF THE DANGER ZONE AND savaged them across the Pacific. For one day, two, three; the main was halved, the storm jib shredded, and in the wildest of jibes the shrouds were stranded and the boom fractured. Towards the end they had lost sense of position and reasonable hope too. Even the danger zone would have been difficult to find again much less an island, any island, in that tumult. They were driven south, and perhaps west. When Stephen tried using Peter's sextant, to determine their position, he came up with contradictory readings. He did not try again. Even the compass could produce surprising news.

Calm took them, and heat, and the distended days began to ooze and fester. Perhaps it was more than a fortnight since Mururoa, perhaps less. Two or three days either way. They were no longer in much condition to count or care. It was vast effort to climb from cabin to cockpit, to take a watch. Difficult enough to open eyes after sleep, to find sight again through eyes gummed with thick yellow discharge. Their skins itched, their scalps. Their faces darkened still more, blackened, and not just with sun. Half rations were no hardship, since they soon ceased to eat much at all. Rex began to vomit less, and remained more and more in his bunk, until arriving at the point where he did not leave it other than to relieve bowels, stomach or bladder unsteadily over the stern; he could no longer take a watch. When Rex was wholly unable to leave his bunk, Stephen began to clean him where he lay, if not always clearing the smell from the stuffy cabin. Blair was next to succumb to the same fatigue; he soon lacked strength to stand at the wheel. His sideburns grew patchy and pale flesh began to show at the back of his head where hair had fallen. Stephen's irritations came mainly from small blisters which spread along his arms and down his body; they became suppurating sores no conventional ointment in the first-aid cabinet could heal. He rigged a stable awning over the cockpit, across the useless boom, to shade himself from the worst of the sun and some of the heat. Though tiring too, he still did his best by the wandering yacht, roping the wheel for self-steer when unable to remain long at the wheel.

For they were still sailing. Sailing as if they had somewhere to go.

Westwards, anyway. Homewards, possibly. Towards sunset after simmering sunset; towards day after scalding day. Never had there been nights with sweeter chill. Hope? Just a game men play at their best and worst, in the best and worst of worlds.

For the world was the danger zone, and life their passport into it, the only permit demanded. All they had to do was find someone able to admit them again before their permits expired. That was all. All? All.

Then, true, there was an island. Suddenly. It was not there and then it was there. Perhaps he had dozed in the cockpit, perhaps he was still dreaming, but those were peaks now improbably puncturing the horizon. And even a dream of land was not to be despised.

So he turned the yacht toward the land he saw, or seemed to see, and roped the wheel; and went down to the cabin to tell the others. Rex first. Stephen grabbed him by the shoulder, tried to wake him. It was some time before Stephen understood that Rex was not to be woken again: not by Stephen, nor any man. So he turned to Blair's bunk. And Blair, though alive, was distinctly beyond him too, with a wandering groan the only response. Peter? For the moment Stephen could not think where Peter had gone, why his bunk should be so empty. He forced a memory, a bag tumbling in a wake, and that made for pain he should have preferred to forgo.

There was no one to tell. No one to share that hope strewn haphazardly against the sky. He climbed out to the cockpit, found clean wind on his face, and a solid wheel in hand again. He willed the peaks higher above the horizon, until they began ruggedly to insist on their own reality, until in an hour or two they were perceptibly towering to port. The place could hardly escape him now. But the island remained a bleak and eroded thing almost entirely of mountain and ridge. A leftover, a forgotten fragment of some larger creation. No sheltering coral; large waves lashed directly against the land, shattering up the cliffs, dispersing and lingering as mists which waited on wind to lift them still higher as shroud for the island.

Rapa? Possibly. No matter. An island in an ocean. A flaw in hell, a now in forever. Any heresy now would do. Any lump of land, any scrap of life, might serve for salvation. Or for final damnation; but any decision also might do. Any end. And for all he knew he might still have been dreaming. His lips were swollen and crusted; his sight was shaky; some of his negroid skin had begun to peel away, showing white again beneath. The last of Blair's whisky was gone; he had finished smoking Peter's pot. He did discover an unbroken bottle of champagne among storm-tossed things in a locker, where Blair presumably secreted it for some celebration, perhaps for first sight of their last landfall, first sight of home again. Not that it was with him now to break out; he had used it, at some length, to sweeten a sour day. His one durable comfort was Rex's gun. He always kept it close by the wheel, sometimes touching it for cool reassurance. Once, the same day he lingered drunkenly on the last champagne, he casually used a clip of ammunition upon a black shark trailing them in the sea. Plainly his aim was poor; the shark survived. No great waste. His only purpose for the gun would require just one round of ammunition, and no precise aim, no skill at all; there could be no greater consolation in any human artefact.

He turned the yacht closer into the island, trying to see what its skeletal shore might tell him yet, in search of a landing. *Moana Nui* responded feebly; there was only the jib to take the wind, tugging the bulk of the boat behind. Each inch of ocean was hugely earned.

Now, he thought. Now.

For the vivid peaks had begun to part at last. There was an opening. There was a harbour. Calm water between long limbs of land. Peace.

He moistened his mouth with rank water from the champagne bottle, still useful as receptacle, as if there were still need to ration its contents with care, conserve it against dry days yet ahead upon the Pacific.

Now. Now. He could hear ragged breathing; his own.

There were rocks rising to port, then to starboard. Broken water. Seabirds circling. He used the diesel, what was left of their fuel, to gun the nose of *Moana Nui* past all hazard, through the tight channel, into the embrace of land, a widening sanctuary of quiet water. A sigh rose within him, as if from sexual release; and it was, after all, no small consummation.

He shut off the diesel; the jib fluttered windless; he was drifting on the afterglow of triumph, drunk with the growing scent of the shore, letting *Moana Nui* take him where it might, since the craft itself appeared to be manufacturing a direction now, and perhaps yet another mirage.

There was a green valley lush with living things. There was a village. There were fires. So he found still another use for the gun after all. He fired it in the air again and again to see if that fantasy of peace might fracture. But the mountains did not split; the island declined to dissolve. The silence of the place was merely pricked, and echoes wandered lazily back from the land. Soon there were dark figures moving along and down the shore. Some waved and shouted; some pushed canoes into the water; others simply stood stricken with wonder.

Then there were canoes alongside, ropes thrown, men with paddles leading the yacht toward shore, and he was trying to tell them things they did not know in a language they did not understand.

202

No matter. They understood enough. The half-shattered yacht was sufficient, the queerly discoloured man aboard, babbling at the wheel; he was giddily detached from himself to see how it all must seem.

But he did call a coherent halt, and for emphasis dropped two anchors into the shallow water. Then, with no delay, he cast himself over the side too. He sank until earth met his feet with elusive impact; he was surfacing wildly, swimming weakly; he was wading waist-high in the water; the shore was twitching before him. As his ankles at last escaped the ocean he began to fall and fall.

Possibly that was where dream stopped, and death began.

Or not yet. The ferment was unfinished. There were hands tugging at him, lifting him up again. There were faces, elderly faces, puzzled, quizzical. Brown muscular bodies. Yet no flowers, no dancing, no song. Just troubled eyes and mouths moving. No way to understand what they were saying. No way at all. But they were surely asking why. Why?

'God knows,' he said, and meant it.

He stumbled forward, out of their grip, as if still going somewhere, still in flight, and fell again to the sand. These strangers knelt about him, insisting on kindness, on taking him in their care. When he looked up, searching out focus, there was a new face grown among the gentle grey-haired islanders. Features distinct and apart. Someone pale, black-haired, and female. Familiar.

'Jacqueline?' he asked.

She nodded.

'Is this it, then?' he said.

She shook her head.

'This has to be enough, he argued. 'There can't be more.'

She shook her head again. An ambiguous answer.

'I understand,' he went on. 'I see what you've been trying to tell me. I got the message; it's all right now. All right. I'm quite ready to die.'

At that point she seemed not to understand. Unless it was he who couldn't.

'What is it, then?' he asked with sudden panic.

She appeared reluctant to say. She just smiled, with some compassion.

'You can't tell me I haven't earned it,' he protested. 'You can't tell me that.'

No, she wasn't going to tell him that. For she still smiled as gently.

'Tell me,' he said. 'For God's sake, tell me. It's only fair.'

She seemed to put out a hand towards him. It was not a gesture of welcome. More one of farewell. And an offering of freedom. He tried not to believe it. Then he had to.

'So that's it,' he said heavily. 'I've misunderstood. That's what you've been trying to tell me all along. That I have the hard part, the hardest part, still to come. That I have to live.'

She didn't disagree. And he no longer saw her in that purple caftan gown, but in casual white slacks and cool green blouse, as if dressed for a summer journey. Even her scent was new, unfamiliar. There was also someone beside her now, vague and shifting, then suddenly as solid. Peter; Peter Lee. Weathered face, unravelling sea-jersey, kitbag slung on a shoulder, perhaps looking for another craft upon an even more pure Pacific. He smiled gently too, quite as compassionately as Jacqueline, before he was gone.

'But why me?' Stephen asked her. 'Why the hell me?'

She shook her head, her smile more remote. Perhaps the answer was in that poem which dream told him he had to finish. But before he could ask, or elaborate, he was falling again, tumbled into a bruising dark. She was no longer with him. Had she ever been? He would never know in this life or perhaps in any other. There was no longer need to know. It was only necessary to know that there was no one at the wheel at all, no one keeping watch. He was drifting, directionless. Only necessary to know that he was hove to just inside the danger zone again.

He woke, reborn, in the warm shade of a hut, among soft and confused sounds and strange smells, sweet liquid between his lips, with tender human hands bathing the unfamiliar body in

204

which he was suffered to finish his life sentence. But his resurrected senses seemed more to say that he was a tentative sculpture, some vestigial memory of man, surfacing slowly from a chaos of lost time and brute pain; or, perhaps, some flotsam and grotesque infant delivered up to the world of man by earth and air, fire and water, the mated elements.

The others? He looked and saw. Rex Stone, or the bitter flesh which had once disguised the man, was also there, everything but his shape concealed under finely woven matting. The old sailor home from the sea? Yes; and the wounded hero at last over the hill, descended to the painless shade on the plain beyond. Just don't let me see the bastard who does it, I don't want to know who: that wish, at least, once more was gratified. Anyone, old man, everyone; anyone and everyone. Rex need no longer hunt for himself in bronze among the high weeds of his garden, carry his heavy warrior's cross again; he was wholly shaped now, wholly finished, for the world to find what it might in such a man. Let his griefs be gone, Stephen thought, let his war be won. A small enough prayer. And better than none.

Blair, withered and dying, had been borne from the yacht on a litter to rest beside Stephen too. What, in that rash beginning, had Blair claimed most to want? To do one good thing with his life. His dying now made that confused wish a prospect of stark and extraordinary substance. Blair might have wanted to make a little history; now history would make him. And Stephen was left with resonance of the tale Blair needed so urgently told; left to trim all detail down to that single vivid shape within which legends reside. And left to live in modest comfort alongside it; he was not without experience.

Blair died then, quite inconspicuously, the slightest of sounds fluttering in his mouth before the silence began, before he left the barricade business behind, before that finest of woven matting descended upon his shape too.

Stephen, risen on a painful elbow, tried to consider the two so long as he was able. At least he saw then that they were safe, beyond all hurt, both as safe as men might ever be. Elsewhere was the fighting and kicking, biting and scratching, grabbing and hating. And the laughing and loving, of course, the better bit too. Elsewhere was all the pain and pleasure. All the living, all the dying, all the joy and peril. Nothing could touch them now; nothing. Only he was in hazard.

So the trick, the ritual, might be not to ask why. Or, at least, to ask it without complaint.

'It's all right,' he announced at length, back on the boat, back at the wheel, looking toward a still lethal horizon.

All right?

That delirious question was his own, of course. That delirious doubt. Yet answer must be made; someone had to keep this watch.

All right?

'Yes,' he insisted. 'It's all right, Rex. It's all right, Blair. Peter too, wherever you are. Everything's all right. Everything's fine. I'm sailing back in again.'